R

MW00930217

Published by Audrey Harrison

This book was proof read by Joan Kelley. Read more about Joan at the end of this story, but if you need her, you may reach her at oh1kelley@gmail.com.

Dear Reader,

This is the book I've always wanted to write. When I'm being sensible, my deepest wish is for my children and wider family to be happy and healthy, but when I'm not being so sensible (which happens more and more the older I get!), my deepest wish is for me to be able to travel back in time.

Anyone who knows me well would not be surprised at such a revelation; I've always been a history geek. I could quite easily choose to go back and meet John of Gaunt and the Plantagenets or even whisper in the ears of some of the wives of Henry the Eighth, assuring them that he really isn't worth it. Perhaps a trip to dance a waltz in one of the many Russian palaces with the tzars, or onto the Victorian era to wear those wonderful full-skirted dresses and see the beasts of machines that made the Industrial Revolution so great. I would also need to travel to the not-so-distant past to visit the two World Wars this country, along with its allies, experienced.

All those periods in history have fascinated me since I was a young girl, but there is one period in time that, if I visited, I could be called back to the present century only by, the lure of showers, availability of good medicine, and food that wasn't already 'off' when it was being served. There are no prizes for guessing which era that would be: my beloved Regency period.

That time of excess, courtesy, complications was when the world we know today really began to emerge. Life was still so different, yet its problems were familiar. The people there wanted the same as we do today: happy marriages, financial security and a belief that things can only get better. Their lives were perhaps more fragile than ours and differed in other ways. We have fantastic medicines at our disposal, we also have divorce. We have the ability to restrict the number of children we have if we should wish, and it's no longer frowned on to achieve greatness through workplace ambition.

Sometimes, though, it feels as if we are as fragile as they were. We want the same happy-ever-after that our ancestors strove for in their often-restricted society. My feeling is that constraint can sometimes bring security; you are aware of what is expected of you. I'm glad I can't see the feminist movement screaming at these words! Call me a traditionalist, but I love clearly defined roles. We live in a far more confusing society today where neither sex knows what is right and wrong for their gender. I'm a simple soul at heart! So send me back to a society that is clear cut, although I admit there were still blurring of roles going on then. Even so, with all its faults I'd love to be a part of that Regency world for just a little while.

Best wishes, Audrey

Please forgive the use of a few swear words in the opening chapters. I hope you'll agree that they are in context for the story. They are there to make a point in the plot and are not there just for the sake of foul language. I don't wish to offend anyone.

This book is dedicated to Martin Salter, alias Mr Bennet, one of the Jane Austen Centre Greeters in Bath. He holds the title of being the most photographed person in England as he carries out his role at the centre.

I met Martin when my husband and I attended our first Jane Austen Festival. Martin greeted us so warmly, giving us useful information, as well as welcoming us to the festival; it certainly helped our nerves in attending an event so out of our comfort zone.

Since that day, Martin has become a friend and someone we both look forward to seeing on our annual pilgrimage to Bath. I don't know how he remembers so many names, faces and details about people, but he does. He's always pleasant, has a kind word for everyone and makes visitors and regulars feel thoroughly welcomed – and he has a great sense of humour too! If you get chance, watch him dance Regency dances — he's very nifty on his feet.

So, thank you, Martin from all the ladies and gentlemen who attend the festival and all the visitors to the Jane Austen Centre. Never underestimate how much of an impact you have on the people you meet.

Chapter 1

She was certain it was going to be a gentle end to what had been a traumatic time.

How wrong could an assumption be?

*

"Mum, come on, or we'll be late!" Megan shouted, running up the stairs.

"I thought the parent was the one to give orders." Catherine said, tying her shoulder-length chestnut hair in a ponytail, giving up on the thought of spending time styling it.

"When you start acting like a parent, you can give the orders," came the response of an all-too-confident fourteen-year-old.

"Do I really have to wait until you are sixteen before I can throw you out?" Catherine muttered.

"I heard that. You won't. I'm too lovable, and you'd only get bored reading all your trashy novels every day," Megan responded with an all too confident laugh.

"They aren't trashy! They're a glance back in history," Catherine responded tartly, rushing around, picking things up as she spoke.

"Funny that they never appear on the GCSE syllabus then," Megan said. "I can just imagine it: 'This year students will be studying Regency romance'. Not!"

"Have you never heard of Jane Austen or the Bronte sisters, you illiterate peasant?" Catherine said, pausing, her hand on her hip.

"Hurry up!" Megan urged, now tired of the conversation. The girl flounced away as only teenagers can, completely unaware of their impact on those around them. Megan wasn't arrogant as some were, but Catherine was sure that would develop as time progressed. Then the hormonal years would eventually end, and her child would turn into a human being once more. She was a pretty girl, not yet aware what impact cascading chestnut hair and clear blue eyes in a beautiful face could have on her male friends.

Catherine shook her head at her reflection in the bedroom mirror as she closed the wardrobe door. The thought of being five minutes late for the Summer Fayre was obviously too much for Megan, but it was something Catherine wished she could avoid completely. She had always helped out at the events throughout her children's schooling, but this year was different. Catherine had avoided their close-knit community until now, and she was reluctant to break her self-imposed isolation.

She sighed to herself; it was supposed to be the children who required counselling after a marriage break-up. In her family it seemed as if her children had moved on and were happy in themselves. She was the one still struggling with the 'whys' and 'how could I have been so stupid' thoughts that were constantly in the back of her mind.

Fabulous at forty the birthday cards had screamed at her not so very long ago. It was almost laughable that a piece of card could mock her at such a low point in her life. She had watched her mother die only six months before her birthday, which would have put a damper on any celebration. Losing the only parent she had ever known had been a wrench; her father had not hung around once the pregnancy had been confirmed.

Catherine would've probably been able to manage the milestone birthday without her mum, if her so-called darling husband hadn't dropped his bombshell weeks before her birthday. She had presumed his distance was because he was planning a nice surprise for her; she had got one thing right: It had certainly been a surprise.

She smoothed down the floaty top, feeling the well-established curves underneath. Catherine liked to think she was average sized, curves in all the right places. She had welcomed the new style that was a nod back to the shift dresses worn in the fifties. If she had anywhere special to go, that was the type of dress she would have worn, but now, school summer fayres were as exciting as life got.

Moving her hand to her forehead, she rubbed at the frown that seemed ever-present these days. When had she become so serious? She sighed; she really didn't need to ask that question. This last year would have tested the strongest of characters. How life could change in such a relatively short period of time was beyond her comprehension most days.

Reaching for her lipstick, she applied a fine layer of red on her lips. She smiled at the irony of the colour — bombshell. It probably would be more fitting if it were called "dropped a bombshell." The colour was needed on her pale lips. These days her complexion was paler than normal, contrasting starkly against her dark chestnut hair.

Catherine sighed. She had to try to return to the person she used to be; if she didn't do it soon, she was afraid her real self would be lost forever. Turning away from the mirror she moved out of her bedroom;

today was the first step in that direction. It was time to start living again, if only a little.

Megan was waiting in the car for her. "And don't think of sticking to the speed limit. Hayley has been there for over an hour." She said before plugging her MP3 into the car charger socket. Once the earphones were inserted it would be the end of any conversation.

Catherine tugged at one of the wires hanging out of Megan's ears as she started the car. "I'm not getting three points for you or anyone else. Text Andrew and tell him to meet us there."

Her seventeen-year-old son would never have agreed to travel with his mum to a school event; that would be far too uncool, but for Megan travelling with a parent was still considered a means to an end. Andrew was attending only because the school demanded that the six formers help set-up and put away the equipment. They got a half day off studies as compensation.

Catherine was under no illusion. She would be abandoned by Megan the moment they arrived, and she would face the gossipers — sorry, other helpers — alone.

They arrived in the busy car park and tucked the car in a corner before entering into the large hall to join the chaos that reigned. As predicted Megan saw Hayley and disappeared with a wave over her shoulder to her mother. Catherine looked around for a familiar face that would not be too keen to bring up the subject of Paul. She saw one or two mums that she knew and although they waved her over, she waved in return but did not move towards them.

Her elbow was touched, and she turned to see a man whom she had not seen for a long time. "Hello," he said with a warm smile. "Welcome back to the fold. I thought you'd given up on us. I'm Deputy Head here now, so I'm the one with the responsibility of trying to make sense of all this."

"You poor thing," Catherine responded with a smile. Adam Jones had been one of Megan's teachers when she'd first arrived in the school. He had helped in all the other fayres, so for Catherine he was a friendly face.

He laughed, "Thank you. I'm sure at some point I will start to see organisation beyond this chaos."

"I'm sure you will, although it may be about five o'clock this afternoon," Catherine said. "I'm normally here earlier, but I'm less organised these days."

"That doesn't matter; there is still plenty to do. We've made a good team in other years."

"Yes, apart from last year," Catherine said, her brow creasing into an all-too-frequent frown. Last year she had been huddled in a corner of her bed, her heart breaking and her marriage in tatters while still recovering from the loss of her mother. The week before the Summer Fayre, Paul had told her that he did not love her anymore. In fact he was wondering if he ever had, and as a result had decided that life with his best friend's wife was a better prospect than a future with Catherine.

"Well, most people are allowed a year off for good behaviour. It was probably because you had heard that I'd been put in charge," Adam said easily. "Anyway, our bring-and-buy stall is lacking a helper." He led the way over to the stall. "Susan is already hard at work, and I wouldn't want her being put off by facing the mob alone."

"That's fine," Catherine smiled with relief. Susan was her best friend and the one that had persuaded her to start facing the rest of the world once more. It was a nice gesture to place her with someone who would offer support if needed and showed a thoughtfulness in the organisation of the event.

"Hiya, are you ready to face the hooligans?" Susan asked with a grimace.

"I'm not sure. I think missing last year has helped the scars to fade a little!" Catherine responded.

"I'm glad you decided to come," Susan said quietly. "I wasn't sure you would."

"I don't think I would've, only Megan needed a lift," Catherine admitted.

"It's the right decision. You aren't the one who's in the wrong."

"I hate to have been the talk of the town though."

"Let them talk. Your mum would've forced you to face the world sooner than this," Susan said gently.

"I know. After she'd beaten up Paul!" Catherine laughed. Her loss still cut deeply, but she was starting to be able to look back at memories of her mother with a smile instead of tears.

"She would have, and he definitely deserved someone punching him repeatedly! I know I've said it before, but I think he only had the courage to leave once your mum died. He might have been double her size physically, but he was definitely scared of her," Susan said with feeling.

"Everyone was scared of her!" Catherine smiled. "Five feet of big opinions if she thought you'd done wrong. Although in some ways it saddens me to think Paul stayed with me out of fear of my mother!"

"You're better off without him. You need someone who worships you not a sleazeball like Paul."

Catherine smiled a little. "I don't think I'll ever be able to trust anyone again."

"In time," Susan reassured her.

"I don't think there is enough time in the world," Catherine said grimly.

The two women worked together to put the stall in order. As they worked, a student approached the table. "Hi, Mum."

Catherine turned and smiled, "Hello, Andrew. Have you come to help?"

"Not likely," Andrew said with a grin. "Have you any money?" He was very like Catherine in ways and looks. Although both children had her chestnut hair, Andrew had her hazel eyes as well. He looked on the world more seriously than even Catherine had when she was a teen. He was the one she worried most about; Megan's sunnier nature would see her through the more trying years of growing up.

17

Catherine groaned, "Hello, Mum. How are you? I'm just here because of your company, and I don't want a single penny from you," she mimicked.

"You'd feel unloved if we didn't bother you all the time," came the quick response.

"Oh, for the opportunity," Catherine mumbled, reaching for her purse.

"By the way, I think Dad's coming," Andrew said quietly.

"Why?" Catherine asked, stunned. Paul had never been anywhere near any of the children's schools since the day they had started, apart from parents evening when Catherine had demanded that he pretend to show some interest in his children's education.

"I dunno. Told him he wouldn't enjoy it, but he's doing the new-man thing with Danielle, isn't he?" Andrew said with derision. "He'll soon get sick of it and crawl back into his hole."

"Andrew! That's your father you're talking about!" Catherine admonished him. Paul may be a complete low-life in her eyes, but she tried her best not to pass the feelings onto Megan and Andrew.

"Just because he's my dad doesn't exclude him from being a top-class pillock, does it?" He laughed at Catherine's shocked expression. "See you later Mum!"

Before Catherine could gather her wits to either laugh or tell him off for his bad language, he had disappeared into one of the smaller halls. She shook her head. He may be seventeen, but very often he seemed older than his years. Perhaps it was because he was the first born and was always encouraged to develop as fast as he possibly could; whereas, when the second child came along, time was at a premium, so she had been left to develop at her own speed.

Catherine was aware that Andrew felt betrayed by Paul far more than Megan. Megan was a happier natured child. The teenage tantrums had not quite started, although there were signs they were on the way. She was the child who was still quick to tears but was also quick to recover, the way a young child was. Andrew was different; he was a natural born worrier and had taken the news of the divorce badly. He had always sought Paul's approval in anything he had done and initially had taken his dad's actions as confirmation that he hadn't been a good enough son, especially as Paul's new partner had two sons.

Then one day he had come home from a visit to his dad's house, announced that his father was an idiot and refused to go again. Catherine had no idea what had happened; they had not fallen out, still speaking occasionally on the phone, but Andrew had not visited since. He had also seemed to grow up a little more, reaching the start of manhood sooner than he perhaps would have in other circumstances. Catherine could see the man emerging, and although she did not count her blessings too soon, she thought he would be fine in the long term.

She turned her attention back to Susan and the stall as the main doors opened and the throng started feeding through the pay booth. It was only a few moments before Catherine could think of nothing apart from prices, change, and preventing items being knocked to the floor. Adam came across a few times during the fair, and one time helped out when Susan and Catherine had their hands full.

Catherine had grinned at him when she realised what he was doing. "Not scared of getting your hands dirty then? I thought that now you were officially in the category of organiser, you wouldn't associate with us lowly helpers." She teased as soon as her sale was complete.

"Only to look good in front of the volunteers as I want to convince you all to come back next year," he replied with a smile.

Catherine smiled but did not respond. She hoped that by next year she could feel something more like herself. She had got lost somewhere between losing her mother and Paul leaving. She wasn't sure how to return to her more relaxed nature, these days tending to get stuck in long periods of introspection. She shook herself — now was not the time for maudlin moods — and turned to the next student vying for attention.

Chapter 2

Two hours later, Susan groaned. "I've not worked as hard as that in years. I'm sure I've aged this afternoon."

Catherine laughed, "It's an experience, isn't it? I'd forgotten how demanding it is."

"I might book a holiday next year," Susan groaned, stretching her back. "Adam Jones is on his way back. He's a bit of a dish, isn't he?"

Catherine looked across at the Deputy Headteacher meandering across the hall. "He's better than most of the teachers here. Have you seen Mr. Bryson?" Catherine asked in a whisper, something about being in the school environment bringing out the naughty schoolgirl in her.

Susan laughed, "I know what you mean. All the kids say he's really scary."

"I think, because he's so small, he thinks he has to scare all the boys. Andrew's still as terrified of him as he was in his first year."

Adam reached the table as Catherine noticed the smile exchanged between her friend and the teacher and was pleased. Susan was an attractive woman who had never settled with anyone for long, always holding out for her version of Mr Right. She worked in the school offices and had always spoken highly of Mr Jones. There was a spark between Susan and the charismatic, handsome teacher, which, in Catherine's opinion, was a good thing. She had never heard anything detrimental about the teacher.

"I'm just checking that you ladies have made us loads of money. And survived, of course," he said.

"Susan is a natural at negotiation. She didn't need me," Catherine said.

"Oh, thanks!" Susan said. "Now I'm lumbered with this stall every year!"

"Believe me, I speak as the voice of experience. The cake stall, the chocolate stall and the games stalls are all ten times worse than this. Hold onto bring-and-buy." Catherine advised her.

"I hate to acknowledge that any of this is anything but a walk in the park, but I have to admit that Catherine's correct. It's mayhem on the chocolate and cakes stalls," Adam said with a shudder.

"And which have you worked on? I don't remember you being in the thick of it even when you were supposed to be helping." Catherine said loftily.

"Just because I haven't worked on them, doesn't mean I don't feel the pain," Adam assured her. "And I helped here with you two ladies don't forget. The fact that I might have picked your stall for fear of my life from the mothers and children at the others is beside the point!"

Before Catherine had a chance to retort she caught sight of Paul out of the corner of her eye. She stiffened involuntarily and took a sharp breath. He was headed towards her, and she did not feel ready to speak to him. There was not enough time or opportunity to make a dignified escape, so she stood rooted to the spot until he reached her.

"Catherine, could I have a word in private?" Paul said, not waiting to see if there was a conversation already going on between the three gathered around the tables.

"I don't think the school fayre is the time to have a private conversation, do you Paul? I'm finishing up here," Catherine responded, trying to keep her voice level when in her head she was screaming abuse at him.

"I'll finish off here," Susan offered, while at the same time glaring at Paul as only a best friend can do.

"You can go into one of the side classrooms if you like. I won't be far away if you need any help," Adam said quietly to Catherine. The school was fully aware of what had happened in Megan's and Andrew's lives; it was only fair that the teachers were informed of two major life-changing events.

Catherine sent Adam a grateful look before setting her shoulders and leading Paul into a corridor off the hall. She opened the door to the first classroom she reached. There was no point delaying whatever conversation Paul wanted to have. She walked over to the teacher's desk and leant against it. It was a vain hope, but she thought that she might feel stronger leaning against the large wooden structure. She folded her arms and waited until Paul spoke.

How things had changed. She would have never considered when she married nearly twenty years ago that the man she had fallen for would betray her in such a cold, uncaring way. Was he really the person who had claimed he would love her until his dying day? He forgot to put in the caveat that he would love her until he found someone better. Catherine shook herself. She was in danger of becoming bitter and twisted; it was an easy trap to fall into when faced with Paul, but she was not going to allow him to do that to her. He had taken everything else; he was not taking *her*.

"Well, I may as well cut to the chase. I'm going to have to stop paying you money for the kids," Paul said, folding his arms defensively.

"What?" Catherine asked in disbelief. The desk behind her offered the support she needed as she sagged into the structure.

"I can't afford it anymore," he shrugged.

"You don't have children and then discard them when they become too expensive Paul!" she responded harshly.

"I knew you wouldn't understand!" he snarled.

"Understand? Of course I don't bloody understand!" Catherine replied, trying to keep her voice low. "How the hell do you think we are going to manage, Paul? Do you think I have a secret stash of money I can just dip into when times are tough? Because I haven't. I'm already working as many hours as I can. We won't be able to manage without your money." As much as she hated having to admit it, she still needed Paul's support. She had worked part-time when the children had been small. It was only when Megan had gone to high school that they had decided it was time for her to go back full-time. She had a job, but any career she had planned had suffered from the years of part-time work, so she was far from earning a healthy salary.

The door opened, and Megan walked in. "Mum, what's going on? Danielle said Dad had some news for us. Oh, hi, Dad."

"Hi, darling," Paul responded, turning on the charm as he did when he felt like it.

"It's nothing, Megs," Catherine said, using Megan's baby name. "Go and find Andrew. I'll be out in a minute." She still wanted to protect her children, even though their father was a complete and utter ass.

"Well, while you're here Megan, you may as well hear what I've got to say," Paul said, holding out his arm for his daughter.

Megan moved across to the embrace. "What is it? Something nice?"

"Well, yes, you could say that. Danielle and myself have decided to take you and Andrew on a trip of a lifetime to Lapland. How do you fancy that? It's only in December, but it'll be a great adventure. But between now and then, I'm going to be out of the country. I'm spending the next few months in New Zealand; we're considering emigrating there and want you and Andrew to join us. All the paperwork is in order, and the visas are in place, but we thought we'd go across and get a feel for the islands, do a bit of travelling before settling in one town. When we come back, we'll go to Lapland, and you can give me your answer as to whether you'd like to come and live with me or stay in rainy England." Paul said with a smile. "How would you fancy living in New Zealand?" He asked Megan, squeezing her.

"Oh my God!" Catherine and Megan said in unison.

Catherine stopped herself from grabbing Megan when she saw the impact of Paul's words on their daughter. She had gone white, and tears were already starting to fall. "Dad, tell me this is a wind-up just to annoy Mum," Megan sniffed.

"No, it's not a wind-up. We've decided there's too much baggage over here for the both of us, so it's time for a new start. Danielle's boys are excited about it," Paul said, oblivious to his daughter's distress.

"So you're refusing to pay maintenance because you're emigrating? Can you do that?" Catherine asked in disbelief.

"The English courts don't have jurisdiction over there," Paul said smugly.

"Which you've already checked," Catherine said bitterly.

"Of course," Paul replied with a smile, completely unrepentant.

The door opened, and Andrew walked in. "What's going on? Mr Jones said you were in here."

Megan used the opportunity to break away from her father and move across to Catherine. She turned to Andrew. "Our Dad, our doting father, has decided that we are baggage and are too expensive. He's not paying anything more to mum, and he's emigrating to New Zealand. He wants us to go and live with him and is taking us on a trip to Lapland in December when we have to give him our answer." The words were said with such despair that Catherine winced. She hated that her daughter was suffering so much pain.

"Mum?" Andrew asked. Catherine nodded; there was nothing she could say that would make the news better for them.

"Andy, it's a land of opportunity. You'd have a great life out there," Paul soothed, for some reason responding to the set of Andrew's face more than he had to his daughter's overt signs of distress.

"Why would we do that when it's quite clear that you don't want us and are travelling as far away as possible to prove it?" Andrew asked quietly.

"Don't be a drama queen, Andy. We're going to New Zealand because it's better for all of us, not to escape you. For God's sake, I want you to come with us!" Paul snapped. "Not everything is about you, you know. Be careful, or you'll start to sound like your mother."

Andrew's fists clenched at his sides, but he remained still. "Why are you making us choose between mum and you? Why can't you live here?" he challenged.

Paul flushed a little, not used to being opposed so openly by his son. "We're giving you the best opportunity we can. It's a new country. It doesn't have the problems you face here. I know it's sudden, which is why we're giving you until our holiday in Lapland to decide. You must be thrilled with at least that part of my surprise?" Paul asked.

"I've always wanted to see the real Father Christmas. That would be good," Megan said quietly, the little girl inside her emerging.

"It's a big decision, Dad. Your timing could've been better," Andrew responded.

"I expected your mother to kick off, but I'd presumed you two would support me in this. I'm really disappointed in your negativity," Paul said sullenly to his son. He had never liked not getting enthusiastic support for his ideas.

"You expected us to be pleased that you are willing to uproot us when we are going through the most important part of our education?" Andrew snapped. Catherine ached for her son; he wanted to train to become a vet, which was a seven year course. She knew he was seeing his dreams disappear. Without Paul's financial support, they would really struggle. She wasn't sure if Paul had thought it through, he was so callous about it, but it appeared her children had a very hard decision to make: stay with her and struggle or travel to the other side of the world and try to make a life over there with a future step-mother but no mum.

"Andrew," she said quietly. She would sell her soul before seeing him not reach his potential.

"Wait, Mum. This joker needs to hear a few home truths." Andrew said his eyes not leaving Paul's face.

Catherine looked at Paul and saw that, for the first time, he did not look so confident. "Come on, Andy. Be reasonable. See this for the opportunity it is," Paul said, trying to pacify his son.

"Do you know something, Dad? We've watched you being a complete bastard with Mum, but we just stood by. Probably selfish on our part because it wasn't really affecting us, but I see now that we've all had a lucky escape. With you out of the country, we'll be truly happy and be able to relax as a family again. I've always tried to make excuses for you, but I can tell you this: You are nothing but a fucking wanker."

"You want to watch your language, mate, or I might just give you the beating you obviously need," Paul snarled, but he stepped back when Andrew moved towards him.

Andrew stood at his full height; he was almost six feet to Paul's five feet eight, and Andrew worked out at the school gym and played sports every day, so he was broader than his father even though Andrew hadn't fully filled out yet. "Come on, Dad. Why don't you try and give me a beating?" Andrew taunted.

"Stop being ridiculous! Grow up, Andrew." Paul snapped.

"Grow up? That's a good one coming from a complete self-centred pig like you. Tell you what, Dad. Why don't you fuck off to New Zealand, and let's hope the plane crashes on the way. Go on, Dad! Get lost!"

Paul moved to pass by his son; Andrew hit him with his shoulder as Paul pushed past the desks, unable to get a clear exit. He only paused when Megan shouted out, "Dad!"

"What?" He said looking over his shoulder.

"Are you still taking us to Lapland?" Megan asked.

"I probably shouldn't if that's the thanks I get for trying to give you both the best chance in life you'll ever have, but yes. The Lapland trip will go ahead. It'll give Andy a few months to settle down."

Paul slammed out the door, making it crash back on its hinges. Catherine held Megan as she shook at the action. She had never been able to deal with conflict, a fact on which her father had never picked up. Catherine held out a hand to Andrew. He took it and then wrapped his arms around Catherine and Megan, resting his head against Catherine's shoulder.

They stood like that for a few moments and then Andrew moved. He looked at his mother, and he suddenly looked like a little boy again, unsure and afraid. "How will we manage, Mum?" he asked, his voice choked.

Catherine held Megan away from her slightly to enable her to look into both sets of eyes. She did not know which was more heart-breaking: the frightened face of her daughter or the strained, almost haunted look in Andrew's eyes. "Listen to me, you two," she said gently but firmly. "I'm not going to lie to you and say it's going to be easy because it isn't, but we'll manage without your dad's money."

"How?" Megan sniffed.

"I don't know. I haven't had time to think, but I'll come up with something," Catherine assured them. "We'll survive this. We're not going to starve, and we certainly aren't going to give up on any of our dreams. Okay?"

Andrew looked at her disbelievingly, but said "Okay."

"Andrew, that's not good enough," Catherine said. "You're going to attend a vet course if I have to sell my body, do you hear me?"

Andrew nodded, and his mouth twitched slightly, "If I have to rely on that Mum, I'm definitely doomed. You're old and wrinkly."

Catherine laughed before becoming serious again. What she had to say next could possibly break her heart, but she owed it to them to utter the words. "Your dad has asked you to consider joining him in New Zealand. I can't lie and say that I'd be over the moon about it if you went, but he's your dad, and you should at least think about it."

"Would you come too?" Megan asked.

"No. I don't think I'd get in. There are restrictions on people who want to emigrate, but I wouldn't want to anyway. Does that make me sound heartless? You two would be over there, and I'd be here," Catherine said with a teary smile.

"We can't leave you," Andrew said.

"The decision you have to make is for your future not mine. I'm sorry it's been dropped on you, and it will take time to sink in, but you should consider it," Catherine said, not wanting to be self-sacrificing, but needing to be fair to her children's future.

They were interrupted by a gentle knock on the open doorway. They all turned to see Susan hesitating at the entrance of the classroom. "I won't ask if everything's ok, but is there anything I can do?"

Andrew pulled away slightly and shook his head. Catherine smiled at Susan. "Thank you. We were just finishing here. Andrew, will you take Megan and wait for me near the car? I just need to collect my stuff and then I'll join you."

Andrew nodded and took Megan's hand, a previously unheard of sign of affection. Catherine felt a lump in her throat as she saw him squeeze his sister's hand.

She had to do something, or she would break down in a wobbly heap in front of her friend, which happened too often these days.

"Oh, and Andrew," she said.

"Yes?" Andrew responded, pausing.

"We will be having a conversation at home about your use of language," Catherine assured him, still reeling slightly from hearing her son use words that were banned in her household.

Andrew laughed and walked out the door, a bit jaunty in his step. They both knew she would excuse his lapse, but she had to maintain the image of the stern parent to bring a more normal feel to the situation.

Susan waited until the children had left the room and walked down the corridor. "I saw Paul virtually fly out of the building. He didn't look happy."

"He wasn't. I always knew he was selfish, but today proved it," Catherine said with a sigh.

"What's he done now?" the friend asked.

Catherine briefly told Susan what had been dropped on them all. Her friend's expression of disbelief could have been funny in differing circumstances, but Catherine was struggling to find humour today.

"What a thing to do to you all!" Susan spluttered.

"Yes. He probably thought that I wouldn't make a fuss about not paying maintenance if he told me in a public place. Which was true, but he didn't expect to have Andrew and Megan coming in half way through. He was surprised that they didn't receive his news with jumps of joy. He just doesn't understand that they have hopes, dreams and lives that have to be considered," Catherine shrugged.

She could not believe now that she had ever loved Paul or that she had been so upset when he had left. His words had brought back other instances when he had dropped decisions on her and had expected no argument or discussion, just expecting her full co-operation. Perhaps she had been the foolish one in taking so long to see what he was really like.

"So what happens now?" Susan asked.

"There's nothing I can do. I have to wait until the kids have thought his idea through. I hope they decide before they go to Lapland with him. I don't think I'll be able to live in so much uncertainty until December. My nerves are frayed enough," Catherine admitted.

"Surely you aren't going to let them decide something as big as that alone?" Susan asked in disbelief.

"I would be selfish if I put my wishes onto them, but of course I'll offer advice if they ask for it."

"Cathy, you can't stand back and watch them leave the country!"

"How can I stop them if it's what they want?"

"Because they're still too young!"

"Megan perhaps, but Andrew has already had to start planning for his future. He's well on the way to completing his A levels. He knows what he wants to do. Perhaps New Zealand can offer an easier route into being a vet?" Catherine responded.

"I don't believe this! Cathy, fight for them!"

Catherine gritted her teeth before answering. She knew Susan was only reacting because she cared, but it wasn't helping. "I'm not guilting them into staying with me. I refuse to do that! Susan, they've been through so much this last year. I'm not adding to their pressure, but, yes, if they choose to go, part of me will never recover."

"You'll be alone, well apart from me. But even I know my limitations as a friend," Susan responded with a wry smile.

"I know," Catherine said quietly.

Susan linked her arm with her friend's. "You definitely need a man!"

"That's the last thing I need!"

"Don't let him win Cathy. You made a mistake. Don't condemn every man because of one idiot, even if he is an idiot of the highest order," Susan said.

Catherine smiled. She wasn't sure she would ever meet anyone who would take away the pain that Paul had caused.

Chapter 3

Paul's news and offer of a trip to Lapland was to cause Catherine additional unforeseen heartache. She had traditionally visited Bath each year with her mother in December to attend the Christmas Market. Even when the cancer was making her mother weaker, they had made the trip, doing a lot less, but it had been important to both mother and daughter to keep the tradition going for as long as possible.

The previous December had been too soon for Catherine to return to Bath, even if she hadn't been dealing with the break-up of her marriage. This year, though, Paul had booked the trip to Lapland on the same week the Christmas Market was being held.

"Don't try and convince me that was a coincidence!" Susan said when visiting in October. Her friend had supported Catherine over the months since the spring fayre while Catherine had supported her children, both financially and emotionally. It had been hard for her, forced into taking another job and trying to be mum, dad and housekeeper all rolled into one.

"I can't ask the kids to choose between the trips. I'm not going to mention that I'd booked a room for the three of us," Catherine said, both sad and annoyed that she wasn't sharing the trip with her children.

She'd hoped to try and introduce some new memories to her favourite place.

"I wish I could get the time off work and come with you," Susan responded.

"I couldn't expect you to use your leave on me when you're busy swanning around the world with Adam," Catherine smiled. Her friend had started a relationship with the Deputy Headteacher soon after the Spring Fayre, and so far, both seemed very happy with the situation.

Susan sighed. "I can't get enough of him."

"I'm glad. He seems like a decent bloke." Catherine liked the teacher. He was just what her friend needed, loving and funny. "Although you've had to kiss some utter toads before finding him!"

"Don't you dare tell him that!" Susan laughed. "I don't want him to get big-headed. I'm breaking every rule in the book with this one, not treating him mean to keep him keen and all that."

"I should think not! All those 'How to' manuals should be burned," Catherine said with feeling. "I know I'm not a good example, but I do believe you should be honest and show how you feel about someone."

"You *were* honest," Susan responded.

Catherine smiled. "I was, yes. I see the flaw in my argument. But you can't go through life not treating everyone decently because you might get hurt at some point. That's no way to live."

"I'm glad the incurable romantic is returning," Susan teased. "A pity you won't put your needs ahead of everyone else's. Ask Paul to change the dates."

"Andrew and Megan couldn't have so much time off school. Having a week was bad enough. They've almost had to sign in blood that they'd catch up with their schoolwork before the school would agree to their absence."

"Which means that you're facing Bath alone."

"I probably should cancel the trip with money being as it is, but I'm selfish. I want to go. I know it'll be hard, but it also might do me good. I've got some time to think without being interrupted and can do whatever I want, putting myself first. I might even book in for a day at the spa. I've not done that for years!"

"Just make sure you have a good time, not a sad one," Susan said quietly, standing to leave her friend.

"I'm sure there'll be tears, but they'll be for mum, not the fool who is now my ex-husband."

"That I can understand. And I don't condemn you for those tears."

*

Bath – December, Present Day

Catherine walked down the stairs to the breakfast room in the large Georgian building. Last night had been a strange evening for all the reasons she could have used to postpone the trip. When it mattered though, Catherine had sat in the driver's seat and, with a deep breath, had turned the ignition key. Nothing would bring back her mum, and she refused to do as Susan had advised and make Andrew and Megan feel guilty. She was not a perfect mother, but that was a parenting tactic she had rejected.

Her home had felt empty once Paul and Danielle had collected the children. Paul had had the temerity to just blast the horn of his car to let them know he'd arrived rather than facing her on the doorstep.

Andrew had been the one who had struggled with the decision to go on the holiday, but Catherine had refused to interfere; it was his decision to make, not hers. He had approached her one evening when Megan was engrossed in one of her nightly telephone conversations with her friends.

"I don't mind not going to Lapland," Andrew had said, coming to sit next to Catherine.

As a boy who was still at the stage of avoiding physical contact with his mother, Catherine understood the seriousness of Andrew's approach. "Do you want to go?"

"I don't believe in Father Christmas and all that stuff, just in case you were wondering," he grinned at his mother.

Catherine smiled back. "I do."

"Yeah, Megan still believes. I'm sure she does."

"It's not a bad thing to still believe in the magic of something," Catherine said gently. Sometimes she wished that they'd stayed as seven and four year olds, still full of wonder at the world.

"Whatever," Andrew shrugged.

"So, you don't want to go?"

"Dad says there's dog-sledging, snow-mobiles and up-close encounters with reindeers and the dogs," Andrew said, struggling to keep hidden the sparkle of excitement in his eyes.

"It sounds amazing," Catherine admitted.

"Bath would be good though," Andrew said, trying to be nonchalant and failing with the parent who knew him better than anyone.

"I know which I would pick," Catherine said quietly.

"Yeah, but you love Bath and all that history stuff."

"I didn't say I'd pick Bath," Catherine responded. She knew she'd uttered the right words when Andrew's eyes met hers, a look of hope in his expression.

"You wouldn't?"

"I still believe in Father Christmas, remember? Why would I miss that opportunity? The other activities sound fantastic for someone who wants to spend his life looking after animals."

"Yeah, I was hoping to see if there was any possibility of helping out with the dogs," Andrew started, his curbed enthusiasm bubbling to the surface.

"I'm sure they wouldn't turn down the chance of having a gullible tourist mucking out for them," Catherine teased.

"It's all part of the learning process," Andrew grinned back.

"And that is why you are going to be a great vet," Catherine said, squeezing her son's hand.

"You're biased."

"I know, but I can't help it." Catherine became serious. "Your dad is going to want a decision from you both about moving."

Andrew sighed. "We've decided not to tell him anything until we're on our way back to the airport; you know what he's like when he gets one of his hissy-fits on!"

Catherine's heart leapt. "You're not going to New Zealand?"

Andrew looked at her as if she had gone mad. "No! It was never an option. Megan wouldn't leave her mates, and she's admitted dad wouldn't indulge her moods half as much as you do!"

"And you?" Catherine probed. She had needed to hear his decision to make sure he was making it for the right reasons.

"I want to study over here. I might want to go and get some work experience after uni, but the British qualification has more weight behind it than anywhere else. I've spoken to a few people about it," Andrew admitted.

"Have you?" Catherine was stunned that her seventeen year old would act so maturely when most of the time she struggled to get a sentence out of him, let alone a whole conversation.

"Course I have. I'm not a numpty, you know! It's a big decision," came the indignant response.

"I know you aren't."

Andrew stood. "Are you sure you don't mind going to Bath on your own? I know it meant a lot to you and Grandma."

Catherine smiled, so relieved that her children were not emigrating that she could face a week alone in Bath with no problem. "Yes, I'm sure."

Andrew nodded and moved to the door. When he was half-way out of the room, he stuck his head around the door. "Mum?"

"Yes?"

"Even if I hadn't wanted to be a vet, I wouldn't have gone. Just so you know."

Andrew had left the room immediately, not waiting for any response, which was for the best as Catherine was incapable of speaking. Tears had filled her eyes, and a lump was blocking her throat as she tried to stem the well of emotion that was fighting for release at her son's words.

She had thought she was losing them, but in reality, they weren't leaving her. She knew they would one day in the future, but that was different – the natural progression of life. This had been an attempt to rip her family apart. Catherine could relax for the first time in months. They were staying, and nothing else mattered.

*

Catherine entered the breakfast room to be greeted by the owner of the guest house.

"Good morning Mrs West. I hope you slept well?"

"I did, thank you," Catherine lied. It was her over-active mind that had kept her awake well into the night, which had nothing to do with the comfort of the room.

"I've seated you with Mr Dobson this morning. I hope you don't mind. I thought you could compare notes over breakfast while you're both visiting alone."

Catherine offered a wan smile but made no objection. In truth, polite conversation was the last thing she wanted over breakfast; she never felt quite human until vast quantities of tea had been consumed. True to her compliant character, though, Catherine sat opposite the stranger without uttering a word of dissent.

The owner bustled around them, taking their orders for breakfast before disappearing into the kitchen. The strangers looked at each other as an awkward silence descended. Catherine tried to look at her breakfast partner without it being obvious. He was a few years older than herself, probably mid-forties. His hair was a rich black, with a few grey flecks emerging; probably a similar amount as Catherine would have if she didn't use hair dye each month.

He smiled at Catherine, and the expression of bashfulness and warmth was appealing. Catherine returned the smile.

"The owner mentioned you'd been here before, and I think I remember seeing you here," Mr Dobson stated. "Was it a couple of years ago?"

"Yes, I was here two years ago," Catherine responded surprised at being remembered. "Do you visit every year?"

"I know it isn't manly, but I love coming to Bath for the whole of the Christmas market. I've been visiting for the last few years and have always stayed here. It's my favourite city," the stranger explained.

Catherine smiled. "I can't argue against that."

"Have you visited often?"

"Yes, we've been coming for years, but this is only the second time in this guest house. It's so central, it's perfect," Catherine answered.

"You were with someone the last time you came," Mr Dobson smiled at Catherine's wary expression. "I promise you that I'm not a stalker! When I travel alone, I entertain myself by studying my fellow guests. It's surprising what intrigue I can attach to the most innocuous of visitors!"

Catherine was reassured by the answer. She had people-watched herself last night in the service stations she stopped at on the journey down. "I usually came with my mother, but she passed away last year. It was too soon for me to even think about coming again. I couldn't face it." She swallowed the ever-ready feeling of despair when she spoke of her mother.

"Oh, I'm sorry for your loss!" came the sympathetic response. "It must be really hard for you. You're being very brave visiting again."

"I felt stupid last night, facing a week on my own," Catherine admitted. "It's been a tough year. I've just reached the end of the year of firsts, first Mother's Day without her, first birthdays."

"It does get easier to bear, I promise you," he said gently.

Catherine looked into the clear blue eyes looking deep into her own hazel ones, and for the first time in a long time, she believed what someone was telling her. Instinctively she knew he was showing genuine concern, and she felt a tug towards a person who did not appear to have any motive other than to be nice to her.

"Thank you. I hope so," she said quietly.

They were interrupted from further conversation by the arrival of their delicious- looking breakfasts. Mr Dobson tucked into his with gusto.

"My doctor tells me I'm at a funny age and should watch my cholesterol, but I can't resist a cooked breakfast when I'm on holiday."

"Well, we could always excuse it by saying we'd walk it off shopping, but I'm not convinced that's true, really," Catherine admitted.

"My ex-wife could certainly walk miles if shopping was involved. Mention a walk in the countryside though, and she suddenly became a cripple. I suppose it was my own fault for marrying a girl fifteen years younger than I was. She was never going to have the same interests at the same time. Especially as I think I was set in my ways by the time I was twenty-five."

Catherine laughed despite normally being reticent in the company of strangers. He certainly knew how to put someone at ease. Surprisingly, for the first time in a long time, she was able to relax and just enjoy herself, which brought out her teasing side.

"I suppose she hadn't reached the big and small swap-over stage then?" she asked with a twinkle in her eye.

"Big and small swap-over? Whatever's that?"

Catherine had the decency to blush before she answered. "I can't honestly believe I've just mentioned that. You're going to think I'm some sort of lunatic!"

"I'm really intrigued now." Mr Dobson smiled in encouragement, leaning slightly forward in expectation of the secret that was about to be revealed.

Catherine put her hands on her hot cheeks, trying to cool the heat. "My friends all say that it's a sign of old age when your knickers get bigger and heels get smaller!"

Mr Dobson burst out with a loud guffaw that was a sound of genuine amusement, which eased some of Catherine's mortification.

After Mr Dobson stopped laughing there was a slight pause in conversation as other guests had entered the breakfast room, and it was small enough for everyone to say their good mornings to each other.

After a few moments, Mr Dobson turned his attention back to Catherine. "No, she hadn't reached that stage, but she was so desperate to maintain her appearance I doubt she would've ever allowed such a thing to happen."

"A perfect match for my ex-husband then. He hated anything that he considered mumsy."

"Yet mumsy usually goes hand in hand with comfort, warmth and security," Mr Dobson responded, seriously.

"Not very sexy though, is it?" Catherine acknowledged.

"Maybe not, but as a kid who started life in numerous foster homes, before I was adopted, mumsy was something I longed for when I was growing up."

"I completely understand from a child's perspective, but it's not usually one of the qualities a young man looks for when he's seeking a wife, is it?"

"I certainly came to appreciate that a good home and happiness was far more important than visiting yet another beach in a faceless resort to top up the tan. She never moved off any of the beaches we visited. We travelled all over Europe, and all Mel could describe of the place was the quality of the sand and what tanning oil she'd used. It very soon became obvious that I'd made the biggest mistake of my life."

Catherine smiled. "I think you had the misfortune of being married to the female version of my husband. You have my complete sympathy."

"Thank you. I'm just glad we didn't have any children."

"We did. And although the split was hard on everyone, I wouldn't be without them or wish away my years with Paul, or the children wouldn't exist. They're the only good things to come out of nearly twenty years of marriage."

"Are you ok?"

"Why do you ask that?" Catherine was surprised at the change of tone, and although she had relaxed in his company, his question made her a little wary.

"You suddenly looked so sad," Mr Dobson said quietly, so that no one else in the breakfast room would overhear.

He knew he had stepped over the boundaries of politeness by uttering such a personal observation, but he couldn't help himself. What Catherine wasn't aware of was that he had been drawn to her when he had first set eyes on her two years ago. Even then there had been an air of sadness around her, but she had chatted jovially enough with her mother as they had planned their days. Hearing today that she was divorced could have been the explanation of her sadness, but somehow he didn't think so.

Catherine's eyes flickered to his briefly before she turned away with a sigh. "I have two children, a boy and girl, and we had planned to come here together, taking them out of school for the first time. I wanted to carry on the custom of visiting Bath. I'm sensible enough to know that the quicker I can introduce new traditions, the sooner the pain will not hurt quite so much."

"But they aren't here."

"No." Catherine paused before continuing. She didn't need to explain to this stranger but somehow she needed to say the words out loud to someone other than Susan. "He offered them a trip to Lapland. He's also asked them to move to New Zealand with him, and they need to give him their answer. Thankfully, they've decided to stay with me. But, understandably, they wanted to experience Lapland far more than they wanted to visit Bath with me."

"Oh."

"Yes, Paul has finally discovered fatherhood, seventeen years too late! There! I've said it! You sit opposite a horrible woman who begrudges her children the trip of a lifetime!" It was easy to confess her true feelings to a stranger.

Mr Dobson smiled gently at her. "I can't condemn you. Not you from what you've told me. For politeness sake I'll not openly say what I think, but you are more magnanimous than I would be in the same situation."

Catherine smiled in return. "You wouldn't say anything my best friend hasn't already said. She has had very strong opinions on everything and has been very vocal about it. So, I thank you for your reserve. I don't think my ego could take another scolding about how stupid I am!"

She took a final sip of tea before pushing her chair away from the table. "I'd better make a move, or I'll sit here all morning. I find it difficult to drag myself away from a never ending supply of tea."

"You're right. It is time to move. I'll walk upstairs with you," Mr Dobson said, also rising.

He was an attractive man, about six feet tall, with broad shoulders. His stride was very confident; Catherine could see him fitting in well on a rugby pitch. His jaw was square; his mouth looked as if it smiled a lot. His clear blue eyes sparkled, but Catherine was not sure whether it was with laughter or mischief. He was not a classical beauty but looked like a real man. Catherine thought he wouldn't be single for long. It was a strange thought to have and almost shook her from her scrutiny.

*

They walked in silence until they reached the ground floor. "This is me," Catherine said, inclining her head to a door at the front of the house.

"You booked wisely. I'm in the gods, up more stairs than should be allowed in any house. The Georgians must have been very fit."

"I booked the room with a separate area for one of the beds. I didn't think Andrew would appreciate being too close to his mum and sister."

"No, I suppose not. It was nice having breakfast with you. I really enjoyed your company."

Catherine smiled at him. He seemed such a refreshing change, a man who was easy to talk to. She had dreaded being on her own in the breakfast room. It was still hard being single after so long being a couple, even when part of that time was a lie on her husband's part.

"If you're downstairs tomorrow, we could sit together again, if you'd like to? I'm Catherine by the way."

"I'm Christopher, but everyone calls me Chris. My mother was determined to give me a grand name and hates that it never gets used!"

Catherine shook the outstretched hand. "Nice to meet you Chris. Hope you have a good day."

Chris squeezed her hand gently before releasing it. "I hope your day is enjoyable and not too difficult."

"Thank you." Catherine opened the door to her room, listening to the steady tread of Chris walking up the stairs. Even on such a short acquaintance, she was sure she had met someone who actually understood.

Chapter 4

Walking the streets of Bath on her own was not as lonely as Catherine had expected. She loved the city, and even after so many years of visiting, she still was overawed by the architecture.

Bath had many of the wooden sheds that represented the traditional European Christmas market stalls now found in many towns and cities. The city was one of the most beautiful she had ever visited, and the Christmas period just added to the magic of the place. The early darkness, crisp air, and lights of the Christmas chalets made it feel as if miracles could happen in the way only Christmas miracles could.

The smells of mulled wine and citrus and the cinnamon decorations only tempted the senses even further, putting Catherine in mind of all the romantic films she had ever watched.

The way people huddled around the small chalets, trying to look at produce could have been annoying at any other time of the year, but the Christmas period seemed to bring out the best in people, and there was good natured banter between shoppers and stall-holders.

Even the homeless people, selling their copies of the *Big Issue*, the magazine those living rough sell in an effort to help them get off the streets, wore Christmas hats and wished everyone a Merry Christmas even if they didn't receive money from passers-by

Catherine stuck to the usual tradition of the first day, exploring the Christmas stalls but not expecting to buy anything; most of her buying occurred on a different day when everything on offer had been seen. When she passed the Salvation Army band and carol singers under the archway in Abbey Green, she had to take a moment to swallow the lump that had formed in her throat; carols would always remind her of her mother. Catherine gave her donations and continued on her journey. Hopefully, one day she would smile with happy memories and not the sense of loss that still filled her.

The areas where the chalets were located were busy but not overcrowded. Catherine and her mother had once visited Lincoln Christmas Market, and the crowds had been almost overwhelming. They had enjoyed their time together but had decided that Bath was their preferred choice and never again deviated from the city.

An avid reader, Catherine always included a visit to the many bookshops Bath had on offer, both new and second-hand. She had visited the shop in Margaret's

Buildings, behind the Royal Crescent and couldn't help smiling to herself as she walked back down the hill towards the city centre by way of the gravel walk. She always felt a sense of achievement when she discovered what she considered a treasure in one of the bookshops, books being excluded from her look-now, buy-later philosophy. Her purchases from her visits burned in her bag; she would be engrossed in one during the evening.

After rejoining the main streets, she walked down Gay Street until she reached the Jane Austen Centre. Catherine paused; her mum had been a confirmed Catherine Cookson fan, hence Catherine's name and had teased her daughter who preferred the stories of the genteel folk of the Regency period about which Jane Austen wrote.

A costumed gentleman standing at the entrance of the centre touched his hat and bowed to Catherine.

"Good morning, Madam. Have you come to visit us?" he asked pleasantly with a Somerset lilt, which Catherine thought charming. It seemed to give his character extra depth. Such was the popularity of Bath that the ears were usually filled with every nationality, so to hear local dialect was refreshing.

Catherine smiled in return; it was lovely to be greeted so formally. "I've been here before, although I admit it was years ago."

"Have you travelled far?"

"Lancashire."

"Ah, and your name is?"

"Catherine. Catherine West."

"Well, Miss Catherine West, it's a pleasure to welcome you back. I think you'll find there's lots more to see. We have all the information about Miss Austen you could wish to know, and there are clothes to try on if you like. I'm sure some of the bonnets would suit a fine lady like yourself! But if that doesn't tempt you, the tea room has some wonderful home-made cakes that I can highly recommend!"

Catherine couldn't help grinning at his words. His friendliness was infectious and, although there to attract customers into the museum, he was waving and doffing his cap at cars passing and smiling at pedestrians, who all seemed to want to take his picture. There was no hard sell from him, just the right kind of welcome.

"I think I will go in. Why not?" Catherine responded on impulse.

"Why not indeed, Miss West? My name is Martin. If I can help in any way, you just let me know. Now let me get the door for you. Enjoy!"

Martin opened the door with a flourish, and Catherine walked in with a smile on her face. She was about to indulge her inner geek as Megan would say, and she was sure she would enjoy every minute.

*

The advice had been correct. Catherine revelled thoroughly in the history and life of Jane Austen. She had treated herself to a Ladies Afternoon Tea in the Restaurant, feeling decadent as it wasn't quite afternoon. She finished off by spending too much in the gift shop before leaving the building.

She felt refreshed as she left. Martin, one of the centre greeters, was being photographed by some very giggly Japanese tourists. He waved at her and said a "Goodbye, Miss Catherine West. I hope you enjoyed Miss Austen's exhibition!"

Catherine returned his wave, leaving him to his photographs. She had not for a moment expected him to remember her name; she had been in the centre for over two hours, and he must have spoken to dozens of people in the interim. His actions had made the city seem a little friendlier; she now had two people with whom she had spoken when, before arriving, she hadn't expected to speak to anyone.

Having bought more than she expected, Catherine decided to detour to the guest house to deposit her purchases. It was just beyond the Abbey, so it was a few minutes' walk away from Gay Street where she stood musing on the issue.

She reached the junction of Gay Street and Old King Street and faltered. A man standing at the opposite end of Old King Street caught her attention. He was holding an advertising board with an arrow pointing down the alleyway to the business he was promoting. That wasn't uncommon in Bath; many of the businesses employed people to stand on the junctions of busy thoroughfares to tempt people into the many side streets the city had to offer.

What struck Catherine as odd was that Old King Street was such a short street, quickly turning into John Street, which was little more than an alleyway running behind Jolly's Department store that fronted onto Milsom Street. John Street contained little more than Mr B's bookshop.

Catherine faltered but frowned when the man holding the sign beckoned her. There was normally no interaction by the sign holders and shoppers. Catherine shook herself; she was being unfair. The poor man was probably earning less than minimum wage, and it wouldn't harm her to use that cut-through. It gave her the excuse to call in at Mr B's.

She hurried down Old King Street, smiling at the sign holder; he nodded in response but said nothing. Catherine passed him and continued into John Street.

Behind her a woman emerged from the doorway of Hall and Woodhouse, the pub and restaurant on Old King Street. She approached the sign holder, a scowl on her face.

"You aren't supposed to interact with anyone," she hissed quietly at him.

He shrugged. "Too many rules. She's on her way. What's the problem?"

"She has to walk down there voluntarily. It might not work!" The woman finished her sentence with a glare and bustled down John Street in Catherine's wake.

Chapter 5

Catherine paused and reached out her hand to use the wall to steady herself. Everything had gone white, and a dead nothingness filled her ears as if she were about to faint, but she remained standing. She shook her head a few times to help clear the fuzziness before leaning against the wall. Rubbing her forehead, she tried to blink to clear her vision, but her frown increased as she looked down the street towards the junction of Quiet and Wood Streets.

Something was wrong. She must have missed the sign saying there was filming taking place; the area she was looking onto was full of people, carriages and sedan chairs, all rushing about.

She had to retrace her steps, or she would cause problems. It was strange that so much activity could be created in the few hours it had been since she had walked along there earlier in the day.

She stood and ran her hand down her front to straighten her clothing. Her hand froze mid-action, and she looked down at her body.

Gone were her jeans, top and thick fleece, to be replaced with what she knew, without doubt, was an empire-waist dress and spencer jacket. Sagging against the wall once more, she felt as if she were losing her mind.

A noise behind Catherine made her look to see a young woman behind her. She was dressed in Regency clothing and wearing a look of concern.

"Are you ill, Mrs West?" came the concerned voice as the young woman halted and picked up a bonnet that had been lying on the ground.

"You know my name?" Catherine asked, numbly accepting the offered bonnet.

"Of course, Madam. I've served you as companion since the death of Mr West, God rest his soul," came the gentle response. "Now, I think it would be a good idea to return to our lodgings and have some tea to refresh you. You'll feel much more the thing. You do insist on going on these long walks of yours."

"I don't understand. This is wrong," Catherine said, struggling to deal with the situation, which seemed so real but couldn't possibly be.

"It's only wrong if you decide it is," came the reassuring words. "I promise you, you are in no danger. Come, let's return to Queen Square."

"Is this some sort of elaborate trick?" Catherine asked in disbelief.

"No. It isn't a trick. It's something for you to enjoy if you wish to embrace it, but there's no pressure. It's completely up to you," the woman replied. "Now, if you'd like to come with me … "

Catherine started to follow and then stopped in surprise. "What the heck?" she started lifting her skirt slightly to look at her footwear. Two metal contraptions were attached to each of her feet.

"Mrs West, please lower your skirt. It would not do to show your ankles in public!" Eliza chastised.

"What am I wearing?" Catherine asked, but had dropped her dress at the instruction.

"Pattens. They protect your footwear on the streets. Nothing to be alarmed about," Eliza responded.

"Easy for you to say!" Catherine muttered.

Catherine followed meekly. She probably should have retraced her steps, but after arguing with herself that something was seriously wrong and she was out of her mind to be trailing a stranger blindly, curiosity overcame fear. Walking slightly behind the young lady, who seemed to be confident in this strange situation, Catherine tried to take in as much of her surroundings as she could.

The noise was unbelievable: carriage wheels on cobblestones; the sound of metal pattens on the feet of young women as they walked along the pavements avoiding dirt and puddles; voices of draymen, carriage owners, and sellers. All added to the noise, creating a cacophony of sound.

The walk to number 13 Queen Square was short, but Catherine felt as if her head were going to explode by the time she reached it. She faltered at the threshold.

"What year is this?" she asked her companion quietly.

"The year of our Lord eighteen hundred and eleven, Mrs West. Miss Austen is not in residence."

"How did you know that's what I wanted to know?" Catherine gasped. She had only just visited the Jane Austen centre, so the addresses Jane had stayed in when visiting Bath had stuck in her mind. Jane had stayed in this house in 1799 when she had stayed in the city with her brother.

"I'm your fairy Godmother, otherwise going by the name of Eliza. I know everything I need to know to make your stay pleasant, although even I could not arrange a visit with Miss Austen."

"Time travel and a fairy Godmother? This is stretching the imagination a little too far! This must be some sort of staged joke, or the strain of the last year has become too much," Catherine said, still expecting to wake up in a crumpled heap on John Street.

"Nothing is impossible," Eliza responded with a smile. "Now, come. We have tea to enjoy."

She led the way into the house. It was quieter than outside, but a rumble of sound could still be heard. Eliza started up the stairs after giving instructions to a maid. "Your rooms are on the first floor. I'll settle you in and you can enjoy some refreshments."

In a daze, Catherine followed Eliza into the two large rooms that filled the first floor of the building. Eliza helped her out of her spencer and bonnet while Catherine took in the space that was apparently hers.

The room facing the front was the drawing room with large windows overlooking Queen Square and the obelisk in the centre of the quadrangle. Catherine looked outside for some moments, trying to make sense of the amount of people and vehicles bustling about.

The buildings surrounding the square were as she knew them, but it felt different somehow. Perhaps it was because the buildings were a different colour not the brightly-cared-for cream of Bath stone, instead being more blackened than the buildings she had passed that morning. Maybe it was the lack of cars; Queen Square always maintained a constant stream of traffic whenever Catherine had visited previously. She had no idea how she knew, but she *knew* she was no longer in her own century, and that thought terrified her. If she hadn't been convinced by the absence of cars, the dirt on the streets would have persuaded her something was amiss. The large number of horses meant there was an excessive amount of manure on the roads. It was being removed by a man with a cart, but it was inevitable that some carriages rode through the muck and spread it further. A build-up of darkened debris on the road made it unappealing to consider crossing. No wonder ladies didn't go outside without pattens on their shoes.

"Here we are," Eliza said, pouring water into the brass kettle that was resting on a brass stand. There was a small, squat taper under the stand, which she now lit. She placed the kettle on the stand above the now bright flame, stepping away from the table it was placed on. She moved to the locked piece of furniture which was a mixture of shelving and a lower cupboard that perfectly fitted into the alcove at the side of the fireplace. Taking a key, which was attached to a chatelaine, she unlocked the cupboard door and took out a wooden tea caddy. She put two heaped teaspoons of loose tea into the waiting teapot before locking the caddy away once more.

Hearing a knock on the door, Eliza answered it and accepted a tray of pastries and Bath buns. "I thought some sustenance was in order," she said pleasantly before arranging the tray to her satisfaction on a sideboard.

Catherine remained near the window, soaking up the room. It was as if she'd stepped into a National Trust property and been allowed to walk beyond the ropes. Unsurprisingly, everything was of the Regency style or older. The chaise longue and chairs were covered in a rich blue material. There were no curtains on the windows, but wooden shutters were opened fully to allow light into the room.

A rug covered the wooden floorboards in front of the fire, which was crackling pleasantly in the grate. Two vases topped the fireplace, a marble structure with a pattern of twisted vines along the mantle front. The room was uncluttered and elegant.

Catherine walked to double doors that separated the front room from its rear and opened one slowly, not sure what she was going to find.

A large bed was the focus of the room with a smaller truckle bed in the far corner. A screen filled the opposite corner; Catherine presumed it held the washing bowl and stand. A chest of drawers, dressing table, large cupboard and two conveniently placed chairs completed the picture.

Catherine turned to Eliza. "I need answers. This is too much."

"Is it not enough just to enjoy your stay here?" Eliza asked.

"No. I'm a long way from my children. I need to return to them."

"You can, whenever you wish," Eliza reassured her.

"How?"

"Did you not say recently you believed in magic?" Eliza asked.

Catherine frowned. "That was a private conversation with my son. How do you know about that?"

"I'm your fairy Godmother. I'm here to give you what you desire most."

"And what is that exactly?" Catherine asked.

"An escape to a time you yearn for, a time when you can enjoy yourself without the responsibilities and worries your present contains."

73

"And how is all this afforded?" Catherine asked, not quite believing what she was hearing but needing to know the practicalities.

"You have a reticule. In that reticule, every day there will be five pounds whether you've spent one penny or four pounds the previous day," Eliza explained patiently.

"And if I empty it out every day?" Catherine asked.

"The funds you take out will still exist."

"Five pounds per day is a lot of money," Catherine had read enough to know that genteel people survived on five hundred pounds a year. At five pounds per day she would have nearly four thousand pounds at her disposal per annum. She shook herself. Was she really considering staying in Regency England for a year? She must have had a bump to the head; it was the only plausible explanation.

"You are here to enjoy. Your reticule gives you the means to do that. Let's have some tea. The kettle is boiling."

"I can't believe I'm listening to you as if this is real!" Catherine said, shaking her head.

Eliza busied herself once more, and soon, her quietly confident movements soothed Catherine.

Catherine accepted the offered tea and edibles. "I shouldn't really be eating these, but I suppose it's been over two hundred years since I ate last!" she smiled. Biting into the buttery pastries she moaned with pleasure. "This tastes good!"

Eliza smiled in return. "You can leave any time you want, but I must tell you a few things. You can only leave the way you came. And while you are here, time will travel twice as slowly as in your time and —"

"You mean I can be here for two days and only be missing one at home?" Catherine interrupted.

"Yes, but this portal, or however you want to refer to it, is only open while the Christmas Market is on," Eliza said.

"Really? And then what happens?" Catherine asked.

"Nothing. The opening disappears," Eliza continued.

Catherine paused. "I'm not sure I want to take the risk and remain here. What if it closes early?"

"It won't. It closes at 5 p.m. on the last day of the Christmas market, exactly when the market closes," Eliza said. "Would you like to visit the Pump Room? Everyone will be gathering, and we've had a visit from the Master of Ceremonies, so your name is in the visiting book."

Catherine was tempted, so very tempted, but before anything else she had to ask a question. "I ... er ... need to, hmm, use the facilities." Her face flushed.

"Of course. You will find the pot in the large bottom drawer in the bedchamber," Eliza said, tidying away the cups and plates. "I'll go to the kitchen and wash these so you will have a little privacy."

"Thank you," Catherine said. The thought of using a chamber pot filled her with horror, but she needed to use something. During the morning she had probably consumed a gallon of tea.

Once Eliza left the room, Catherine opened the drawer and took the pot behind the screen; there was no way she was going to sit on it in the middle of the room. She took off the lid that fitted snugly on top of the pot and was relieved to find some dry cloths inside; that answered her unspoken question.

Catherine quickly found out that so many layers of Regency clothing were not easy to cope with while also manoeuvring over a chamber pot. She suddenly began to appreciate having open drawers, something that had been quite a shock to find when she had first lifted her skirts.

Once finished, she replaced the lid and thought she would be unable to face Eliza if it were her responsibility to empty the pot, but Catherine realised it would be wrong for her to try and sort it out. She righted her clothing and washed her hands.

Moving to the dressing table, she sat on the small stool, which made it easier to look at her reflection in the mirror. Twisting her head this way and that, Catherine wondered how anyone ever knew what they truly looked like. The glass gave an uneven reflection. It wasn't long before Catherine smiled; at least it hid any sign of wrinkles.

Eliza re-entered the room and approached Catherine. "Would you like to visit the Pump Room?"

Catherine sighed. "I'm probably going to regret this until my dying day, but, no. I want to return to John Street. I'll be able to relax only once I know I'm back where I should be."

Eliza frowned. "That's a real shame, but of course you can return. Come, I'll get your spencer and bonnet, and we can be on our way."

Eliza helped Catherine into her outdoor clothes, and the ladies left the premises. The throng of people made Bath seem as busy as it was in modern times. The difference was, there were no tourists stopping every few seconds to take photographs or selfies. Instead all ranks of people filled the streets from those who were obviously from the more genteel society to vendors loudly selling their wares.

Although she tried not to be affected by the sights, Catherine could not pretend to be unmoved. A love of history made her want to stop and stare; only the strangeness of the situation made her wish to hurry back to normality.

She looked behind her a number of times during the short walk to John Street. After the fourth time, Eliza looked at her.

"What's troubling you?" Eliza asked.

"I'm sure I'm being paranoid because all of this is surreal, but I feel as if we are being watched," Catherine said.

"I doubt it. It's probably just the strangeness of the situation," Eliza reassured. "Here we are." They paused at the bottom of the street. "Are you sure you want to return?"

"Yes. I'm too far away from my children," Catherine said with conviction.

"They are in a different country," Eliza pointed out.

"I'm not comfortable with you knowing so much about me," Catherine said. "But, yes, they are in a different country. But at least I can communicate with them if we're in the same century. I'm sure I want to return."

"You will be able to visit until the end of the Christmas Market. Remember that," Eliza reiterated. "I'll bid you good-day."

"I'm sorry about leaving the chamber pot," Catherine said, embarrassed.

"It is no problem. The maid will have sorted it out. It is a function of the body, nothing to be ashamed about," Eliza said easily.

Catherine watched Eliza turn away from her and return to Queen Square.

Catherine took one last look around before heading back along John Street. She took only a few steps before she staggered and reached out for the support of the wall as everything turned blindingly white, and the dead nothingness returned.

After a few moments of discomfort, Catherine was able to focus on the sounds of car engines and even heard a gaggle of American voices. She opened her eyes to see the same scene she had left in what appeared to be only moments before.

Picking up her bags, which had remained untouched on the ground where they had been dropped, she walked back into the city slightly dazed.

Chapter 6

Entering the breakfast room, Catherine smiled at Chris who was already seated. "Good morning!" she said cheerfully. It had taken her a long time to fall asleep, and when she had, she'd dreamt of carriages and long dresses, but this morning she was determined to put whatever madness she had experienced to one side and enjoy her day.

"Good morning, Catherine. Did you have a good day yesterday?" Chris asked, indicating she should join him.

"It wasn't the day I was expecting," Catherine answered honestly.

"That's Bath for you, always full of surprises," Chris answered with a grin. "What have you planned today?"

"I explored the bookshops yesterday. I'm concentrating on targeting the markets," Catherine responded. "How about you?"

"I think I'm going to spend some time in the Pump Room. It's a great place to people watch," Chris said, tucking into his bacon and eggs with relish as he'd done the previous day.

Catherine was struck again at how confident he appeared. Sometimes, even at her age, she felt she had retained the uncertainty of her teenage years, especially in anything to do with Paul. He'd certainly hammered at her confidence.

"We always had afternoon tea there." Catherine confessed one of the traditions she had shared with her mother.

"If you'd like to join me …" Chris offered.

"Thank you, but no," Catherine said quickly. "I'm taking one step at a time, but I think for the moment I'm not ready to face the Pump Room quite yet."

"Of course. I should've been more considerate. If you were to change your mind, I'd happily accompany you. The unknown can sometimes seem scarier than it is in reality," Chris said with sympathy.

"Thanks. You're right. And I'll do it. Just not quite yet."

"How are you coping with the visit?" Chris asked gently. "It's different being in a place alone isn't it?"

"It's fine," Catherine assured him, although yesterday she hadn't really been alone; Eliza had been with her. "And I skyped the kids last night. They're having a brilliant time, which frees me up to enjoy myself."

And go to the Pump Room, came the unbidden thought.

Catherine wasn't sure if she meant with Chris or Eliza, and didn't wish to dwell on either scenario.

"Good plan. With the markets being here only for a little while, I try and pack in as much as I can, and saying that, I'm going to desert you now. Hope you have a good day," Chris said, standing just as Catherine's breakfast arrived.

Catherine felt a sense of disappointment that Chris had seemed in a hurry to go. She hoped he hadn't been offended by her refusal to join him in the Pump Room, but she wasn't quite ready to face afternoon tea there.

*

Walking through the market stalls Catherine was distracted. She'd made a few purchases, but her heart hadn't really been in shopping. She'd passed the Pump Room once to see if she could spot Chris, but there'd been no sign of him.

Unable to stop herself, she walked to Queen Square and stood outside the building she had been in yesterday. There was a plaque to the left of the doorway stating that it housed solicitor's businesses.

Unsurprisingly, there was no outward sign of what she had experienced when she'd walked over the threshold.

Catherine walked away from the corner of the street wondering what she had expected to see. Eliza peeking out a window? The only thing that made her smile was that the wooden shutters looked to be still in working order. It pleased her that the building had not changed or been modernised too much on the inside.

"I must be going mad," Catherine muttered to herself, but as she approached the opposite corner of Queen Street, she turned away from Quiet Street and headed up the hill towards Gay Street.

She wasn't going to go down John Street. She argued with herself until she reached the corner of Old King Street and looked towards John Street. The man with the sign was there as he had been the day before.

Catherine set her shoulders and walked over to him. "Hello," she started.

"Hello," came the wary response.

"Did you see what happened yesterday?" Catherine asked. There was no point beating about the bush.

"I didn't see anything."

"Oh, come on! You must have. You beckoned me over!"

"Only because I want paying, Mrs. The more people I get walking to the shops the better."

Catherine didn't quite believe what she was being told. He'd definitely encouraged her, but she also didn't want to appear to be bullying him. "Did you not see me stumble?"

"No. Sorry, Mrs. I didn't see anything."

Catherine turned away from the man but then paused. He looked a little alarmed, as if he expected her to carry on questioning him, but she had no intention of that. She turned back towards the top of John Street.

The Pump Room.

In 1811.

She started to walk.

*

Eliza stepped nimbly down the steps of Hall and Woodhouse. "Well done, Eric. You were very convincing."

"She was scary. I don't envy her kids," Eric said with feeling.

"It's our job to support our people. She's been through a lot and isn't quite ready to receive her good fortune. It's my job to steer her a little and yours to support me."

"I'm sure I'm only here to get a tick in the box," Eric grumbled.

"Whatever do you mean?" Eliza responded, already following Catherine.

"The powers that be get a tick in the box because they've got a male fairy godmother. I'm nothing more than a statistic!" Eric said loudly at Eliza's retreating form.

Eliza turned around slightly. "You're a fairy godmother-in-training. Let's not get carried away just yet," she responded with a smile before continuing.

Eric mee-mawed at Eliza's back. "As if I'm going to get experience doing this lark, standing holding a sign, not allowed to talk," he muttered, before seeming to disappear into the fabric of the wall he was standing near.

A passer-by blinked twice as if trying to focus, but then he shrugged and carried on walking. For a moment, his sight had gone fuzzy, but when it had come back into focus, all he could see was a blank wall. He had no idea why the wall had caught his attention in the first place; there was nothing special about it. Going on his way, he would never recollect what he'd seen: Eric disappearing into thin air.

Chapter 7

Catherine stumbled against the wall as she had the previous time she'd experienced the disorientation. Blinking to clear her vision, she ran her hands down her dress.

"Please enjoy yourself," Andrew had insisted last night when they had spoken over the intermittent Skype connection.

"I don't want to be an overprotective parent, but I like being in touch," Catherine had said with a laugh. It had felt ridiculously good to talk to Andrew and Megan.

"And your children will be happier knowing you're having a good time and not worrying about us the whole of your holiday. Go out and enjoy yourself, Mum. We're fine, honestly," Andrew had assured her.

Had she been just seeking a way to remove her guilt? She wondered as she took in her bearings once more. Andrew had indirectly given her permission to go and indulge herself. Her concern of becoming cut-off from them had proved false. She had been reassured that she could return to the present.

There was still a small part of her that didn't believe what her eyes were seeing, but the larger part of her wanted it to be true, wanted the opportunity to explore Regency Bath.

She heard footsteps behind her and wasn't surprised when she saw Eliza approach her. "Good morning, Mrs West," Eliza said pleasantly.

"You promise I can return at any time?" Catherine asked, needing further confirmation.

"Yes. While the Christmas Market is on, you can come and go as you please," Eliza said with a smile. "In the meantime, shall we go to the Pump Room?"

Catherine grinned. "Yes. Let's."

*

She should have tried to blend in, but she couldn't. She was walking around in full regency dress in 1811 for goodness sake! Who wouldn't be staring in awe at their surroundings?

She knew that by this point in history, Bath was not the popular place it had been, but to her untrained eye it was far busier than she had expected. Clouds of smoke billowed from the numerous chimneys on the rooftops. She half expected to see Dick Van Dyke running across the ridge tiles with his sweep's brush over his shoulder, singing his heart out about Mary Poppins even though that story was from a different time in history. She wouldn't have been surprised at anything anymore.

The pair soon turned into the Square in front of the Pump Room, and Catherine hesitated.

"Are you well?" Eliza asked.

"Yes. It's just a little overwhelming," Catherine admitted. The view was the same that she had looked upon a hundred times, and yet it was so different.

The main noticeable change was that there were carriages passing in front of the Pump Room, there being no pedestrian square as there was in the future. The large entrance to the Roman Baths Museum was also missing; instead a library, shop and inn filled the area.

She could see the White Hart Inn which no longer existed in its original form, in the building being used for shops. People were arriving and leaving the building. Horses and a carriage stood near the entrance.

She stepped out of the way of a Sedan Chair which entered the Pump Room without depositing its occupant outside the building.

"They really took people inside?" Catherine asked.

"Yes. The invalids or the lazy," Eliza responded. "It's not a very comfortable ride."

"Oh, I have to try it!" Catherine said with a laugh.

"Come. Let us make some new acquaintances," Eliza said, relieved that Catherine actually seemed to be relaxing into the experience.

They entered the Pump Room, and again Catherine was struck with the differences. No tables filled the large area; instead people milled around. There was not a steady stream of society walking in a circle as she had imagined when reading her regency stories. It was a more disorganised promenade around the room as friends moved to speak to others with whom they were acquainted.

Eliza left Catherine at the side of the room but soon returned with the Master of Ceremonies.

"Good day, Mrs West. I'm pleased to make your acquaintance. Miss Cuthbert has informed me you don't have any acquaintances in Bath at the moment," the Master of Ceremonies said.

"Not that I'm aware of. Since the death of my husband, life has been very quiet," Catherine said, enjoying the formality of being bowed to. She dreaded the thought of needing to curtsey to others, knowing she would be stiff and awkward, but she hoped her lack of experience wouldn't be noticed. As for killing off Paul, it gave her a small feeling of satisfaction. She was not violent, nor wished harm to anyone, but she excused her words by knowing divorce was not an option in Regency times unless in very special circumstances. In any case, divorce would have rained scandal on her head and made it impossible for her to enter Society.

"Understandably so," came the sympathetic response. "There are two ladies I would like to introduce to you, if I may?"

"Y-yes, of course," Catherine faltered. Meeting people was a little nerve-racking. The chance of her making a mistake in this society was high; she wasn't enough of an expert on the time to be comfortable at interacting with anyone.

She was taken to the two ladies who were seated, both trying to drink the waters and pulling comical faces every time they took a sip.

"Mrs Edwards, Mrs Hayes, please allow me to introduce Mrs West to you. She is recently come to Bath and is in similar position to yourselves. I thought you were the ideal candidates to welcome her to the area," the Master of Ceremonies said.

The ladies stood, seeming relieved to be able to hand their drinking cups to a waiting footman.

Pleasantries were exchanged and questions asked. Catherine felt a little uncomfortable but decided to stick as close to the truth as she could, hoping that would prevent too many mistakes.

"I've never been to Lancashire," Mrs Edwards said. "I was born near Sidmouth and have only travelled here because of my good friend, Mrs Hayes. She wanted company."

"My doctor is concerned about my malady since my husband died. He prescribed a month of the waters," Mrs Hayes explained.

"And how are you finding Bath?" Catherine asked.

"It's overcrowded with widows and invalids, so we fit in perfectly!" Mrs Hayes responded with a laugh.

"It seems I have come to the right place," Catherine smiled. The two women appeared older than she. She was curious about their backgrounds but didn't want to pry too early in the acquaintance. She didn't want to make any social errors.

The ladies chatted, easily accepting Catherine and Eliza into their group. "How long is it since your husband passed?" Mrs Edwards asked. She was the prettier of the two, her intelligence shining through clear green eyes. She wore the cotton cap under her bonnet which all older ladies did, something that Catherine realised she should start wearing. It wasn't an attractive prospect; she wanted to pretend she was a young lady not a middle-aged one who was passed her best.

"Almost two years," Catherine answered, almost doubling the length of time she had been separated.

"Two years, and you are just now returning to society!" Mrs Hayes declared. "Have you been well provided for that you are not keen to find another husband?"

"Muriel!" Mrs Edwards chastised. "Mrs West does not need to explain her circumstances to us!"

"I beg your pardon," Mrs Hayes responded, a slight blush tinging her cheeks. Her curls were grey, and her clothing not quite as fine as Mrs Edwards'. Her words were perhaps uttered because of the constraints of her own situation.

"It's fine. I don't mind," Catherine assured both women. "I have been provided for." In this life, she mused silently. I've no idea how we'll manage when Andrew goes to university even with student loans, but she was determined to think of something to give her children the life they deserved.

"You're lucky. Mr Hayes was a little too fond of card games for there to be many funds left over after he passed."

"I'm sorry about that. How long is it since your husband died?" Catherine asked, glad to be given the opportunity to ask.

"Nine months. I've come out of mourning early as Mrs Edwards kindly accompanied me to Bath. At one and thirty I can't waste any time in finding another husband," Mrs Hayes said. "I know the truth is that most men see us as completely in our dotage by the time we reach thirty. I'm still hoping to find someone who will consider me eligible."

Mrs. Hayes was thirty-one, Catherine swallowed. Nine years younger than herself, and yet she looked and acted years older. It was a good thing Catherine was not here to find a new husband. At forty she would be seen as quite elderly.

"You'll find someone. You are a good person, Muriel," Mrs Edwards said soothingly.

Mrs Hayes smiled at her friend. "As you are a whole two years younger than me, it's easy for you to say," she said with a sad smile. "I know I'm beyond being considered a good age to bear children, and with no fortune, there is little to recommend myself."

Mrs Edwards tsked, but Catherine was aware it was probably the only response the friend could make. Mrs Hayes didn't have much to recommend her in the Regency way of looking at things. She didn't think it was appropriate to suggest that women still had children into their forties. With poor conditions and equally poor medical expertise, it was perhaps for the best if Mrs Hayes didn't have children.

Catherine looked around the room. She had the same feeling of being watched as she had the previous day, but when she turned, there was no one who seemed to be finding her of any interest. Not surprising really, she mused. She'd read somewhere that the women outnumbered the men in Bath something like four to one. She ached a little for Mrs Hayes. With those odds, no fortune and older, her chances of attracting a husband were slim at best.

"Are you ladies attending the Assembly Rooms tonight?" Eliza asked.

"Oh yes, we wouldn't miss any of the entertainments on offer," Mrs Edwards said quickly. "Shall you be there?"

Eliza looked at Catherine in question; it was her decision.

"Yes, we shall," Catherine responded with a smile that betrayed a little of the excitement she was feeling.

"Excellent! We shall see you there!" Mrs Edwards responded. "I think it's time for our constitutional," she said to Mrs Hayes.

"Oh, dear! The hills around Bath are excessively steep," Mrs Hayes said pitifully.

"We need to build our strength if we are to spend the night dancing," Mrs Edwards responded briskly.

"More likely we'll be joining the chaperones," Mrs Hayes replied darkly.

Catherine smiled as she said her goodbye. When the ladies had moved out of earshot, she turned to Eliza. "Which Assembly Rooms is it? Upper or Lower?"

"Lower," Eliza responded.

"Excellent! I get to visit the Lower Assembly Rooms. I wish I could say my children would be jealous, but they won't. At least I'll know how special it'll be," Catherine said with a laugh. She hadn't come to terms with what was going on, still not quite believing the whole experience, but she was going to enjoy herself nonetheless.

"Might I suggest a walk over to Sydney Gardens next?" Eliza suggested.

"Oh, yes, please!"

*

The two women walked from the Pump Room, bypassed the Abbey and went around the building and gardens that made up the Lower Assembly Rooms. Catherine was not tempted to stop only because she would be seeing the building later that evening.

They walked over Pulteney Bridge, Catherine pleased to see the tiny buildings lining the bridge thriving as they were in her present. It was a little daunting walking along the narrow pathway with carriages trundling very close by. Catherine had never been at ease near horses, especially if they were attached to large moving vehicles. Her unease increased at the closeness of the pedestrians to the animals. She followed Eliza dutifully, relieved when they crossed the bridge and the road widened once more.

As they left Argyle Street behind and started through Laura Place, Catherine faltered. The Bath stone of the buildings was dazzling in the afternoon sunshine.

"It's beautiful," she said involuntarily.

"What is?" Eliza asked in amusement.

"Bath, with its buildings. It is truly beautiful," Catherine responded.

"I'm glad you are enjoying it," Eliza said.

"These buildings are cleaner than the ones in Queen Square," Catherine commented about the dazzling stone.

"They're newer," Eliza explained. "So have had less time to be polluted by the smoke." She continued to walk down Great Pulteney Street.

"Of course," Catherine said, following in Eliza's wake. She was too busy looking around to be able to keep up with her companion. Catherine saw some of the chimneys bellowing with smoke even though the day was quite mild. Yes, Bath of 1811 was vastly different.

Catherine was delighted with the gardens. She liked to wander around them when she visited, imagining that if she ever travelled to Bath in summer, she would enjoy sitting and reading in the gardens.

Now, though, she looked on the area with fascination. Once more the place was crowded. For a place no longer fashionable, it was extremely busy. Eventually, after walking along the pathways, seeing the entrance to the labyrinth, and watching the others enjoying the outside space, Catherine agreed to take refreshments in the hotel.

She was seated at a table with Eliza, happy to watch everything going on around her when her cup clattered to its saucer. "Chris?" she asked astounded.

"Mr Dobson!" Eliza responded quickly, giving Catherine a warning look.

"Oh, yes. Mr Dobson. I didn't expect to see you here!" Catherine said, recovering from her mistake of using Chris' first name.

Chris stood stock still, looking as if he would rather be anywhere else but in front of Catherine's table. Eventually, he sighed and bowed. "Mrs West," he said. "How delightful it is to see you."

"Really?" Catherine asked, rising to curtsey. She couldn't help the disappointment in her voice, and it seemed to stir Chris.

"I beg your pardon, Mrs West. This is an odd situation, but I am indeed pleased to see you," Chris said.

"If you would like to join us, Mr Dobson, I shall arrange some more refreshments," Eliza said, standing and moving towards a member of staff.

"Very sensitively done," Chris said, before taking a seat next to Catherine. "Forgive my rudeness?" he asked quietly with a smile.

"I don't understand any of this," Catherine said raising her hands in a shrug.

"I could tell it was your first time yesterday," Chris said.

"You saw me?" Catherine asked.

"Yes, in Queen Square," Chris explained.

"I thought someone was watching us! You were in the Pump Room this morning!"

Chris smiled ruefully. "Yes. I'm sorry. I was trying to keep out of your way. I found it quite hard to come to terms with it when I first came through."

"How long have you known about this?" Catherine asked intrigued and relieved that someone else was involved. She was reassured at his presence. She

101

couldn't be hallucinating if a stranger was part of the adventure.

"A few years now," Chris admitted. "It's the real reason I come to Bath every year. I can't resist it."

"Why didn't you mention it this morning at breakfast?" Catherine asked.

"Would you have done if our roles were reversed? I wasn't sure if you'd put it down to having a bad dream or a funny turn," Chris explained. "I suppose I was afraid you'd think I was completely mad."

"Possibly at first, but now I'm just reassured that I'm not having some sort of breakdown, which is what I thought for most of yesterday," Catherine admitted. "Do you not have a person like Eliza accompanying you?"

"No. I did for the first two years, but after that, I was more than happy to make my own way," Chris responded with a smile.

"Why does it happen?"

"I've no idea. I was told at the beginning, that there was a reason I'd been picked, but it was up to me to find out what that was. I haven't looked very hard to make sense of it all. I've just been enjoying myself," Chris said with a wide smile.

"I expect you have, with being grossly outnumbered by young ladies!" Catherine said primly.

Chris laughed. "I've been the perfect gentleman, but I admit to being quite in demand in the assemblies. My footwork would certainly surprise some of my rugby team!"

Catherine smiled. "I knew you played rugby!" She coloured at the realisation she'd just revealed that she'd been pondering about him.

"I do, but now I'm perfectly happy dancing a cotillion, as you will find out if you will dance with me for the first two in tonight's assembly. I'm presuming you are staying?"

"Yes, I am. I was worried I couldn't get back, but Eliza has reassured me, and for some reason, I believe her."

"She's your fairy godmother. Of course you believe her," Chris said, as if it were the most natural thing in the world to utter.

Catherine rubbed her hands across her face. "It's still a little hard to take in."

"It's all very new. Just enjoy it," Chris said softly.

"You make it sound so simple," Catherine responded.

"It is, if you let it be," Chris answered with a smile.

Chapter 8

Catherine looked out of her window before she allowed Eliza to help her prepare for the evening. The building opposite had been made to look like a palace, although houses stood beyond the grand facade. The square in the middle was surrounded by fencing she had seen before, and the centre of the square was made up of gravel pathways, with formal, low level planting. It was completely different than the garden area that was there in the twenty first century. The obelisk somehow looked taller, but it was the same one that stood tall more than two hundred years later.

She turned away from the window; it was time to prepare for her first assembly.

Her soap was scented with jasmine, which smelled delicate and fresh. It was quite uneven to the touch, but using the abrasive cloth at the side of the water bowl, Catherine was able to create enough lather that, after washing, she felt clean and refreshed. She dried herself off with a towel. She wondered idly how she would cope in the depths of winter, as her skin was already covered in goose bumps. Thankfully, it appeared to be a mild December.

Catherine took hold of what was clearly a toothbrush. The handle was made of bone. The bristles were very stiff, and Catherine wasn't too sure about putting it into her mouth. She popped her head around the screen and indicated that Eliza should come to her.

"What is it?" Eliza asked quietly, making sure the maid, Florry couldn't overhear her.

"Is this toothbrush going to do my teeth permanent damage if I use it?" Catherine asked. "What are these bristles made from?"

Eliza smiled. "It won't damage you in the short-term," she responded. "I'm not sure what the bristles are made from, but it'll be a natural product."

"Natural. As in from an animal?" Catherine asked, paling a little.

"Yes."

"Ergh," Catherine groaned.

"What's wrong? You aren't a vegetarian," Eliza pointed out.

"Eww. I just don't fancy putting it into my mouth," Catherine said with feeling, retreating back behind the screen.

She picked up the small pot which was clearly some form of tooth powder. Putting the brush in it, she grimaced when putting the concoction into her mouth. It was the quickest teeth clean she had ever performed, and she swilled out her mouth excessively before patting her face dry.

"That was lacking any sign of a minty fresh taste," she muttered quietly to herself.

Florry moved the screen slightly to enable her access to Catherine. She was helped into a linen chemise that reached down to her knees. Then her knitted stockings were handed to her, which Catherine, although dying of embarrassment at being dressed, was grateful to be putting on something warm. The stockings were secured around her thighs by garters. Next she was handed a pair of drawers. The legs came down to the knees, no high leg briefs here. Catherine examined the open crotch with raised eyebrows; she wasn't sure she would ever get used to some regency items.

When Florry fitted Catherine into her short stays, she actually felt that she was turning into a Regency lady. It felt different actually being dressed in the clothing, item by item. When she had walked through the portal she had been fully dressed. There had not been the opportunity to examine the clothing in detail. The pull of the corset, although not as restrictive as a Victorian one, certainly lifted her posture and gave her bust a shelf-like look. Then the petticoat was fitted over, reaching down to her ankles, ending with a feminine frill. Finally, she was helped into the blue taffeta dress. It had short sleeves for evening wear.

Catherine sighed when the dressing was over. She had not taken so long, even on her wedding day, and had never had anyone to help her. Being a lady was a far more complicated process than she had imagined.

"How would you like me to do your hair this evening Mrs West?" Florry asked, indicating that Catherine should sit at the dressing table.

Catherine rolled her eyes. This getting dressed was like a marathon. "Surprise me, Florry. I shall let you decide." Catherine said, not having a clue what to suggest.

Florry smiled in the mirror and got to work, braiding Catherine's hair after brushing it. She gave Catherine a centre parting, which she had not worn since she was at school. The braid was tied into a bun and pinned on the crown of her head. Curly wisps of hair were teased out of the braid and positioned around the edge of Catherine's face.

"That's lovely, Florry. Thank you," Catherine said, turning her head from side to side.

Catherine picked up her shawl from her bed and decided that she was as ready as she was ever going to be.

*

Catherine decided she needed to walk to the Lower Assembly Rooms. She could have justified employing a Sedan Chair, but she was nervous and thought walking would relieve some of her apprehension.

Once engaged for the first two dances after their encounter with Chris, Eliza had insisted that they return to their rooms and practice dance steps. Catherine had soon come to the conclusion that learning the footwork was impossible, but learning the movement of the dances would hopefully be enough to get her through the evening.

"We really need to employ a dance master," Eliza had said with feeling after watching Catherine move woodenly around the drawing room.

"I'm British. I don't do extrovert!" Catherine insisted in defence of the criticism of her ability.

"You are a member of the twenty-first century when anything is possible!" Eliza retorted.

"Don't be fooled by the hype," Catherine muttered darkly. "We can be as restricted as a woman in this century."

"Every woman in this century can dance," Eliza said, deciding that being a fairy godmother perhaps wasn't as easy as she'd imagined.

"Have you listened to the music in my century?" Catherine asked. "It's all about dancing around handbags — when I was last on the nightclub circuit anyway — not flinging oneself half-way across the room as this type of dancing seems to require! And what's the big deal with skipping? I thought my skipping days were over until I became a grandmother!"

Eliza took a steadying breath. "Come. We need to get to a certain proficiency for tonight."

By the end of the session, Catherine wasn't sure who was the most exhausted, herself or Eliza. One thing was for sure, they were both sick of dancing.

The pair walked through the streets in silence. Catherine was already exhausted mentally and physically, and there was another five hours before the ball ended. She wasn't sure she would be able to keep awake that long.

The front of the assembly rooms was bustling. People arriving on foot, by chair or carriage meant there was a hustle and buzz about the area that lifted Catherine's spirits.

They walked into the room, and Eliza waited with a smile on her face for Catherine to process what she saw. "Do you approve?" she asked quietly.

"It's wonderful!" Catherine breathed.

The main room was filled with people dressed in all levels of finery. Catherine was beginning to realise that Bath society was a lot more mixed than she had imagined, the rich and the less wealthy seemed to mingle far more than she had anticipated.

The room itself was large and rectangular. Huge chandeliers hung from the ceiling, candlelight already flickering high above everyone's heads. Full-height windows ran down the longest sides of the rectangle, bringing in as much natural light as possible. On the wall opposite the entrance doorway, a gathering of musicians was warming up. Although the room was large, it didn't feel big enough to house the number of people who were wandering into it.

"It's going to be very busy tonight," Catherine said, feeling a little overwhelmed.

"It is," Eliza responded. "You'll come to appreciate the amount of space you enjoyed this afternoon while dancing."

They were interrupted by the arrival of Mrs Hayes and Mrs Edwards. When greetings had been exchanged they moved to the edge of the ballroom.

"I do hope I dance at some point this evening," Mrs Hayes said wistfully.

"I'm sure you will," Catherine said reassuringly. "I met an acquaintance when we walked to Sydney Gardens earlier. He expressed his desire to dance. I'm sure he'll be keen to be introduced to ladies as eager as he is."

"Excellent!" Mrs Hayes said with pleasure. "And if he's handsome, it will be a real treat!"

Catherine laughed. "Yes, he's handsome."

"I hope you're referring to myself, Mrs West," Chris said with a smile at Catherine's flush at him joining them.

"Not at all," Catherine responded quickly, but she knew the lie had not fooled Chris by the laughter in his eyes. "Mr Dobson, please allow me to introduce my friends to you."

The introductions took place, allowing Catherine to surreptitiously appreciate Chris. He was wearing a navy blue frock coat, golden waistcoat and cream breeches. His muscular frame filled his jacket, and his legs suited the revealing stockings. He really was impressive to look at.

Mrs Hayes and Mrs Edwards clearly admired Chris as he could hardly separate himself from them when the master of ceremonies called the start of the first dance.

Catherine forgot her nerves when they lined up in the dance as she laughed at Chris' scowl. "Before you take me to task, you were the one extolling your dancing expertise this afternoon!"

"I didn't expect to be dancing the first six dances in a row though! I wanted to take you on a walk along the terraces and pathways of this building," Chris said, still grumbling.

Catherine smiled warmly. "That's kind of you, but would it be appropriate for us to be seen in such a fashion?"

"It's a place to see and be seen. I'm not the type of gentleman to try to compromise a lady. Not in this century anyway," Chris said, raising an eyebrow.

Catherine flushed. His meaning wasn't completely clear, but she had noticed from the first that his eyes seemed to look deep inside her. It was a new and strange feeling — one that, at the moment, she didn't have time to analyse. The music started, and she had to focus on keeping up with the other dancers.

There was no time to talk; full concentration was required. As the half hour progressed that the dance lasted, Catherine found herself unable to speak. The activity was lively enough, but with the concentration, the crush of the bodies and the heat of the room, she could barely function. At the end of the dance, she visibly sagged.

Chris moved towards Catherine and took her hand, threading it through his arm in an act of support. "Come. Let's miss the next dance," he said, gently leading Catherine away from the dancers.

"I'm sorry," Catherine said. "I'm obviously not as fit as I'd thought!"

"It does take some getting used to," Chris assured her. "I spend quite a few weeks on the aerobic equipment in the gym before I come here. I find it helps!"

"Now you tell me!" Catherine breathed heavily. Her cheeks were red with exertion. "I could do with a large drink!"

Chris led the way into one of the refreshment rooms. He sat Catherine down before obtaining two glasses of Negus.

"I'm sorry there's nothing more refreshing," he said, handing Catherine a glass.

"It's too much to hope for a glass of iced water, I suppose?" Catherine asked with a smile.

"I'm afraid ice would be too expensive, and the water would probably see you not leaving your bed for a week if you were to drink it. I dread to imagine the consequences of that," Chris said with a shudder.

Catherine smiled. "I suppose alcohol it is then! I do wish it was chilled though!"

They sat in companionable silence while Catherine cooled a little. There were enough coming and goings for them not to attract any attention.

"It's still very unreal," Catherine said quietly.

"I know. Just enjoy it."

"I'm half afraid to go to sleep here tonight."

"You'll still be able to go back," Chris assured her. "I don't know how or why, but it never falters."

Catherine nodded in acceptance of his words. "There's one thing that bothers me," she said.

"What's that?" Chris asked.

"If I have nearly four thousand a year, why on earth am I staying in Queen Square? Shouldn't I at least be living in Laura Place?" Catherine asked, laughing. "I'm a respectable widow, and Queen Square isn't what it used to be!"

Chris chuckled. "Perhaps you'd better raise that with your companion? I'm more than happy with staying in the White Hart."

"Do you enter and leave down the same alley as I?" Catherine asked, lowering her voice, as two gentlemen stood quite close by.

"Union Passage?" Chris asked, just as quietly.

"No, I go near Mr B's bookshop on John Street," Catherine responded. "It's strange that there are two places."

"There could be more," Chris said with a nonchalant shrug. "I'm too intent on enjoying myself to worry about it."

"As I should be," Catherine chastised herself. "Come, shall we join Mrs Edwards and Mrs Hayes again? I think they'll soon be smitten with you, if they aren't already!"

"Lead me to my fate!" Chris said, over-dramatically.

The pair left the room, and the gentlemen who had stood nearby started to speak. "Four thousand a year and a widow. Arthur, I think this visit has just become interesting," the first man said quietly.

"You were convinced there would be someone here who'd be suitable," Arthur responded to his friend.

"I think I've just found my next wife. As a widower, I understand completely how she has suffered. I think ours will be the perfect pairing."

"Are you sure she won't find out in what a sad way the last Mrs Chorlton met her end?" Arthur said warily.

"Not at all. It was an accidental death after all. Anyone can fall down the stairs in the middle of the night when not carrying a candle. Now, let's go and find the Master of Ceremonies, so he can perform the introductions. I feel like love is in the air tonight, Arthur. Or is it money I smell?"

"For your sake, I hope you find happiness and money this time," Arthur said, following his overbearing friend into the ballroom.

Chapter 9

The group was interrupted by the Master of Ceremonies. "Mrs West, Mrs Edwards, Mrs Hayes, these gentlemen would like to make your acquaintance," the Master of Ceremonies said with all the formality of his position.

The three ladies all turned towards the newcomers. "Mr Chorlton, Mr Parker, please allow me to introduce the ladies to you."

Each dropped a curtsey as she was introduced.

"This is Miss Cuthburt, Mrs West's companion, and Mr Dobson, an annual visitor to Bath," the Master of Ceremonies continued. With the introductions completed, he left the group to help someone else expand their acquaintances.

"Mrs West, if you aren't currently engaged, please would you do the honour of dancing the next two with me?" Mr Chorlton asked.

"I'm not, but I'm not a very good dancer," Catherine admitted. Faltering with Chris as a partner had been fine; a stranger potentially caused more difficulties.

"I'm sure you're all modesty," Mr Chorlton said with a smile.

"I'm sure she's not," Chris muttered, half to himself.

"I apologised to your toes!" Catherine said with a laugh. "I've not danced for so long that I'm very out of practice."

"That's what comes of two years mourning, my dear," Mrs Edwards said sympathetically.

"If you are not engaged, I'd be delighted to dance with you," Mr Parker asked Mrs Edwards.

"I'm not," Mrs Edwards said with a smile. "How lovely! With Mr Dobson dancing with Mrs Hayes, Mrs West with Mr Chorlton, we'll all be entertained. Oh! Apart from you, Miss Cuthbert!" Mrs Edwards said, embarrassed that she'd overlooked the companion so easily.

"I don't mind at all," Eliza responded with an easy smile. "I'm not inclined to dance. I take much more enjoyment in watching the dancers."

The three pairs moved to the dance floor as a group and were only split-up at the contrivance of Mr Chorlton.

Catherine felt as if the heat had increased substantially in the half-hour she hadn't been dancing. She took a deep breath but managed to smile at Mr Chorlton. She was sure he was younger than she. He had quite a slender figure but a pleasing face. He perhaps was not as handsome or as tall as Chris, but he suited the clothing he wore and carried himself in a dignified way.

The dance started, and it was some time before Mr Chorlton spoke. "I can see you weren't uttering false truths when you expressed your lack of dance practice," he said as they stood at the bottom of the set.

"Oh! Have I stepped on your toes? I'm so sorry! My husband didn't care for me to dance," Catherine decided to utter a little falsehood.

Mr Chorlton smiled. "No! Not at all. You just seem to be concentrating fully on the steps."

"I can see everyone chattering as they move, and I really don't know how they do it!" Catherine admitted.

"You will soon become accustomed once more," Mr Chorlton replied. "Your husband didn't enjoy entertainments then?"

"Not really," Catherine admitted. "We had quite a limited social life." She wasn't telling lies. Paul had hated most of the things she'd enjoyed, so they'd very rarely socialised together once the children had arrived.

"I'm a widower, so I understand what you've been through," Mr Chorlton said, his brow creasing.

"I'm sorry to hear that," Catherine said with feeling. "Have you any children?"

"Yes, four. They are all small, so they stay with my mother."

"The poor things, to be motherless so young," Catherine said with feeling. She wasn't able to continue the conversation as they re-joined the set, and she had to concentrate on her steps once more.

At the end of the first dance, Catherine used her fan vigorously. "My goodness, the heat is excessive!" she said with feeling. She refrained from mentioning the strong odour in the room, which wasn't very pleasant and would probably only increase as the evening wore on.

"Would you care to take a walk on the terraces and the pathways?" Mr Chorlton asked.

Catherine would have liked for Chris to show her the area, if she was honest, but he was engaged to dance for the next couple of hours. She could insist to Mr Chorlton that they take part in their next dance but the heat was oppressive. She had no idea how the gentlemen were coping with their frock coats on. She was suffering in a short-sleeved dress.

"That would be lovely, thank you," she responded after a short hesitation.

She was led through a door at the rear of the room and joined a throng of people milling about the area in varying sized groups.

Mr Chorlton offered Catherine his arm, and they walked slowly along the pathways. "How long will you be enjoying the pleasure of Bath?" he asked as they walked.

"I'm not sure. Possibly the next two weeks," Catherine said, multiplying the remaining days of the Christmas market by two.

"So soon? That's disappointing!" Mr Chorlton said with feeling.

"I'm sure there are other ladies who can dance as poorly as I," Catherine said with a smile.

"I think I would have to search far and wide before finding someone as perfect as you," Mr Chorlton said seriously.

"I doubt that very much," Catherine responded with derision.

"A charming companion, and a beauty at that! I'm almost overawed by your charms, Mrs West. What more could a gentleman ask for in a new acquaintance?" Mr Chorlton asked with feeling.

"Please, Mr Chorlton!" Catherine said, immediately pulling her arm from his. "Your flattery is unrealistic! We have only just met!"

"Forgive me," Mr Chorlton said quickly. "It is too soon since your loss."

"It isn't that," Catherine admitted truthfully. "Half an hour's acquaintance is a little too soon for any form of flattery, never mind such strong words. I assure you, I'm not so unique!"

Mr Chorlton smiled. "And your words are said in an effort to dissuade me? Mrs West, your modesty does you credit, I will cease in my flummery. Perhaps if I complain bitterly about your dancing ability, you will feel more comfortable?"

"Maybe, but don't be too bitter," Catherine said with a smile. His words made her feel distinctly uncomfortable, but she reminded herself that this wasn't real and felt easier about it.

Mr Chorlton smiled. "I have a box at the theatre tomorrow. Would your party like to join me there? I'm longing to watch *The Rivals* whilst in Bath."

"Oh! I saw it last year! It would be wonderful to see it in the place where it is set," Catherine exclaimed in delight.

Mr Chorlton frowned in confusion. "But I thought you said you hadn't come out of mourning until recently?"

"I hadn't. I meant the last year of my husband's life. Forgive my foolish way of speaking," Catherine responded, recovering quickly. Megan and Andrew had given her tickets for the play for her birthday, and Susan had accompanied her to Manchester to watch it.

"There is nothing to forgive," Mr Chorlton said with a smile. "We all have ways of coping with our loss. I find I struggle with my children. They miss their mother, and when I gaze upon their tiny faces, I'm reminded of what we've all lost."

"You poor things," Catherine said, reaching out her hand to squeeze Mr Chorlton's arm in sympathy. "I can only imagine how you all must be suffering."

"Thank you for your sympathy. I appreciate your words. It isn't easy, and when one is a man, it isn't the done thing to admit one feels a failure to his children."

"I'm sure they wouldn't agree with your sentiments," Catherine said with feeling. "You are trying to do the best by them."

"I am," Mr Chorlton said.

His eyes were a little brightened with moisture, and Catherine smiled sadly at him. She could not help but be moved by his words.

"How old are they?"

"Five, four, three and two," Mr Chorlton.

"They are babies!" Catherine said with surprise.

"They are, and they won't remember their Mama. It's a great sadness, but we are not unusual in our loss, so I can't claim any more disadvantage than others in the same situation. To you, I admit it is hard to bear sometimes, and it would be nice to be able to share my load with someone who understood." Mr Chorlton turned them so they were returning to the assembly. "Come, I have kept you from your party. Help me forget my woes, Mrs West, join me at the theatre tomorrow."

"Are all the ladies invited?" Catherine wasn't sure about the etiquette and needed to confirm before she returned to her group and made a blunder.

"Of course! We shall be a jolly party!" Mr Chorlton said easily.

The group were eager to form a party to attend the theatre. Only Chris hung back a little in his enthusiasm. Catherine failed to notice his reticence, but she did notice Mrs Hayes looking in alarm at Mrs Edwards.

Catherine waited until it was appropriate and spoke to Mrs Hayes when they would not be overheard. "Does the trip to the theatre cause you any difficulty, Mrs Hayes?" she asked gently.

Mrs Hayes flushed. "No! Well, that is, not really, not while Mr Chorlton is providing the box and interval refreshments," she said quietly.

"What is it then? I'd like to help if I can," Catherine coaxed.

Mrs Hayes sighed. "You wouldn't understand, having a fortune of your own."

Catherine spoke quietly, but there was deep meaning to her words. "I understand a lack of money completely. I know what it is like to struggle. I really do."

"It's embarrassing," Mrs Hayes said, not meeting Catherine's gaze.

"If it is causing you such concern, we are not yet close enough friends. True friends can be honest without shame," Catherine said with a smile. She began to suspect she knew what was amiss with her new friend. "I have the perfect plan for tomorrow. I have some money that is burning a hole in my reticule for want of spending. We need to go shopping together!"

"I don't think shopping is a good idea," Mrs Hayes responded, looking uncomfortable enough to make Catherine convinced she had guessed correctly; Mrs Hayes did not have the funds to dress herself appropriately for many entertainments.

"You misunderstand me, Mrs Hayes. I want to treat you to a shopping expedition," Catherine explained quietly.

"I don't want charity," Mrs Hayes said primly.

"And when you marry a rich man, I expect to be taken to the finest of entertainments at your expense!" Catherine said. "Until then, while I have good fortune, let's both enjoy it!"

"You really don't need to," Mrs Hayes said, looking a little overwhelmed.

"You have welcomed me without restraint and made my stay here far more pleasurable than I was expecting it to be. Let me share my good fortune with you," Catherine said quietly.

"Thank you," Mrs Hayes said in a whisper.

*

Later that evening as most of the revellers walked or were transported through the streets of Bath, Mr Chorlton and Mr Parker stood in the recess of a door, sharing a cigarillo.

"So, how did the wooing of the wealthy widow progress? You were outside some time," Arthur asked.

"She isn't going to be the pushover I hoped," Mr Chorlton admitted. "She didn't respond well to flattery, but she did respond to the stories of my poor motherless children."

"So that's the way to her heart is it?" Arthur asked. He was a little daunted by his friend but found it best to agree with his schemes. It was less painful that way.

"It's the route to her money. I couldn't give a fig whether her heart is involved or not," Mr Chorlton responded with derision. "I'm going to have to move quickly though, she's only staying for two weeks."

"That's not a very long time. What if you don't convince her to marry you? What will you do then?" Arthur was worried his friend was becoming very desperate in his search for funds. Two weeks to form an attachment was a tall order, even for someone as confident as Mr Chorlton.

"There's a means to achieve anything," Mr Chorlton said, quietly confident. "I need that four thousand a year she has at her disposal, and that's all there is to it."

Chapter 10

Catherine awoke and groaned. The beds in 1811 were definitely not of the modern pocket-sprung variety. She had slept, but her body felt a little worse for wear, although to be fair, it could have been the level of dancing that had occurred the previous evening. It had been better than any gym workout she had ever done and had lasted a substantial amount longer.

Eliza was already up and about. She offered Catherine a cup of hot chocolate while she was still in bed.

"This is very decadent," Catherine said, accepting the warm drink.

"It will help put you over until you break your fast. I thought a public breakfast in Sydney Gardens might be in order."

"Oh, yes!" Catherine said, immediately rising from the bed. "I wish I could have a shower," she said, looking mournfully at the porcelain washing bowl.

"I doubt you'll see any rain today," Eliza said, as Florry walked into the room, carrying fresh water.

Catherine realised she would have to be more circumspect when speaking. It was clear she was unaccustomed to how servants worked. It was quite intrusive to someone unused to being cared for in such a way. Florry busied herself with preparing Catherine's clothing while Catherine washed.

Her skin felt as if it had been thoroughly scrubbed by the time she finished. One shock of the previous evening had been the way the smells in the assembly rooms had increased as the night progressed. By the end of the evening, Catherine could hardly bear to be in the room, the odour was so pungent. Only a heavily scented handkerchief regularly applied to her nose had stopped her from pretending illness, so she could leave the room. She was fully aware that she must be contributing to that smell, and although insisting on washing before she had climbed into bed, she still felt unclean from the lack of water running over her body.

Eventually, she was dressed in a lilac day dress decorated with cream flowers. A cream spencer fitted snugly over her dress. Pulling on her gloves, she watched Eliza affix lilac flowers to the bonnet Catherine had worn the previous day.

"You mean I haven't got a bonnet for every outfit?" she asked when Florry left the room.

"I'm afraid not. Although you have got a number to choose from. I would imagine the Mrs Hayeses of this world have to do with a single bonnet," Eliza said.

"It's a shame her husband didn't leave her some money to live off," Catherine said.

"She is not unique, unfortunately, but it's a kind thing you are doing."

"If I can help her while I'm here, I'm happy to do as much as I can. I don't need the money," Catherine responded, putting the bonnet on her head. A flicker of unease about the lack of money fluttered in her chest as she remembered her own predicament, but she pushed it down. That worry was for another day; today was for helping Mrs Hayes. After a large breakfast in Sydney Gardens, of course.

*

Catherine and Eliza walked to the bottom of Milsom Street to meet Mrs Hayes and Mrs Edwards. Catherine had suggested she walk to their accommodation, but Mrs Hayes had been quick to dissuade her.

"She must be living in an area she's ashamed of," Catherine surmised to Eliza.

"Probably," Eliza responded.

"Well, with my ten pounds collected over two days, I'm hoping she will have some souvenirs that will be practical for her," Catherine said. She had taken out her unused five pounds last night as soon as they had returned to Queen Square, and as Eliza had predicted, there was a replacement in her reticule as soon as she opened it.

"I have the funds you need for the practical side of living in Bath," Eliza said quietly.

"That feels excessive," Catherine said. "I already have more money than I could possibly want," she reasoned fairly.

Eliza smiled. "It's only for a short time. It's important that it's perfect for you."

Mrs Edwards and Mrs Hayes were already waiting for the ladies to join them. They shared their good mornings before Catherine tactfully directed the shopping.

Two hours later the ladies entered the premises of Sally Lunn's, laughing and ready to eat their fill of Bath buns to fortify themselves after a serious bout of spending.

"Your generosity knows no bounds!" Mrs Hayes exclaimed when Catherine directed Eliza to pay the bill.

"If I can't share my good fortune with friends, who can I share it with?" Catherine said with a smile. "I'm happy to have enjoyed a good day with you both, and we have the theatre to look forward to tonight."

"Yes. And I shall be wearing my new shawl and gloves. And what excitement to know I have three new dresses to plan!" They had bought the material, but Mrs Hayes had insisted on making the dresses herself, she would not let Catherine spend the money on hiring a modiste to complete the task.

"Mr Chorlton seems drawn to you, my dear," Mrs Edwards said to Catherine.

"He's very charming," Catherine admitted. "But I'm not looking for a replacement husband." She pushed away the inner image of Chris that emerged; she could not think of anyone as husband. She didn't dare risk her heart getting hurt again. It still felt battered.

"Every woman needs a husband. How else can we be secure?" Mrs Hayes said with feeling. "I, for one, wish to be able to sleep soundly at night instead of worrying about the cost of everything and anything!"

Catherine reached over and squeezed Mrs Hayes' hand. "I'm not being flippant, truly. I just can't see me becoming attached to someone else."

"Who needs to be in love?" Mrs Edwards asked. "A good character, a reasonable income, anything beyond that is a blessing."

"Of course it is," Catherine muttered, but her smile was false. Such a life would be, in some ways, as restrictive in her own time. She was not so different than Mrs Hayes with her struggles while she supported Andrew's university life, but Catherine could never see a time when she would accept a proposal without love being involved.

The ladies separated after having their fill of the local delicacy, each wanting to prepare for the theatre. As Catherine settled on the chaise longue in her room, she pondered about Mrs Hayes' fate.

"Perhaps it is my goal to help her, and that's why I'm here?" she wondered aloud.

A slight frown crossed Eliza's forehead, but it soon disappeared. "You can only do so much. Mrs Hayes needs a husband."

"Perhaps I could encourage Mr Chorlton?"

"I don't think he would be interested in Mrs Hayes. Mr Dobson could be though," Eliza suggested.

"No! He's as temporary as I am. That wouldn't do," Catherine said quickly.

"Is that the only reason?" Eliza asked, watching with a smile the dark expression on Catherine's face.

Catherine glanced at Eliza. "Of course! No. We need to help Mrs Hayes in her search for her next husband."

"This is a fool's errand!" Eliza muttered to herself, but her comment was unheard.

*

Catherine was delighted that Eliza agreed to them taking a Sedan Chair to the theatre. They engaged two, and the small convoy moved through the streets at a speedy pace. Catherine held onto the leather straps inside the wooden box, laughing as she was jolted around.

She was helped out of the chair at the entrance to the theatre. Still laughing, she waved to Mrs Hayes and Edwards who were arriving on foot.

"That was the best one shilling and sixpence I've ever spent!" Catherine said. "What an adventure!"

Mrs Hayes and Mrs Edwards smiled politely, clearly not understanding why Catherine would be so enamoured of her trip. Catherine noticed their restraint and tried to curb her enthusiasm. When the ladies brightened, she turned to see who was approaching and was pleased to see Mr Dobson.

"Did you see my grand arrival?" Catherine asked with a smile as they made their greetings.

"Yes," Chris said with a secretive smile. "The first time is always the best."

"I don't know how the infirm cope with it. I was thrown about like a ragdoll," Catherine said, taking the opportunity to speak while the arrival of Mr Chorlton and Mr Parker distracted the ladies.

"Time costs money, so the quicker you are unloaded, the quicker the next customer is collected," Chris said.

"I'm glad you're joining us tonight," Catherine said quietly.

"I'm not," Chris responded. "It was made very clear that the invitation didn't extend to myself."

"Really? That isn't very polite!" Catherine said, trying to hide her disappointment. She had been looking forward to experiencing the theatre with Chris close by.

"Maybe not. But when a gentleman is intent on ingratiating himself with the ladies, he doesn't want competition," Chris said quietly, smiling in amusement at the sharp looks he was receiving from Mr Chorlton.

Catherine didn't have the opportunity to respond as Mr Parker approached her. "Mrs West, if you're ready to enter?" Mr Parker asked, offering his arm.

Catherine took it with ill-grace. She didn't like rudeness, and even putting her own feelings aside, excluding Chris had been poor behaviour on the part of the other gentlemen.

The party seated itself in the private box. Although Catherine was not at the front of the space, Mrs Hayes and Eliza taking those seats along with Mr Parker, she had a clear view of the theatre.

The room was lit quite brightly, enabling the guests to look around and see who was in attendance. Catherine was amused to see Chris seated in a box with a party of ten, directly opposite the one in which her party was settled. The theatre was narrower than she had anticipated, the boxes appearing a lot closer than imagined, enabling her to receive an answering smile when she first noticed Chris.

She settled down to watch the play with relish. This was going to be an experience she wouldn't forget in a hurry.

Hours later Catherine was delighted that she had actually experienced something so ridiculous that it had been hilarious. There had been hardly any cessation of noise when the actors came on stage. The audience in the stalls had supplied their opinions with unrestraint about the play, the actors and the audience.

The lights had never dimmed, so trying to concentrate on the stage had been increasingly difficult. Added to that, the intervals at the end of each act meant that the usual single interval in modern productions had been replaced by four in this particular play.

Each interval had consisted of food and drinks being served in the boxes and in the stalls and circles. It had also meant a steady stream of people moving around the theatre, seeking out those they knew.

Catherine had enjoyed the drinks but had looked at the food with suspicion. The lighting to the rear of the boxes was not bright enough to see exactly what was being served, and she didn't trust it. Especially as the same items seemed to be served at each interval. Food hygiene standards were clearly a thing of the distant future.

Chris had entered their box at the third interval and had managed to speak to Catherine for a brief moment. "Enjoying it?" he'd whispered.

"It's chaotic!" Catherine had laughed. "I've hardly any idea how good or bad the play is. It's all been about the audience!"

"Everything is about society. Who's with whom and what they're doing. Didn't you know that?" Chris teased.

"I did, but being a part of it is completely different than reading about it!"

"I shall leave you to enjoy the next act," Chris said, moving to speak to the other ladies before leaving them once more.

She settled in her seat next to where Mr Chorlton had positioned himself. He had been very attentive throughout the evening, and although Catherine had thought him handsome and charming on their first meeting, she was beginning to feel a little overwhelmed by his attentions.

He approached her as soon as Chris moved from her side, offering a smile that didn't reach his eyes. "Your friend is very particular in his attentions," he said, nodding towards Chris who was making Mrs Edwards blush.

"He's a very friendly person," Catherine responded noncommittally.

"Has he designs on either of your friends?"

"I've absolutely no idea," Catherine said sharply. "Can one not be personable and charming? Does one always have to have an ulterior motive?" For some reason she didn't like the thought of Chris chasing either of her new friends. Never usually one to be selfish, she had the overwhelming urge to be the one closest to Chris, and the feeling unnerved her.

"I suppose not. But it would be quite a novelty if that was the case," Mr Chorlton said. He would be having a conversation with his friend later about the feelings his chosen one had for another. They would need to consider encouraging Mr Dobson to leave Mrs West alone.

Chapter 11

Waking on the third morning, Catherine knew she had to return to her modern world. Two days for one Eliza had said, and this was her fourth day. She wasn't sure at what point to return, but in some ways she wanted it to be sooner rather than later. Even after so few days, she was missing some of the modern luxuries – the main one being she couldn't wait to wash her hair. Having shoulder length hair with a mind of its own meant she normally washed it every day. This would be another day she could not, and her head was beginning to feel itchy with grease.

She clambered out of bed to start her morning routine of trying to have a decent wash that satisfied her modern sensibilities.

Eventually, dressed in a terracotta dress edged in cream lace, she joined Eliza in the sitting room. She walked over to the window to enjoy the bustle of the Regency city.

"I need to work out other ways to help Mrs Hayes," Catherine started. "I can't take her shopping every day. There must be other things I could do."

"You are here for a limited time, as will she be. She has a home elsewhere," Eliza advised.

"I know, but it makes me feel frivolous to be enjoying five pounds a day when she is struggling," Catherine responded. "Perhaps if I saved as much of my money as possible and then, on the last day, gave it to her as a present. Almost two weeks of five pounds would give her about sixty pounds, give or take a few pounds. That would surely help her in the long-term?"

Eliza sighed. "I don't think that's why you're here," she said gently. "The reason is usually more to do with yourself."

"So this happens often?" Catherine asked in surprise.

Eliza looked as if she was cursing inwardly. "It can happen and not always in Bath."

"How wonderful!" Catherine said with a laugh. "I could spend years travelling through time!"

"This is a once-only experience for you," Eliza cautioned.

"Is it? Oh, that's a shame," Catherine said, the wind taken out of her sails. She was going to point out that Chris had been more than one time but didn't wish to sound ungrateful for the experience she was having.

"Which is why it's important you don't get sidetracked."

"Yes, okay. I will concentrate on enjoying my time here. But if I can help someone else along the way, all well and good," Catherine insisted.

*

Catherine and Eliza walked to The Royal Crescent. Catherine had been keen to see the people promenading. They were soon joined by Chris, who after greeting them both, offered his arm to each of them. When Eliza declined, he insisted with a smile.

"Don't deprive me of the chance of walking along this fine crescent with two handsome ladies at my side. The pavement is wide enough to take our three. Everyone else will have to jump into the road to avoid us!"

Eliza acquiesced, looking pleased at Chris' insistence, and the three walked along.

"What time do you normally return?" Catherine asked quietly. "I'm presuming you do return regularly?"

"Yes. It avoids questions being asked at the guest house," Chris responded. "I usually try to go back during the afternoon. I've always thought leaving it to the evening is complicating matters."

Catherine nodded her head in agreement. "Yes, I think I want to return once we have walked here."

"Keen to leave?" Chris asked a little surprised.

"I think I need the reassurance of physically stepping back. It's all well and good being told you can do something, but I don't think I'll totally relax until I leave and come back once more," Catherine admitted.

"I could be offended that you seem to disbelieve everything I say," Eliza said primly.

Catherine laughed bitterly. "After the last few years I disbelieve everything, including my own judgement."

"Just because you were married to a fool doesn't mean that there's anything wrong with you," Chris said gently.

"It certainly feels it."

"No one else sees it that way," Chris reassured her.

"That's very kind of you. I wish I could," Catherine said with feeling, but for once she believed Chris' words, and they warmed her.

*

Catherine had sent a note around to Mrs Edwards and Mrs Hayes, excusing herself from the card party they had promised to attend that evening.

She approached John Street with trepidation, but with one last nod to Eliza, she fisted her hands and walked into the alleyway.

A whoosh of breath left Catherine's lungs when she stood and heard the sounds of engines driving along Quiet Street not so far away. The dead nothingness had happened as on her other times, but instead of alarming her, it had come as a relief. She took a few steadying breaths while leaning on the wall for support.

She walked slowly up the alleyway. It was the long way round to her accommodation but she wasn't sure she could walk the full length of John Street without being transported back to 1811.

She tried to work out her feelings as she walked. She felt as if she didn't belong to either world. Nodding to Eric as she passed, she looped down Old King Street and onto Queen Square continuing to walk towards the guest house, the draw of a shower forefront in her mind.

*

Eliza followed Catherine a few minutes later. Eric was still standing; he tried to remain passive, but couldn't stop the slight smile forming on his lips.

"Not an easy case?" he asked, amused at the glare Eliza gave him at his words.

"No. It appears not," Eliza said with a sigh. "Why can't these people see what's right under their noses?" she asked in exasperation.

"If they could, we'd be out of jobs," Eric reasoned.

"I suppose so, but she has two choices of beaux and instead is running off down a completely blind alley!"

"She's trying to do some good. I don't suppose there's any harm in that," Eric defended Catherine.

"You know we can't change the life of someone who isn't connected to the one we're trying to help. It will complicate the timeline too much," Eliza pointed out.

"Yes, yes, I've read the manual!" Eric said heatedly. "I still think offering her an option in the wrong time period is cruel. What if she falls in love with that one? Does he come here? I don't think she'd leave her children if he couldn't join her in the future."

"She won't. We have to give them choices to make. Otherwise it's too much like we're interfering," Eliza defended her actions. "We can only provide possible solutions. They have to find their own way to happiness."

"It sounds like hard work to me," Eric muttered. "It'd be a lot easier if we just told them what to do, and you never know, they might appreciate it more."

"And that, Eric, is why you are still holding a sign," Eliza responded tartly before disappearing.

*

Catherine opened the door to the gentle knocking. She was dressed in her pyjamas after enjoying the longest shower she had ever taken. Her hair was wrapped in a fluffy towel and piled on her head.

She blushed to see Chris standing in the doorway. "H-hello," she stuttered.

Chris grinned. "I see you've done exactly what I did the first time. Tell me. Were you in the shower for more or less than half an hour?"

Catherine burst out laughing. "Slightly less I think, but only just! My teeth have never been scrubbed as much before, once I prised myself from the shower."

"I thought I'd make sure you got back okay. Have you enjoyed it?" Chris asked.

"Yes. Look, I know you'll want to do the same as I've just done, but when you're ready, would you like to have a drink in the Crystal Palace?" Catherine asked, referring to the pub in the square near to where they were staying.

"That would be lovely. Shall we say an hour?" Chris suggested, his smile warming Catherine's insides.

"Yes. Perfect. Just give me a knock when you're ready," Catherine said, closing the door. She felt daring. She'd never asked a man out before in her life and, although she was under no illusion that her suggestion could be construed as a date, it still felt as if she'd been bold. It created a good fizz in her insides, and she smiled to herself at her body's reaction.

Checking her phone, she found no texts or messages from Andrew or Megan. She was relieved; the guilt would have been great if she hadn't immediately replied to contact from them. She sent them each a message saying she was hoping they were having a good time. She didn't want to be a possessive parent, but she had a strong urge to always make sure they were fine; she supposed it had come from having to deal with everything to do with them without Paul's support.

She pushed thoughts of her ex to one side as she blow-dried her hair, taking care to make it shiny and smooth. It felt wonderful to be clean again. She dressed in smart trousers and a loose strappy top. She had loved the Regency clothing once she had become accustomed to the layers, but it felt liberating to wear lightweight clothing once more.

Applying some eyeshadow, blusher and lipstick, she cursed her vanity, but wanted to look good. She pushed aside the reason why, still unable to analyse her feelings too deeply.

The listened-for knock came eventually, and Catherine opened the door to reveal a still slightly damp Chris. His hair curled close to his head, drying naturally. He had shaved, and his face looked slightly reddened from the effort. He was wearing trousers and an open-necked shirt underneath a sports jacket, looking casual but smart. It was a big difference from the formality of his Regency outfits, but he was still striking. He was a man who attracted appreciative looks.

"I'm ready for a decent drink, but part of me wants to drink a gallon of clean water first!" Chris said with a smile, his eyes warming as he looked at Catherine.

"It's funny what I've missed," Catherine said, grabbing her coat, locking her door and popping the key in her pocket. "Showering is an obvious one, but comfortable shoes are definitely high on the list. Walking in pattens is a test all on its own!"

Chris grinned. "It's disconcerting, speaking to someone in the street and then meeting them later and realising they are three or four inches smaller than you thought because of that strange piece of footwear," he said.

"The good part is that the clothing hides a multitude of sins!" Catherine said with feeling.

"You don't need to worry about that, but I bet there are some unpleasant surprises on wedding nights!" Chris chuckled as they entered the pub. "Would you like something to eat? I'd like some decent food."

"Yes, I'm sure I can eat something light. They don't believe in salads, do they, in 1811?" Catherine responded, trying to hide her flushed cheeks, the flush caused by the compliment Chris had given her. She wasn't used to flattery, but it was pleasing to receive it from him.

"No, but I can't criticise them for that!" he said with feeling, leading the way through to the covered terrace, which had heaters scattered about.

It was early evening, so it was still quiet. They easily secured a table away from the other early diners. They chatted about the menu as they made their choices, commenting about the different food from two centuries ago. Chris eventually ordered the food, ordering lots of sides of salads and vegetables. He came back holding three drinks.

"I couldn't resist a glass of sparkling water," he said, shamefaced.

Catherine laughed. "Completely understandable." She accepted her glass of white wine and lemonade mixer and took a welcome mouthful. "Everything seemed to be very rich or very heavy."

"I think it was. Rich sauces hide the fact the food is sometimes off when it's served. And Bath was supposed to be one of the best places to eat," Chris said.

Catherine shuddered. "They must've have had strong stomachs."

"Perhaps not. The mortality rate wasn't brilliant," Chris responded.

"Do you know why you're allowed to visit there?" Catherine asked.

"No. I was told on my first visit that there was a reason I'd been allowed in, but since then, there's been nothing to suggest why," Chris admitted.

"Eliza's said it's my one and only visit," Catherine explained.

Chris' face fell. "Really? That's a shame. I was looking forward to seeing you there every year. We could've caused all sorts of trouble!"

Catherine was pleased at Chris' reaction. "We could! I think I know why I've been allowed access."

"Oh? You're smarter than me in that respect. You've only been there a couple of days, and already you know. I must admit though, I've been intent on enjoying myself rather than finding out," Chris admitted.

"I think it's to help Mrs Hayes. She's in such need of assistance. I really feel sorry for her," Catherine said, warming to her topic. "She's desperate to remarry, which is really strange to me after my experience, but I do understand her reasoning."

"Do you not want to remarry at some point?" Chris asked.

"Well ... I thought not, but after speaking to Mrs Hayes and Mrs Edwards, I'm not sure anymore. I don't need to marry the way they do, but perhaps one day …" Catherine admitted for the first time. "I'm not sure I'm ready just yet though. What about you?"

"Oh, I was only off marriage for a short while," Chris said with a smile. "Like you, I'm not sure when, but I'm not averse to meeting that special someone and taking things further."

"It's a hard decision to make isn't it? Acknowledging when you're ready to risk your heart again when it's been so battered in the past," Catherine said quietly.

Her words received a sympathetic smile from Chris, but he didn't say anything in return.

A companionable silence descended between them, which was only ended when their food arrived. They busied themselves with commenting about the food before Chris brought the subject back to their shared adventure.

"I'm not sure you're right about helping Mrs Hayes. What I was told was that it was to do with myself in some way. I can only presume that your transportation would be for the same reason," Chris said, tucking into his steak with enthusiasm.

Catherine smiled at Chris. She had the feeling he did everything with vitality and relish. Somehow, he always seemed so *active*. "What other reason could there be? I don't need anything," she said.

"We all need something," Chris responded.

"I could do with another job to help put Andrew through university, but apart from allowing me to turn every modern day into two days, I don't see how that could be achieved. I already have two jobs. I'm trying to build up a reserve of cash. This will be my last self-indulgent treat for a long time," Catherine said honestly. She wouldn't normally confess such a thing to a virtual stranger, but their relationship had gone beyond normal boundaries.

Chris didn't respond immediately. Eventually, he looked at Catherine. "That's it," he said simply.

"What is? A way of changing time in the present?" Catherine asked with a grin.

"No. It's a way of meeting your needs," he said, lowering his voice slightly. "You need money, and this has given you the perfect opportunity to get it."

"I don't understand," Catherine admitted.

"You have access to brand new, untouched Regency antiques. Plus, you have five pounds a day to buy them," Chris explained. "If you buy the things that antique dealers are paying top money for, your problem will be solved."

"Can I bring things back?" Catherine asked, not totally convinced of Chris' plan, but willing to hear more.

"Yes. Well, I can. I've brought souvenirs back each year. As long as I'm holding them in my hands, they've come with me," Chris explained. "You can make a start by selling the stuff I've already brought back."

"No!" Catherine said forcefully. "Those are yours!"

"I bring them back to Bath with me every year. It's a bit of a ritual, to be honest, that I can't explain fully. But apart from that, I never even look at them on a day-to-day basis. You can try them out this afternoon. There's a top-class antique dealer in the city centre. Let's go investigate what my trinkets would bring," Chris said.

"I can't," Catherine said, withdrawing from Chris a little. "It's too much."

Chris paused before speaking. "You're willing to help Mrs Hayes. Why is this any different?"

"It isn't," Catherine admitted with a flush. "And it's arrogant of me to try and justify it any other way. I should be as grateful as she was when I took her shopping. I suppose I'm too quick to become defensive. It is very good of you. Do you think it could work?"

"We can only try. I've even still got the receipts. I think I feel a distant aunt of mine dying in the not too distant past," Chris said with a smile. "Fortunately she didn't suffer, but we have a lot of things to get rid of."

"You are a disrespectful nephew," Catherine chastised.

"The worst," Chris agreed with a grin.

Chapter 12

Catherine had never been as nervous as she was when she walked into the antique shop later that afternoon. She let Chris do all the talking to the shop manager and watched with amazement as a deal was done in a relatively short period of time.

As they left, Chris took hold of Catherine's hand and steered her in the opposite direction away from the shop. Catherine had stiffened at the contact but forced herself to relax as Chris turned a few corners and entered the Raven pub.

"I need a stiff drink after that," he muttered, only releasing Catherine's hand as he reached the bar. "A brandy please, a large one," Chris said, before looking at Catherine in question.

"Vodka and lemonade, please," Catherine said.

In silence, they took their drinks to an empty table in the small atmospheric pub, and Chris sat down heavily. He took a large mouthful of the brandy, letting it slowly trickle down his throat. "I'd never have guessed they'd be worth so much," he said quietly.

"They were trinkets in Regency times," Catherine said, equally as stunned.

They had taken a box of vinaigrettes, snuff boxes, card holders, tea spoons, silver rattles, tooth pick holders and two tea caddies. The shop had been delighted with the perfect items along with the receipts of the shops in Bath in which they'd been purchased more than two hundred years previously, or over the last few years in Chris' case.

The money that had been transferred to Catherine's account had made her feel lightheaded. It totalled over five thousand pounds — an amount she could not ignore.

"I don't know what to say," she said quietly, overwhelmed at Chris' generosity.

"He said he'd be interested in more items," Chris said, still astounded himself, but trying to make Catherine feel better.

"How can I repay you?" Catherine asked.

Chris placed his hand gently on Catherine's. "I don't want anything. Honestly. If this takes pressure off your finances, all well and good. That's enough for me. I've enjoyed your company these last few days and, hopefully, we'll continue to have a good time until the end of the Christmas Market. I've no hidden agenda, I promise."

Catherine looked into Chris' eyes and smiled. "You are a Regency hero even in modern clothes," she said quietly.

"I'm not sure my mates would believe that, but I'll accept the compliment. I'm that egotistical," Chris said with a smile. "Now, we have to make a plan and see how many things we can bring back with us. If you can do this every year your kids are at university, it should really help."

"Eliza said I'd only be allowed through once," Catherine pointed out.

"Well, if that's the case, I can still bring things through. Although, it won't be as much fun if you're not there," he admitted.

Catherine laughed. "What did Mr Chorlton say the other day? Something about flummery. I think you both went to the same school of flattery!"

Chris rolled his eyes. "Don't compare me with that dandy!" he muttered roughly.

"He's not that bad," Catherine defended their acquaintance. "Although I do think he was rude not inviting you to the theatre."

"He couldn't stand the competition," Chris said with a growl.

"Probably knew he hadn't the looks or charm to win!" Catherine said and burst out laughing at Chris' pleased expression. "When are you returning?"

"Tomorrow after breakfast," Chris said without hesitation. "I like spending every moment there, but I will be taking a long shower in the morning before I venture out."

Catherine was reminded of how he'd looked when he had first knocked on her door after his last shower, and she felt a warm sensation flood her body. She didn't meet Chris' gaze; she hadn't felt such a response in a long time. She didn't want to betray her inner emotions to a man she was beginning to realise she would find extremely hard to resist if he were ever to decide he was interested in her.

*

Catherine received replies from both Andrew and Megan, assuring her they were having a good time. That meant that she could enjoy her evening. She flopped on the bed, switching the television on for background noise while she mulled over the day's events. She hadn't expected quite so much excitement once she'd returned to the present day, but it seemed her whole time in Bath, whichever century she was in, was going to be an adventure.

She suddenly sat up with a curse. Something had dawned on her, and she had to let Chris know. Locking her door, she started up the stairs, feeling a little brazen at interrupting his evening. He might not even be in, she mused as she trod up the plush carpet.

Chris had told her which room he was staying in, and Catherine understood what he meant when she had walked up too many stairs to reach it. She tried to catch her breath, knocking on the door gently. She didn't want anyone in the other rooms knowing she was trying to get into a single man's room, whether she was forty and unattached or not.

Chris opened the door, and although he was clearly surprised, he smiled his welcome. "Come in! Would you like a drink? I've only got red wine, I'm afraid."

"A small glass would be lovely, thanks," Catherine said.

Chris indicated she should sit on the two-seater sofa that ran along one of the walls in the bedroom. The room was a lot smaller than her own, but it was tastefully decorated and furnished. A large double bed dominated the room with bedside cabinets at either side. A television was fitted to the wall above a chest of drawers where a fire would once have been. A wardrobe fitted one of the alcoves, while the sofa ran along the other wall, stopping before the other alcove. A tea tray was on the chest of drawers. Chris was using the tea cups as wine glasses.

He shrugged as Catherine smiled when he handed her a tea cup. "I suppose I could ask for glasses, but I somehow excuse it as less alcoholic if it's served in a tea cup."

"That excuse will do for me," Catherine said with a smile.

"Is this a social call?" Chris asked, perching his large body on the edge of the bed. Catherine could see he had been sitting on the bed, with the slightly rumpled sheets, but was relieved he didn't take up such an inviting pose while she was in the room.

"I realised a flaw in the plan for buying all the silverware in Bath," she started.

"Oh?"

"I'd decided I was going to use my money to help Mrs Hayes. I can't do that if I'm spending all my money on myself," Catherine reasoned.

"It's what you should be doing," Chris pointed out.

"Possibly, but the money would benefit her more than it would me," Catherine said. "I might be struggling, but it's nothing to the difficulties she will face in Regency England."

"I can use my money to buy things for you, but I do think you should spend some of yours as well."

"Are you sure you don't mind spending your money on me? You could be using it to have all sorts of fun with so much money available to you every day," Catherine asked.

"Yes, I'm sure. It's not as if it's my first time and I want to try everything out. I just go because I thoroughly enjoy it," Chris explained. "This will give me some focus."

Catherine smiled. "Thanks." She finished the wine and stood. "I'd better go."

Chris stood. "Shall I see you at breakfast?"

"Yes. Although if you can't prise yourself out of the shower, I'll see you in the Pump Room," Catherine said with a smile.

Chris opened the door for Catherine, and in a moment of brazenness, she reached up to touch Chris' cheek with her hand. "Thank you," she whispered, standing on her toes to reach his cheek, kissing it lightly with her lips.

Chris looked surprised but smiled. "You're welcome. Especially if that's the reward I get. Can I expect that every day?"

Catherine looked bashful but smiled. "Don't push it," she responded and left the room with Chris' chuckle ringing in her ears.

Chapter 13

When Catherine returned to 1811, she was excited and nervous at the same time. She hadn't seen Chris at breakfast, and she was keen to seek him out. She walked with Eliza to the Pump Room, looking forward to seeing Chris once more in his Regency finery.

Mrs Hayes and Mrs Edwards were waiting for Catherine in the meeting place and greeted her warmly.

"Are you attending the dress ball at the New Assembly Rooms tomorrow evening?" Mrs Edwards asked. "We've made a new acquaintance who is keen to dance with us!"

"And one of my new gowns will be ready," Mrs Hayes smiled. "We've been working on it non-stop, haven't we, Lucy?" she asked, turning to Mrs Edwards.

"We certainly have!" Mrs Edwards agreed.

"I would like to," Catherine said, looking to Eliza for confirmation. When she received a nod, she smiled. "Yes. We will be attending. I look forward to seeing your new gown."

"Who's got a new gown?" Mr Chorlton asked from behind Catherine.

"I have," Mrs Hayes said with a blush. "We're attending the dress ball tomorrow."

"In that case, I would be delighted if you would agree to dancing the first two with me," Mr Chorlton said with a flourish.

Mrs Hayes responded with delight.

Catherine smiled at the gesture. It was a generous thing to do for a woman who had been expecting to sit out most of the dancing because of her position in life.

"It seems we are to make a happy party, Mrs West," Mr Chorlton said, turning to Catherine.

"Indeed!" Catherine said, her eyes lighting-up when she saw Chris approaching their group.

Chris made his bows to the group. Catherine was surprised when Mr Chorlton greeted Chris warmly. "I introduced these ladies to my sister yesterday. I'd like to introduce her to yourself and Mrs West. She's a lovely woman who enjoys dancing."

"She's a pretty young thing," Mrs Hayes gushed.

Catherine was ashamed that her smile faltered when she saw Miss Chorlton approach their party when Mr Chorlton beckoned. Catherine curtseyed as the pretty, slim, twenty-something entered their mix, smiling at Chris in appreciation.

"I thought while my sister was visiting friends in Bristol, it would be the perfect opportunity to see each other," Mr Chorlton explained to Catherine and Chris.

"He persuaded me with the temptation of fine company and lots of dancing," Miss Chorlton responded with a laugh.

"You will have to wait until my first two dances at the ball have been danced. I couldn't resist Mrs Hayes," Mr Chorlton said with a nod to the blushing woman.

"Oh," Miss Chorlton said, looking downcast.

"If I could have the honour of the first two?" Chris offered gallantly.

Jealousy surged through Catherine, but she inwardly cursed herself. She had no right to feel such irrational emotions. He was not hers. She didn't want him to be. Didn't she? He was free and had suggested he was open to romance. Catherine was not. She certainly couldn't compete with a pretty young thing even if she were. No. Romance was not an option.

Trying to deal with overwhelming feelings of regret, she turned to Mr Chorlton; he had offered to dance the next two with herself. She smiled. "Thank you, yes." That would be hours separated from Chris. The adventure suddenly seemed less appealing.

The group eventually went their separate ways, with Catherine and Eliza leaving the party first. They had crossed Pulteney Bridge before they turned, hearing hurried footsteps behind them.

Chris was approaching, looking relieved. "I thought I'd lost you," he said. "Aren't we going shopping today?"

Catherine flushed. "I didn't know if you'd still want to."

Chris frowned. "Whyever not? We've got a plan."

"You don't have to spend your time and money on me. It's very kind, what you've already done," Catherine said, trying to be the martyr and hating herself for it.

"I don't understand. I thought we'd cleared this up?" Chris asked in confusion.

Catherine sighed. "I'm sorry. It was the green-eyed monster speaking. Can you ignore what I've said, and let's start again?"

Chris smiled but a frown still troubled his features. "You were jealous. What of?"

"She's very pretty," Catherine said, trying and failing to carry off a nonchalant shrug.

"That bit of a kid we've just been introduced to?" Chris asked in amusement, his expression clearing. "Give me credit for having some sense! I know my ex-wife was substantially younger than me, but I don't chase young girls! Although, there is some positive to come out of this morning," Chris continued with a grin.

"What's that?" Catherine asked, half dreading the response.

"It's definitely a good sign if you're jealous about me dancing with other women! I shall make sure I'm introduced to every newcomer!" Chris said with a raised eyebrow.

Catherine flushed. "I seem intent on blurting out every thought I have to you!"

"Good," Chris responded. "Now, will you take my arm and come shopping with me, my dear, Mrs West?"

Catherine did as he bid. She wasn't sure what was happening to her, but since she'd been introduced to Chris, she was experiencing feelings she hadn't had since she was a teenager, and she wasn't sure where it was going to lead.

*

Chris entered the White Hart pleased with how he had spent the afternoon. He felt almost addicted to Catherine, wanting to spend as much time with her as he possibly could. He smiled when he thought back to her consternation at being jealous; it had boosted his ego enormously.

He worried about showing too much feeling. He was fully aware she'd been hurt and was still recovering from the wounds her experience had caused. He wasn't going to rush anything with her. She'd confirmed she was attracted to him; that would be enough encouragement until she was ready to embark on what Chris hoped would be a long relationship.

He was dragged from his pleasant thoughts by the sight of Miss Chorlton heading in his direction.

"Mr Dobson! How lovely to meet you! My brother has abandoned me, and I'm desperate for company," Miss Chorlton said with a fluttering smile.

Chris wanted nothing other than to return to his room, but politeness forced him to respond. "In that case, would you join me for coffee in the public room?" he asked, ever the gentleman.

"Could I not persuade you to accompany me to Molland's? I've heard the pastries served there are delightful!" Miss Chorlton responded. She was extremely pretty, fully aware of how her blonde curls and pale blue eyes appeared. That she was unmarried was more to do with ambition and an eye on the next opportunity than want of admirers. With little dowry to speak of, she was aware it was her looks and charm that would secure an attachment. She, like her brother, had a clear idea of what she wanted.

"I'm afraid not today," Chris responded with a smile. "I'm a little exhausted after my shopping expedition."

Miss Chorlton looked stunned at the words. "Shopping? Isn't that a pastime we ladies enjoy?"

"I was in company with a lady," Chris supplied.

"Oh? And who is the lucky lady who can wear out her favoured gentleman?"

"Ah, that would be revealing a lady's secret, which would be very ungentlemanly of me. I'm afraid, my lips are sealed on the matter. I would enjoy a coffee with you nonetheless," Chris said smoothly, refusing to indulge Miss Chorlton in her games.

"In that case, coffee it is!" Miss Chorlton said. She indicated to her maid that she could retreat back to her room.

They were soon seated in a busy public room. Miss Chorlton sat on the seat which would put her in the direct view of anyone entering the building.

"My brother abuses his sister, Mr Dobson! He promises all sorts of entertainments and then leaves me to my own devices," Miss Chorlton pouted, sipping delicately out of her cup, while looking over the rim of the china.

"I'm surprised a trip to Bath tempted you," Chris pointed out, not unreasonably. "There are other places that are far more entertaining for a young, unmarried woman."

Miss Chorlton lowered her voice, leaning closer to Chris. "I think my brother wanted my approval of his chosen lady. He wrote nothing but praise about her. Something he has never done before. What could I do? There are only the two of us, so I must give him my support if I can."

Chris stiffened but tried to disguise it. "And who is the lucky lady?" As if he didn't already know, he thought bitterly.

Miss Chorlton smiled. "You expect me to divulge a secret when you kept yours? Oh, come, Mr Dobson. I am not so naïve!"

"Touché," Chris smiled.

"I will reveal that she's of both our acquaintance."

"That isn't exactly a revelation," Chris said, his teeth jarring on the words. Chorlton had been hankering after her from the start of their acquaintance.

"Now don't go miss-ish on me, Mr Dobson! Let me enjoy being a tease. As you've pointed out there are little enough amusements in this place. I'm surprised at your own attendance," Miss Chorlton responded.

"I find I like the quieter life. The season in London has never appealed to me," Chris answered honestly.

"I wish I could spend the season in London!" Miss Chorlton said with feeling. "I'm hoping after my brother marries, he will start to take part in the more exclusive side of society."

"So he is hoping to marry a fortune?"

"Yes, but that is betraying too much of the lady in question," Miss Chorlton responded. "Please don't hint to my brother of what we've been speaking! He'll be very angry," she whispered as the aforementioned gentleman approached their table.

"Chorlton," Chris said standing and placing some coins on the table. "I've been enjoying your sister's company, but please excuse me. I must prepare for the party I'm attending tonight."

Mr Chorlton nodded and didn't delay Chris' withdrawal. Once safe to do so, he sat next to his sister and smiled. "So, what have you wheedled out of the tiresome, Mr Dobson?" he asked.

His sister smiled. "He's definitely not pleased about your pursuit of Mrs West. Oh, he tried to hide it, but he couldn't. A pity he's already love-struck, it would have been nice to have a flirtation with him."

"I thought he had the same idea as me about her. I'm depending on you to keep him out of the way. If Mrs West is leaving soon, she'll have to agree to marry me one way or another," Mr Chorlton said. "I hope it's sooner rather than later. Hanging around with blasted simpering women all the time is driving me to distraction! My brandy consumption has increased dramatically since meeting a gaggle of Bath widows!"

"I can and will distract the handsome Mr Dobson. He won't be able to resist what I have to offer, if the need arises," Miss Chorlton said confidently. "He will get a little push in the right direction when the time is right. If Mrs West doesn't succumb to your charms, we'll show her that Mr Dobson is as gullible as the next gentleman!"

Chapter 14

Chris entered the New Assembly Rooms and spotted Eliza alone. He approached her quickly. "Can I have a word please?" he asked, his tone low.

"Is there a problem?" Eliza responded but moved to the side of the room, so they could have a semblance of privacy.

"There might be," Chris answered grimly. "Are you aware Chorlton has serious designs on Catherine?"

"I know he's attracted to her, but that isn't a surprise is it?" Eliza responded, her tone prim.

"No. It isn't. But is it wise, bearing in mind there are only a few days left of the Christmas Market?" Chris asked.

"It's my job to give Catherine opportunities," Eliza said.

"And you consider him an option for her? Surely you can't be serious?" Chris was astounded that someone who was supposed to know Catherine could get her so wrong.

"Her confidence needed lift. She needs options in how to move on with her life, but I don't need to explain any of this to you," Eliza said, turning away.

Chris grabbed Eliza's arm. "I won't let you put her in a position that will break her heart again! Her husband's already done that. You can't have her falling in love with someone who existed over two hundred years ago!" he hissed, trying not to lose his temper.

"Keep your voice down!" Eliza snapped back. "As I've said before, she'll make her own decisions."

Chris was left rubbing a hand over his face in frustration. How could something that had seemed so harmless suddenly be turning into a nightmare? If Catherine wanted Chorlton, it would break Chris. He felt so much for her already, it scared him, but he could ultimately accept her choice. What he couldn't face was her falling for Chorlton and then being hurt. It wasn't fair. This was no longer the amusing diversion it had started out as.

*

Catherine approached Chris when he entered the large assembly room. "Here you are. I've been dying to see you! Have you seen this room! It's amazing!"

The room was a large rectangular shape. There was a balcony where the musicians were seated, playing a minuet. People milled around the dancers in the middle of the room.

"I've been in here before but never with so many people and for such an occasion!" Catherine continued. "I can't believe I'm here! I want to play a card game for money. Although I've no idea of the rules. Would you guide me?"

Chris smiled, unable to resist her enthusiasm. "Just wait until it fills. It's a heck of a crush. Apparently, it's a sign of success, but to me, it just increases the odd odours that fill the room!"

Catherine laughed, but then became serious. "I'm so jealous you've had this for so many years," she said wistfully. "If it wasn't for the overwhelming body odours I could live here forever!"

Chris laughed. "I'm glad it's not only me who struggles with the lack of deodorant. Posies of smelling herbs just don't get rid of the underlying pong!"

Catherine chuckled. "I feel I could make my millions on the cards."

"Try Vingt-et-un. It's like the modern day twenty-one or black jack. The other games are too complicated to pick-up quickly, and you don't want to draw attention to your lack of knowledge," Chris instructed. He loved the way Catherine was sparkling with mischief. It seemed she was finally losing that air of sadness he'd noticed when he first saw her.

"I shall have a try, although I'm only spending a few pennies," Catherine assured him. "I'm not becoming selfish. I'm still saving my pounds for Mrs Hayes."

"I'd never think you were selfish," Chris said, turning serious. "Please be careful."

"I'm only teasing about gambling," Catherine said with a reassuring smile.

"I didn't mean that. Just promise me you'll be careful."

Catherine looked at Chris, knowing he was trying to send her some meaning. "Can you not tell me more?"

"Probably not. They could prevent me from being here with you. Just remember that I'm here day or night, if you want me," Chris said seriously.

"Now there's a thought!" Catherine said before bursting out laughing. "Did I really say that out loud?" she asked in mortification.

Chris grinned. "Yup."

"Oh! Look! Let's join the others!" Catherine said quickly.

"Coward," Chris whispered. He was rewarded with a look that warmed him more than words uttered in a public ballroom could ever have done.

*

Dancing in the New Assembly Rooms was a treat Catherine was sure she would remember forever. She had visited the modern-day museum and marvelled at the separate rooms which made up the space, but to be there, for it to be filled with Regency people dancing and enjoying an evening out was beyond comparison.

Her only regret was that she had hardly spent any time with Chris. It seemed strange that she had not known him for very long, but he affected her as no one else had ever done. She sometimes wished she could talk to Susan about her feelings, but how could she describe the experience she was having? She wouldn't have a clue where to start.

Mr Chorlton came to claim his dances after he had danced the first two with Mrs Hayes.

"My friend seems to like Mrs Edwards a great deal," Mr Chorlton said, nodding towards Mr Parker who, after having two dances with Mrs Edwards, was now escorting her into one of the rooms serving tea.

"She's a lovely lady," Catherine responded with a smile. It was true. Mrs Edwards was far quieter than the exuberant Mrs Hayes, but it didn't render her company any less valuable.

"If only we could find someone for Mrs Hayes, it would be a perfect grouping," Mr Chorlton said as they passed in the set.

"I thought I detected some favouritism on your part," Catherine said, refusing to acknowledge about what Mr Chorlton was suggesting.

"Me? Goodness, no!" Mr Chorlton laughed. "I thought I'd been clear who my attentions were aimed at. Perhaps I need to be clearer?"

"I don't think there's any need for that," Catherine responded, not wishing to have the conversation with Mr Chorlton that he was hinting at. She began to feel a tad uncomfortable.

"My dear lady, are you so blind, you cannot see what's right in front of you? Have I not been open enough?" Mr Chorlton asked at his first opportunity when their paths crossed again in the dance, and they could not be easily overheard.

"All I know is that I'm emerging from a difficult time," Catherine responded truthfully.

"I hope there will be only happiness for you from now on," Mr Chorlton said.

Not with you, Catherine thought to herself, but this time, managed to keep her inner voice from speaking out loud. "I do too," she muttered.

"We should plan an excursion!" Mr Chorlton said, changing tack. "My sister would like to get to know you better. Why don't we arrange a trip out of Bath?"

"I'm afraid I'll be unavailable for the next few days. I have to leave Bath on family matters," Catherine said quickly. She was going back to the modern world. Catching up with Megan and Andrew came before everything else, even Regency Bath.

"Ah, that's a pity," Mr Chorlton responded, looking put out. "Perhaps the day after you return?"

"Yes, if everyone else can attend," Catherine agreed. It would be nice to explore the wider Bath area while she could.

Once her dances with Mr Chorlton had finished, she had danced two with Mr Parker and only then could she enjoy Chris' company. She had managed to play a few games of cards and had lost the pennies she had gambled but had felt it worth the expense, just for the experience.

Falling into bed late that night, she turned to Eliza who was preparing herself for bed now that Catherine was sorted. "I'm going to be at my hotel in time for breakfast," she said.

"Missing modern food?" Eliza asked with a smile.

"I never thought I'd miss anything so basic, but there are some strange tastes to stomach here!" Catherine said with feeling. "Most of it I don't even recognise. Part of me doesn't want to be told what it is!"

"Yes, it takes a while for the palate to get used to the difference," Eliza acknowledged.

"If there wasn't so much activity in this era, there'd be many more weighty people than there are," Catherine said. The average person was a lot smaller physically, although not necessarily in height. She had expected to tower over everyone but, in reality, most people were of an average height.

"It's all the dancing and walking," Eliza responded.

"Yes, my calves have never ached as much before!" Catherine said with feeling. "I wish I could wear a pedometer. I'm sure I'd be doing far more than my ten thousand steps a day!"

"Probably! Are you enjoying the experience?" Eliza asked, settling herself onto the truckle bed.

"Oh, yes!" Catherine responded with feeling. "I'm loving it!" She lay her head on the feather pillow, punching it into shape. Closing her eyes, she fell asleep thinking of how clear blue eyes had smiled into her own when she had spoken aloud her risqué thoughts.

Chapter 15

Yawning, Catherine entered her bedroom in the twenty-first century, feeling full of bacon, sausage and eggs. Normally she would have curbed the amount she had eaten but not on this holiday; she was ravenous for decent, uncomplicated food.

She flopped down on her bed not having any plans other than to contact Andrew and Megan, which she would do at a more reasonable hour.

Hours later, Catherine was disturbed by a persistent knocking on her door. She clambered off the bed, and running a hand through her hair in a vain attempt to calm it into some sort of acceptable style, she opened the door.

"Morning," she greeted Chris with a yawn.

"Afternoon!" Chris said with a smile. "I'm sorry for disturbing you, but I just wanted to check that you'd returned okay."

"Yes, although I think this two days to one is taking its toll!" Catherine said with a smile. "I'm going to be back at work next week needing another holiday!"

Chris smiled. "It is a bit full-on, isn't it? Look, I'm not going to pester you all day, but would you like to go to dinner tonight? The Pump Room does delicious evening meals with the musicians playing. I know it's not authentic, but it is a lovely experience, if you haven't already done it."

"No, I haven't. It sounds wonderful," Catherine said.

"Good. Should I book it for half seven?" Chris asked.

"Yes, it's a date!" Catherine responded.

"Is it?" Chris asked quietly.

Catherine paused. "Do you want it to be?"

"I do, but what about you?"

The silence stretched between them. Chris shifted uncomfortably. He looked about to speak when Catherine looked at him. "Yes, I think I do."

"You think?"

"I want it to be a date," Catherine said, trying to stop the flush spreading across her cheeks. She cursed herself. She was forty, for goodness sake! Teenage years were far in the distant past, yet this week, she seemed destined to re-enact them.

"Good. I'm really glad," Chris said, his smile lighting up his face. "I'll give you a knock about seven fifteen."

Catherine leaned on the door when she'd closed it. Her stomach was churning with fear and excitement. She knew without a doubt she wanted it to be a date, but it would be the first one she'd been on since meeting Paul over twenty years ago. Her cynical side wanted to mutter 'and look how that turned out', but she refused to let her mind wander down that path. Chris was different; she was sure of it.

Catherine couldn't resist sending Susan a text. She simply put 'Got a date' and waited. Two minutes later she answered her phone as the expected call came through.

"You've what?" Susan asked without preamble.

Catherine laughed. "I've got a date! And he's a hunk!" She allowed the giddiness to break free that had been bubbling since her conversation with Chris.

"Well it's about time!" Susan said with feeling. "Tell me more."

Catherine told her friend how they'd met. She hinted that they'd been spending a bit of time together without going into too much detail. Catherine didn't want to start lying to her friend.

"That's brilliant!" Susan said. "Text me when you get in."

"Yes, Mum," Catherine teased.

"But if you invite him back, don't worry about the text!" Susan said with amusement.

Catherine laughed, saying her goodbye and finishing the call. She had a date to prepare for.

*

Catherine looked at her face in the mirror, turning this way and that. She had dressed in the only dress she had brought with her, which with black tights, looked smart enough to have a date in a lovely setting like the Pump Room.

She had left her hair down, appreciating the opportunity after so many days of it being pinned to within an inch of its life. She had blow-dried it so much, it shone. Catherine promised herself she would never tire of the feeling of being well showered as the aroma of her shower gel wafted into her nostrils.

Applying more make-up than she would normally wear, she grimaced at herself in the mirror. He had seen her without make-up. She didn't know why she was trying so hard, but she added another layer of mascara just for good measure.

The knock came at precisely quarter past seven, and Catherine grabbed her long black woollen coat. Being used to lots of layers in Regency Bath she didn't want to catch a cold with so few days left to enjoy.

Chris whistled as Catherine opened the door. "You are very pretty dressed in empire dresses and dancing around a ballroom, but I think I prefer tonight's attire," he said with an appreciative smile.

"That's because there's a trowel full of make-up on as well," Catherine said, batting away the compliment.

"I don't think so! Come, my lady. Let us adjourn to the Pump Room!" Chris said with a bow, offering his arm.

Catherine was glad she was in contact with him. Although in Regency times there was more restraint in many cases, she had become used to holding onto Chris' arm when they were together. To have stopped on this night especially, would have made her feel a little distant from him, which she didn't want.

They walked chatting through the Abbey Churchyard and turned into Abbey Chambers, approaching the Pump Room. The Christmas chalets were all closed for the night. It was dark, and the lights from the Pump Room shone out onto the stone pavement in front of the building. A large Christmas tree stood in front of the Abbey.

"It's so much quieter these days," Catherine said in hushed tones. People intent on a night out in the city were passing through the area, but there was little sound.

"It is," Chris agreed. He stepped back as Catherine entered the Pump Room through the revolving door before following her inside.

Catherine paused in the doorway to the large room. It was as elegant as it was in Regency Bath, but this evening, the tables that filled it during the day welcomed the evening visitors within its walls.

They removed their coats, and they were shown to their table. People were being placed at discreet distances from occupied tables to prevent any overhearing of conversations. It was all very delicately done.

Once they'd ordered drinks and accepted menus, Catherine smiled at Chris. "This feels more decadent than all we've been experiencing this week!"

"I know. I came here a couple of years ago and loved it, although it is a little sad when you're here alone, watching everyone else enjoy a tete-a-tete."

"Don't try the 'oh, woe is me!' I've seen how the ladies flock around you!" Catherine said with a smile.

"None of whom I would wish to take out, except you," Chris replied honestly.

Catherine smiled, pausing before she replied. "I don't know how to behave. I'm very out of practice," Catherine admitted, glad their drinks had arrived and she could fiddle with the stem on the wine glass.

Chris noticed her agitation and responded to it. "I could entertain you with many stories of disastrous dates, but I refuse on the grounds that my street credibility would be lost forever!"

"As Megan assures me, I'm far too old to have any street cred. I'm afraid you can't claim any. You being older than me," Catherine responded.

"I know where your teenager gets her cutting remarks! Ouch!" Chris moaned, taking a long drink of his beer. "I'm definitely not divulging any stories after that insult!"

"Aw, don't be miserable!" Catherine laughed. "It was only my unsubtle way of asking how old you are."

"Please use subtly in future. My battered ego insists," Chris said with feeling.

Catherine was pleased that he was laughing with her. Having someone who didn't take offence at silly comments was definitely a new experience. "You know my age, it's only fair."

Chris sighed, dramatically. "I'm forty-six. Does that make you feel better?"

"Yes," Catherine said with a grin. "I was terrified in case you were going to say you were younger than me. Mrs Hayes and Mrs Edwards are both babies in comparison to my age. They make me feel positively elderly. It's reassuring that you're older!"

"Can we change the subject now, before I start to cry?" Chris moaned.

They paused to order food and a bottle of wine with the meal before Catherine continued her interrogation. "Did you never want children?"

"I suppose I'd always presumed I'd have them at some point," Chris started, relaxing into his seat. "But with meeting my ex-wife and her not wanting any, it sort of sealed my future. I think, in the main, it's decided by the wife isn't it? After all, it has the biggest impact on her life."

"It was Paul who drove the decision in our marriage," Catherine admitted. "Oh, I don't want to seem as if I regret having them! I don't! Not for a millisecond! But I wouldn't have had them when I did. I was on the promotion ladder at work, and I wanted to leave it a few years. But Paul had decided he wanted children, so that was it."

"Phew, I really can't see why you were married for so long to a caveman like that. He doesn't do the new-man image any good whatsoever," Chris responded. "I could easily spend the evening criticising your ex. In some ways I think I ought to in order to reassure you we aren't all the same, but I don't want to. I'd rather spend my time in a more pleasurable occupation and get to know you better."

Catherine smiled. "I'd rather not talk about him either. But going back to you. Do you not want to find someone to settle down with and have a family now?" She needed to know if he wanted children, because although she had not known him for very long, it was becoming more important for him to be in her life for the long-term. She didn't know if that would be a possibility, but if he was longing for his own family, she couldn't offer that. Complications after Megan had forced a sterilisation on Catherine. She couldn't be that open; it was too soon, but she needed to know if he wanted a family of his own.

"I will find out about you, you know," Chris said with a smile. "But no, I don't want children of my own. I don't want to be in my sixties with teenage children. I think there are a lot of people who couldn't cope with that, and I'm definitely one of them!"

"I can understand that," Catherine said, smiling with relief.

"Now, what was this career ladder you were talking about and where do you work?" Chris asked, refusing to be sidetracked any further.

They chatted throughout the delicious meal, hardly noticing the other diners. Lingering over coffee, Chris stifled a yawn. "Oh, excuse me!" he said mortified. "I haven't caught up yet."

"It's ok," Catherine assured him. "I had a long sleep this morning after breakfast, so I'm fine. But I would be doing the same if I hadn't. Let's go back."

Chris asked for the bill, and although a whispered heated discussion took place over who was paying, eventually Catherine gave in ungracefully. "This isn't fair. You've helped me so much this trip. I feel like I'm always taking something from you," she grumbled as they put on their coats.

"Believe me, your company is worth a thousand meals," Chris assured her.

"Well, you're very kind, but I still feel as if I'm taking advantage."

"Any time you want to do that, just let me know," Chris responded with a smile, making Catherine blush.

They walked into the cold evening, which was even quieter than when they had arrived. Chris held out his hand for Catherine's instead of linking arms. Catherine acquiesced with an increased heart rate.

Chris paused at the Christmas tree and lifted Catherine's hand to his lips. He kissed her fingers gently, looking into her eyes. "I want to kiss you in front of this tree, so you'd better say no, if you'd rather I didn't."

Catherine's breath hitched. "I'd rather you did," she said quietly.

Chris wrapped her in his arms, pulling her against his body. Catherine wrapped her hands around his neck without needing encouragement. She had wanted to kiss him for so long, but until this moment, hadn't realised just how long it had been since she had been kissed by someone she had feelings for. Deep feelings.

They stayed entwined for an age, each relishing the opportunity to explore the other. Eventually they were disturbed by a couple of homeless men passing the Abbey.

"Hey, mate, want to rent a sleeping bag?" one yelled good-naturedly. "It's big enough for two!"

Chris smiled onto Catherine's lips and opened his eyes to stare deeply into hers. "We must be making a spectacle of ourselves."

"I hope so," Catherine said in response, loving how she could see the colour change in his eyes, even in the dim light. They had changed to a deeper blue, and it warmed her that she had caused the change.

Chris chuckled. "I think we'd better return, but I want to say something before we do."

"Oh?" Catherine asked, a flicker of wariness reaching through her relaxed state.

"I'm not going to ask you to spend the night with me. Not tonight. That doesn't mean I don't want to be with you all night, because I really do," Chris explained.

Catherine had pushed away the thoughts of where their kissing might end, but she was a little disappointed and relieved at the same time. "What's stopping you?" She had to ask even though it would seem very forward.

"You. I don't want to push you too fast. I want this to be a long-term thing, Catherine. I want to spend a lot of time with you, if you agree? Would you see me again when we return to our normal lives?" Chris asked, searching her gaze in an effort to anticipate her answer.

"We live so far apart," Catherine pointed out, not unreasonably. She wanted him so much but had to be sure he was thinking it through.

"I know, but there're always weekends and holidays, and who knows? If this works out, I could get a transfer north. Please say that I'm not moving too fast," Chris said, knowing that he would never want anyone other than Catherine. It was happening at great speed, but he had never felt so strongly about anyone, even Mel.

"You'd do that?" Catherine asked in surprise. "Move your life such a distance away?"

"Yes, of course I would. You couldn't uproot your children, especially when they're staying with you in this country. Your life is with them, so I'll follow you. As long as you want me in your life, I'll be there. It's that simple," Chris assured her.

Catherine was touched by his words and surprisingly unwary of how much he had thought about their future. "I hope it is because I want you to stay in my life," Catherine said. "I never dreamed I'd feel this way. And so suddenly."

"I'm glad you do," Chris whispered. He wanted to say more, but it was too soon. He was more than happy that she seemed to have started feeling the same way about him as he did about her. It was a start. An excellent start.

They walked back to the hotel, hardly speaking, Chris wrapping his arm around her shoulders, keeping Catherine close to him. They entered the hallway, and Catherine stopped at her room.

"Thank you for tonight," she said, facing him.

"I've thoroughly enjoyed myself and can't wait for the time I don't have to be restrained with you," Chris said pecking her on the lips.

"I'll see you in the past," Catherine said with a smile.

"Goodnight," Chris said, managing to pull himself away from her. Just.

Chapter 16

Seeing Chris across the Pump Room for the first time since they'd kissed, it was inevitable that Catherine blushed and felt butterflies in the pit of her stomach. She smiled shyly at him and was rewarded with a cheeky wink.

Mrs Hayes nudged Catherine, slyly. "I think Mr Chorlton is going to be disappointed," she whispered as Chris joined their group.

"He never had a chance even without Mr Dobson," Catherine whispered in return.

"He thought he did," Mrs Hayes said with a smile before attending to the conversation going on around them.

"We could travel to Blaise Castle and return if we kept a steady pace," Mr Chorlton was saying about their planned day out, which had been talked about the last time they had met.

"We would need four phaetons," Mr Parker said. "We'd best travel in pairs."

Chris held his hands up. "I'm afraid I'm no phaeton driver! I'll need a carriage with a coachman."

"You jest!" Mr Chorlton responded. "Every man can drive a carriage."

"Not this one," Chris responded with an unconcerned shrug.

"That's unique," Mr Chorlton said, looking at Chris with suspicion. "What gentleman doesn't drive his own vehicle?"

"Quite a few, I would imagine. I don't ride a horse either. Just so you know," Chris responded. There was always going to be an undercurrent between the pair. Chris was fully aware he was wished a thousand miles away but was intent on staying close to Catherine, more so after what they'd shared the previous evening.

"Well that is singular!" Mr Chorlton said, clearly pleased with his own superior abilities. "We shall have to hire a barouche. I expect Mrs Hayes, Miss Cuthbert and my sister can join you. That will leave two phaetons for myself and Parker."

"I'll travel with Miss Cuthbert," Catherine said quickly. "I'm sure Mrs Hayes would like to see the view from a phaeton."

"Not at all. I'm more than happy with a covered seat. A phaeton is too adventurous for me at my age!" Mrs Hayes responded with feeling.

Catherine wanted to point out that she was older than Mrs Hayes but thought it prudent to hold her tongue. She would seem completely averse to spending time with Mr Chorlton, and although it was a fact that she didn't want to encourage him, it would have been unexplainable to push the situation.

Mr Chorlton and Mr Parker soon made their excuses and left the group to arrange the transport for the following day.

Catherine was able to spend the day with Chris, shopping with their combined funds and enjoying each other's company. Although they could not openly touch while in public there was a lot of subtle contact between them.

Preparing for the ball in the evening, Catherine mulled over her adventure. She was dressing in yet another beautiful gown, a jade green taffeta which floated around her figure. Tiny silver flowers had been embroidered around every edge, adding to the dress's elegance.

Eliza approached Catherine once Florry had fixed her hair and left the room. "Are you looking forward to your last ball?"

"It's still very strange visiting the Lower Assembly Rooms," Catherine admitted. "It's the one area that no longer exists. Everything else is still there although used in a different way, but the rooms have vanished. Yet, here I am, attending another ball within their walls," Catherine said with a smile.

"You smile a lot more than when you first arrived," Eliza said gently.

Catherine looked at her companion through the mottled surface of the looking glass. She wasn't ever going to confide her deepest feelings to Eliza, but because they'd lived together for the better part of two weeks, a closeness had developed between the pair.

"This has done me the world of good," Catherine admitted. "I finally feel I'm coming alive again, returning to who I used to be."

"That's good to hear," Eliza said, handing Catherine a shawl.

*

Mr Chorlton looked over to where Catherine and Chris were dancing. His sister stood next to him. "There's something going on between those two," he ground out.

"It appears so," Miss Chorlton responded. She always had an eye on the next opportunity but had never had any serious hopes pinned on Chris.

"You'll need to entertain him tomorrow. It's my chance to seal my fate," Mr Chorlton responded.

"I shall do my best, dear brother. Just don't forget my help when I'm wishing you happy!"

Mr Chorlton smiled. "With the amount of funds she brings, we'll all be in the lap of luxury."

"Will you be able to tolerate her once you're wed?" Miss Chorlton asked.

"Probably not, but it didn't stop me marrying Bertha, did it?" Mr Chorlton responded.

"No, I suppose not. She was very dull. I hope Mrs West is more entertaining," Miss Chorlton said with hope.

"I don't particularly care," came the unfeeling response. "Four thousand a year can make even the most tedious woman attractive."

Catherine prepared for the trip to Blaise Castle with mixed feelings. It would be an adventure to travel in a phaeton, but she would rather be with Chris. Selfishly, she wanted to be with him all the time. They had discussed staying over in Bath for an extra night once the Christmas Market had finished. She knew without a doubt she would be spending the night with Chris. She was ready to take the next step with him.

The party set off at a fine speed, everyone excited at the prospect of a day out.

Catherine felt a little nervous at leaving the streets of Bath. Moving too far away from her route home would always make her uneasy. Having Eliza in the barouche helped her calm down; she was sure Eliza wouldn't have let them go on the trip if there was any risk of not returning.

Mr Chorlton kept up the conversation as they rode. Catherine had found him attractive and entertaining when she had first met him, but now he seemed false and a little overbearing.

She was developing a headache and was freezing cold by the time they reached Blaise Castle two hours later. She was helped down from the phaeton by Mr

Chorlton, who held onto her a little longer than was comfortable.

"Come! The gardens have been laid out by Repton. I've long admired his work. Let's take a stroll," Mr Chorlton said.

The group followed him through the public parkland before leaving the greenery behind and seeking refreshment in an inn. Catherine seated herself nearest the fire, shivering with cold.

Chris approached her. "This is madness! You need to travel with us on our return. At least the number of bodies in our carriage creates some warmth!"

Catherine smiled. "It sounds tempting. What a day! It's not even a real castle!" she said with feeling.

"He's a coxcomb!" Chris growled.

Catherine smiled. "Is that a real word?" she asked.

Chris chuckled despite his annoyance at the situation. "It must be. I heard someone using it and have looked for an opportunity to use it ever since!"

"It does seem to fit," Catherine said quietly.

They were unable to continue their conversation due to the arrival of the food. A steaming hot stew was just what was needed to warm the chilled travellers.

During the meal Chris said that Catherine should travel with his group on the return journey.

"I've already arranged an alternative carriage, with a cover, hot bricks and rugs. We shall be delightfully cosy," Mr Chorlton said smoothly.

Catherine's heart sank. She would rather not be in a carriage for two hours, especially with Mr Chorlton, but it wasn't appropriate to speak. She decided she would speak to Eliza quietly. As her companion, Eliza should be travelling with her in a closed carriage. Catherine was determined to force the issue. She was not an innocent debutante, but she did not feel comfortable being alone with Mr Chorlton out of everyone's sight.

The grouping split after lunch, some seeking to freshen up, some wishing to stretch their legs before the return journey. Catherine used the facilities available in the inn and returned to the private room where they had eaten. She stood in front of the fire, trying to absorb as much warmth as she could before stepping outside. Thankfully the day was fine, or she would have considered the outing a complete disaster.

A sound behind her made her turn, and she was dismayed to see Mr Chorlton approaching her after closing the door behind him.

"Mrs West, I need to speak to you," Mr Chorlton stated immediately. "I can't restrain myself any further. You must allow me to speak with the most sincere affection."

"I'd rather you didn't!" Catherine said quickly.

"My dear lady, you cannot be blind to what is between us. The attraction we shouldn't be denying," Mr Chorlton continued, now standing in front of Catherine and snaking his arms around her waist.

Catherine put her hands on his chest in an effort to push him away, but he pushed against her, pressing their bodies together and partially trapping Catherine's hands.

"I want you, Mrs West, and there's nothing you can say that will convince me you don't feel the same."

Catherine wriggled her hands to free them. "Stop this!" she pleaded. "This is madness."

"Isn't that what love is?" Mr Chorlton asked before pressing his lips to Catherine's.

Before Catherine had a moment to even think about pushing Mr Chorlton away, she was startled by a sound at the now open door.

"Oh, brother! Am I to wish you happy?" came the clear voice of Miss Chorlton.

Catherine forced the kiss to stop and looked in alarm at the young woman standing in the doorway, looking delighted. "No!" she said.

"Mrs West, of course, you are to marry my brother! One can't go around exchanging kisses in such an amorous way without there being consequences," Miss Chorlton said with a smile.

Catherine felt sick. "No! Stop this!" she appealed to Mr Chorlton.

"You can wish us happy, indeed sister!" he responded. "We are to be married and very soon!" He forced another kiss on Catherine.

Catherine used all her might to push against Mr Chorlton's chest and separate herself from him. He managed to keep an arm around her and pin her to his side. When Catherine turned back to the doorway, she realised there was a crowd now standing there. Her eyes flew to Chris, who was standing with Mrs Edwards, Eliza and Mr Parker. Only Mrs Hayes was missing from the scene.

Chris looked pale with fury, but after one look of disgust aimed at Catherine, he moved away from the doorway and stomped down the hallway.

Catherine and Mr Chorlton were surrounded by their friends, wishing them happy and offering congratulations. She struggled to leave the grouping, needing to try and make them understand it was all a mistake, but for some reason no one seemed to be listening.

It was as if she were in a living nightmare. Every time she said something, Mr Chorlton or his sister contradicted her. It felt as if she would never be able to make them cease.

Eventually, when Mrs Hayes had joined the throng and Mr Chorlton had once more started to spout how they were to marry, Catherine snapped.

"Stop!" she shouted, louder than she had ever done. "This is madness! I'm not marrying you, ever!" she said, looking directly at Mr Chorlton while the others looked on in silence.

"You were found in a compromising position," Mr Chorlton said, his voice low.

Catherine had the feeling the real man behind the façade was about to emerge. "You forced a kiss on me. I refuse to marry as a result of that!"

"You kissed more than once," Miss Chorlton pointed out. "You were kissing when I entered and then once again after the marriage had been announced."

"A kiss, by itself, means nothing, especially when it was forced on me!" Catherine snapped, knowing without doubt that to Chris, a kiss meant everything.

There were shocked gasps from Mrs Edwards and Mrs Hayes.

"It doesn't mean anything, believe me," Catherine said, turning to her friends. "This is all a mistake! I'm not marrying Mr Chorlton! Why on earth would I marry him? I've only just come out of one horrific marriage. I'm hardly likely to enter into another in which I know I'd be unhappy!"

"You'll marry me or be ruined!" Mr Chorlton spat.

"I'll take ruination any day!" Catherine said flaring at the threat. "Now, if you'll excuse me, I need to find Mr Dobson."

"That buffoon will hardly touch you now," Mr Chorlton said. "You'll find he no longer moons over you the way he has been doing."

Catherine paused on her way to the door. "Was this planned?" she asked, a sinking feeling in her chest.

"How could I plan it?" Mr Chorlton asked.

"I've no idea, but it seems a little contrived, doesn't it? You suspect me of having affection for another, so I'm caught in a compromising position by your sister and then him," Catherine said. "Oh, good grief! This is like some sort of poor gothic novel!" She turned to Eliza. "I need to find Chris."

"Who the hell do you think you are?" Mr Chorlton snapped, moving forward and grabbing Catherine roughly by the arm.

"Hey, now Chorlton! There's no need for roughing up a lady!" Mr Parker said heatedly.

"She's no lady!" Mr Chorlton snapped. "I'm going to show her exactly who she's dealing with!"

"Get off her!" Mrs Hayes, pushed Mr Chorlton.

He released Catherine and turned as if to strike Mrs Hayes, who cowered, but Mr Parker moved quickly.

"Enough!" Mr Parker said, pulling Mr Chorlton away from Mrs Hayes. "What madness has possessed you?"

Mrs Edwards and Eliza moved to comfort the distraught Mrs Hayes.

Catherine faltered. She should go to her friend, but she needed to sort the mess out with Chris. Leaving the room she hurried down the hallway. Seeing the innkeeper, she approached him.

"A Mr Dobson was with my party. I need to find him. He will have passed you a few minutes ago. Do you know in which direction he went?" Catherine asked, no longer caring how she might appear by seeking out a man.

"You've missed him, madam," the innkeeper said. "He left almost as soon as I saw him. With all the carriages waiting for you, he just jumped in one and left."

Catherine's face paled. "Thank you," she said before returning to the private room.

Walking into an atmosphere that was uncomfortable she looked at Mr Chorlton. "I refuse to travel back with you," she said.

"You're a fool!" he snapped. "This isn't the end!" Storming to the door, he motioned that his sister should follow him. The pair left without looking back.

Catherine had gone to Mrs Hayes' side and took hold of her hand. "Thank you for coming to my rescue," she said quietly.

"He was so gentlemanlike at the beginning," Mrs Hayes said, her tear-streaked face showing how the episode had affected her.

"They usually are," Catherine said grimly before turning to Eliza. "I don't know how we're going to get back to Bath, but I suggest the sooner we go the better. I need to find Chris."

Eliza nodded and left the room.

"Have you an understanding with Mr Dobson?" Mrs Edwards asked.

"I honestly don't know," Catherine said, finally voicing her fears. While she was separate from Chris, she couldn't explain the truth of the situation.

"It's just with you using his given name so freely ... "

"Where I come from, it isn't unusual to do so," Catherine said, for the first time sick of the constraints that surrounded her.

Mrs Edwards looked shocked but didn't pursue the subject any further. An uncomfortable silence descended on the room.

Eliza eventually returned. "Mr Dobson took a coachman and one of the phaetons. He left us the barouche," she explained. "It is ready for us now. A driver is waiting."

The party moved through the building and out into the coach. The group, which had been so comfortable with each other, now seemed like strangers during the strained two-hour journey back to the centre of Bath.

Chapter 17

Catherine was glad the carriage had come to a stop at the White Hart Inn. She wasn't sure if Eliza had arranged it, but she jumped out of the vehicle and entered the inn without waiting for escort.

Approaching the innkeeper, she spoke. "Could a message be sent to Mr Dobson's room please? I need to speak with him most urgently."

"That's not possible," the innkeeper said.

"Why not?" Catherine demanded.

"I'm afraid he's not here, madam," the innkeeper responded.

"Has he gone out? Has he not returned?" Catherine felt she was talking to a teenager, only being fed a little information at a time.

"He's left the inn for good. Left in a hurry actually. I'd have thought he was doing a runner, only he pays in advance when he visits every year," the innkeeper said, pleasantly.

"I see. Thank you," Catherine said, turning to leave.

She met Mrs Edwards at the doorway. "I'm going to take Mrs Hayes to our rooms," Mrs Edwards said. "I don't think she'll want to go to the card party we've been invited to tonight. She's a little overwrought."

"I'm sorry I've caused her upset," Catherine said with feeling. "She, of all people, who is here for health reasons, didn't need to be upset further."

"She will rally," Mrs Edwards said. "She's stronger than she acts. She's had to be. But she's a gentle soul at heart and doesn't like people being treated ill. Mr Chorlton has made an enemy, and although she doesn't hold much influence, I doubt he'll be looked on favourably by those who know us. Gentlemen are expected to act in a certain way, and threatening to strike a woman isn't up to snuff, as they say!" Mrs Edwards said with feeling.

"I don't want her life being made uncomfortable because of my lack of character judgement," Catherine said with feeling.

"We all thought him a gentleman," Mrs Edwards said reassuringly.

Catherine followed Mrs Edwards out of the White Hart and approached the small group of Mr Parker, Mrs Hayes and Eliza.

"I'm sorry today has turned out so poorly," Catherine said taking hold of Mrs Hayes' hands. "I didn't want any of this upset."

"He threatened you," Mrs Hayes said, still clearly distraught.

"He was speaking in haste," Mr Parker said consolingly. "I'm sure, once he calms down, he will be ashamed of his actions."

"I'm not as convinced of his good character as you are," Catherine responded, not sure whether Mr Parker was hiding his own character as his friend had done.

"He's just bound by circumstance," Mr Parker responded.

"How so?" Catherine asked.

"He needs to marry someone who has wealth," Mr Parker said, shamefacedly admitting the callous motive of his friend but speaking the truth to those he had come to regard.

"I see. He thought I was the route to money, did he?" Catherine asked.

"Yes," Mr Parker admitted.

"And you were willing to help him?" Mrs Edwards asked, her colour heightening.

"I was at first, I admit. But when he brought his sister over and was talking of compromising either yourself or Mr Dobson or both, I realised he had gone too far," Mr Parker admitted.

"That's easy to say now," Mrs Edwards responded primly.

Catherine saw Mr Parker's expression drop and felt sympathy for him. "Thank you for standing up to your friend. It must have been a struggle."

"It was," Mr Parker admitted. "It was easy to let him babble on about his plans before I was introduced to you all. Getting to know you has been the best thing to happen to me." He looked shyly at Mrs Edwards.

Catherine was touched. Mr Parker was clearly a little younger than Mrs Edwards, but he was no schoolboy. He was probably in his late twenties. His actions were one of someone who was smitten, and she liked him for it. Mrs Edwards was a lovely person and deserved to be happy.

"And we appreciate the support you've given us, especially today. Mr Parker, I need to follow Mr Dobson. Could you please escort the ladies home? I would be happier to know they are protected," Catherine said.

"I shall be delighted to act as protector," Mr Parker said, once more looking to Mrs Edwards. His smile lit his face when she gave him an encouraging nod.

Catherine said her goodbyes and walked away from the White Hart. She was not sure what the best course of action would be, but she was sure of where she had to go.

Eliza caught up with Catherine and started to talk. "I thought you liked Mr Chorlton?" she asked, as they walked towards John Street.

"At the beginning he seemed charming, and it was flattering to receive attention from him, but it wasn't too long before whatever mask he was wearing began to slip. It was my own fault for being caught up in the romance of this situation. I normally wouldn't have spent so much time in his company if I'd met him in the present day. It didn't seem as important in Regency England. It's as if it were all make-believe, and there were no consequences," Catherine explained as she walked.

"He seemed to care for you."

"It appears he cared about my money, when in reality I have very little. It's ironic that he would have run away from me if we'd met in my real life. He had me feeling sorry for his children! What a fool I was! Does he even have children?" Catherine asked.

"Yes, I believe so," Eliza replied.

"But you don't know?" Catherine asked in astonishment.

"No. I only know the details about the person I'm meant to help," Eliza admitted.

"Well, even with the help of my so-called fairy godmother, I've managed to hurt one of the most decent people I've ever met!" Catherine said with feeling.

"What are you going to do now?" Eliza asked.

"I'm going back and hoping to goodness I'm not too late to rectify this."

They both hardly paused as they walked onto John Street. Catherine still needed the support of the wall when she transferred from one time to another. She envied Eliza's unfazed approach to it all.

When the dizziness eased, Catherine stood straight, touching her clothing as always, as if she still couldn't believe that she could time travel. "I don't know if I'll see you again. I'm not sure I'll be returning," Catherine said.

"Really? It would be a shame not to enjoy the last few days," Eliza responded with concern.

"Parts of it have been amazing. But, if it means I've lost Chris' good opinion, it won't have been worth it," Catherine said seriously. "Please excuse me. I've got to find him."

Catherine walked briskly away from Eliza, nodding in recognition when she passed Eric. She wondered idly why he was still there. After all, she knew the way to the portal, or whatever it was, by now. She might be geographically challenged, but even she could find her way to 1811. Striding along briskly, she headed back to her hotel.

*

Eliza leaned on the wall near Eric and blew out her cheeks.

"Not going to plan?" Eric asked.

"It's a disaster!" Eliza said with feeling.

"She was hardly going to fall for that creep Chorlton, was she?" Eric asked, wondering how Eliza could have been so easily fooled.

"I thought he was perfect for her. Just what every Regency heroine needs," Eliza said. "I never for a moment thought he was a fortune hunter!"

"Don't we get a full resume on each person? She doesn't seem the type to fall for your stereotypical hero," Eric said with a shrug. "It looks like I've even more to learn than I thought."

For once Eliza didn't come back with a smart retort. "It looks like I've caused problems instead of helping her find happiness," she admitted.

"There's still a couple of days left," Eric offered hopefully.

"After today, I'll need more than a couple of days to sort out this mess!" Eliza said with feeling.

Chapter 18

Catherine ran straight up the stairs to Chris' room. He had to be there. She was desperate to make things right.

Knocking quietly so as not to disturb the other guests; she waited impatiently. When no answer came, she knocked again a little louder.

There was still no reply, but Catherine was convinced Chris was behind the door; she sensed him there. Knocking for a third time, she put her mouth near the door, saying, "Chris. Please."

A moment passed, and the door opened. Chris stood in the doorway, his face a blank mask.

"Why are you here?" he asked roughly.

"It wasn't what it seemed," Catherine gabbled.

Chris sneered. "It never is. So, you weren't kissing him? Can you really explain such an action to make it right?"

"He was kissing me. That's a big difference!"

"Semantics," Chris shrugged.

"Do you think after the evening we shared, I would do that to you?" Catherine asked in disbelief. She had been convinced he would see sense if she explained, but when faced with Chris' intransigence, she didn't know how to reach him.

"I've honestly no idea. I just know what I saw."

"Chris, I never wanted him to be near me, let alone kissing me!" Catherine said with feeling.

"I understand. It's an adventure. You want to experience everything. It's fine. I don't want to be involved though. Do what you want. Just leave me out of it," Chris said coldly.

"No!" Catherine snapped. "It's not like that. *I'm* not like that! Please let me explain!"

"There's nothing to explain. I've seen it all before," Chris said.

"I don't understand," Catherine whispered, his immovable stance knocking the fight out of her.

"My ex. She was keen on sharing herself with others. It was never how it seemed, obviously. She took me for a fool. I'm never going to get involved with anyone remotely like her," Chris finally explained. "This isn't an overreaction on my part. You can do what you wish, Catherine. I just want no involvement with it … or you."

Catherine stepped back as if he had struck her. The colour had gone from her face. She blinked as if struggling to focus.

Chris could have gone to her. Perhaps should have gone to her, but instead he sighed. "There's nothing more to say. We obviously want different things. Goodbye Catherine." He closed the door softly, leaving Catherine alone on the landing.

She wrapped her hands around her waist, trying to contain the emotion welling up inside. She was afraid if she let it out, she would never be able to stop.

Taking a breath, she turned away from the door and took hold of the banister rail. She had to get away. He didn't want her. Stepping down the first step, she faltered and sank to the carpeted floor, unable to support herself. She couldn't walk. Couldn't move. He had rejected her.

Leaning her head against the wooden rails, she squeezed her eyes tight, but the tears forced their way through. She made no sound but remained on the top step, shaking, crying, unable to move.

*

Chris opened the door two hours later. His first reaction was one of anger that she had waited for him, but then he paused, Catherine wasn't Mel; he knew that deep down. He had felt unsettled as soon as he'd closed the door on her. Wanting to get away from the expression of hurt in her eyes, he'd needed to withdraw before he had chance to weaken. But once the door had closed he had felt lost and bereft. She was not Mel.

He had lashed out at her, and instead of the huge drama Mel would have caused in such a situation, Catherine had betrayed the hurt inflicted on her in the quietest way possible.

He sighed. He had reacted in anger. He had never felt jealousy like it when he'd seen her in Chorlton's arms. He hadn't stopped to consider for a moment if Catherine had been against the action. He had transferred Mel's personality onto her.

She hadn't moved at the sound of him opening the door, so he moved to the top of the stairs. She was holding onto the rail as if for dear life, her tear-streaked face pale and drawn. Her eyes were closed; her body showed no signs of recognising that he was there.

He'd hurt her deeply.

Chris crouched down and sat next to Catherine. It was a bit of a squeeze, but he managed it. Slowly he took hold of her, and although she did not come willingly, he eventually enveloped her in an embrace.

"I'm sorry," he whispered into her hair.

Catherine started to shake as a fresh bout of tears overwhelmed her. She couldn't respond to him, couldn't do anything but shed more silent tears.

Chris stroked her back, kissing her head, making soothing noises, until eventually her silent sobs subsided once more. When she was quiet, Chris held her close not saying anything. He was accustomed to anger and recriminations, not real sadness.

When he felt she'd calmed, he started to speak.

"I was deeply in love with Mel. She took over my whole world. I wanted to give her everything and anything," Chris started, needing to explain. "I realise now I was ignoring the signs even at the beginning. She was a social butterfly. It was one of the characteristics that attracted me to her, but I failed to recognise she needed the buzz of being the centre of attention. And she'd do anything to get it."

Catherine made no sound, nor did she move, but Chris knew she was listening. It was somehow easier to speak of his foolish mistake when he wasn't in danger of seeing pity in her eyes.

"I didn't realise at first what was going on. I just thought she was the life and soul of the party … which I suppose she was in a way," he said with a bitter laugh. "She saw sex as a means to keep her as everyone's darling. There were times when she'd overstep the mark in my company, and I'd challenge her; I wasn't a complete pushover. What I failed to appreciate was how much of an expert she was at playing mind games. It was never how I thought it was. It was always me who'd misread the signals. Never her. Like a fool I believed her time and again."

Chris rested his head on the wall in an act of defeat. "It was only when I caught her in a situation that she couldn't talk her way out of that things came to a head. Although, she even tried to turn it on me then, which was when I saw what a fool I'd been. She'd used me as a means to an end. Providing a decent lifestyle and not much else really. Our marriage had been a complete sham and a waste of years of my life."

Chris stroked Catherine's hair. "I don't deserve your forgiveness, but like an arrogant pig, I want it. I acted like an idiot today. I should have punched him and then asked questions. I should have waited before running off like a kid who can't handle life. I know you aren't anything like Mel, but I forgot that important fact in a temporary moment of madness."

Eventually Catherine began to speak. Her voice was barely a whisper. Chris had to strain to hear it, but she made no move to pull away from him. He supposed she did not want to look at him.

"I loved Paul when we first met. I really did. He was attractive, funny, rich, older than me, worldly-wise. I thought he was some sort of God. We hadn't been married for very long when I realised I'd made a mistake," she confessed for the first time to anyone.

"I was pregnant by then, so I put my thoughts down to a change in hormones. By the time I knew it wasn't the pregnancy, Andrew was born, and I was filled with so much love for him, I can hardly explain. I knew my role was to protect this sweet little boy, and part of that protection was providing a secure upbringing for him. I wouldn't leave. But I wasn't being a martyr. I was just being a mum."

Chris squeezed her tenderly.

"After Megan was born, the affairs became less hidden. We went to counselling for months. Each time, I would say I would be a better wife, and he would promise to be faithful. It never lasted, of course," Catherine said bitterly. "We should have separated years ago."

"You had a young family. I understand why you didn't," Chris said gently, unable to stop himself from defending Catherine — something he should have done with Chorlton.

"We muddled along. I suppose that's the best way of describing our marriage. But then mum became ill. By that time we weren't living as man and wife. Yes, we shared the same bedroom but nothing else. He had stopped hiding the fact that he was having affairs. Oh, the kids didn't know, but I did. I was to find out later that the affair Paul was having while mum was dying was to be the one that lasted," Catherine continued.

"When mum died, I suddenly realised how adrift I was without her. I'd relied on her over the years so much, and she'd gone. Then Paul announced he was leaving to set-up home with his mistress, and the world spun out of control."

"You must have been devastated," Chris consoled.

"Yes and no," Catherine responded. "I was still grieving for mum, but I wasn't devastated over Paul. I was relieved in some respects. I don't think I would have ever had the courage to leave him, you see. His timing could've been better. It hit the kids really hard, which cut me deeply. But there was no love left between Paul and me. None at all. I reeled from the shock and the fact that I'd failed at something I'd tried so hard at." It was the first time Catherine had been truly honest with herself.

"You probably couldn't have done anything to change him," Chris said knowing it had been the same with Mel.

"I never expected to feel anything for anyone again. I didn't think I could," Catherine said, pushing herself into a sitting position away from Chris. He moved to stop the change in position, wanting to be in contact with her, but her hands stayed his. "From that first breakfast we shared, I felt something for you. A pull. A connection. Call it what you like, but it was real. It took me by surprise, and I tried to push it aside."

"And yet, I'd spent the week lusting after you when you visited two years ago," Chris said, trying to cause a smile.

Catherine's lips lifted, but the smile didn't reach her eyes. "At the start, when Paul began having affairs, I was devastated. I might have thought I didn't care but I did, it ripped through me. After a time, though, I managed to harden myself against the feeling, which is why I thought I'd never be able to feel for anyone again. I thought I was switched off."

"I didn't see that when I first saw you, but I did notice there was an air of sadness surrounding you," Chris admitted.

"This 'thing' between us has meant more to me than years of my marriage," Catherine said quietly. "I was flattered when Mr Chorlton seemed to prefer me, but I think it was my ego needing a boost. As shallow as that sounds. It felt like it didn't matter because it wasn't real. It was in the past so how could it be harmful? Which is no excuse, I know. Within a couple of days though, I didn't really like him. He made me wary."

"Justifiably so, with the trick he pulled," Chris said through gritted teeth. "Seeing you with him …"

"I would never have done that to you. Led you on while chasing another. I'm sorry you saw what you did," Catherine said. "I was trying to sort the situation out, but everyone just appeared, and it all became an even bigger mess. The stupid thing is, he thinks I'm a wealthy woman! It's laughable, knowing the reality of my situation!"

"His sister was desperate for me to follow her," Chris admitted.

"It stank of a set-up," Catherine said. "The whole thing was so sudden and so ridiculous!"

"Ridiculous was not the first word that sprang to my mind," Chris ground out.

"When I discovered you'd gone from the inn, I was nearly beside myself with panic," Catherine admitted. "I just needed to get to you."

"It reminded me too much of what I've already been through. I just couldn't face it. Not with you," Chris said quietly.

"I would never be unfaithful. It isn't in me to cause so much hurt. I know first-hand what devastation it causes," Catherine said. "I didn't know what to do to make it right. I can't explain fully what I mean. I'll look like a fool."

"Try," Chris urged.

"I've never felt so desolate since mum died. It was as if I'd lost the best thing in my life, after the kids of course," Catherine said quickly.

"Of course," Chris repeated with a smile. "The best thing?" he asked quietly.

"Yes. It's too soon. I'm too old to fall so quickly. But Chris, if you can't forgive my stupidity in not screaming the moment that man pulled me into his arms, you need to tell me now. I don't know how I'm going to get over you not being in my life, but I'd rather do it now than in the future if you can't forget what happened today," Catherine said seriously.

"Hey, you're not the only one who's fallen quickly and hard. I was talking about moving up north, wasn't I?" Chris asked gently.

"Yes, but that was before Mr Chorlton," Catherine pointed out.

"Let's forget him. Let's forget the whole sorry episode. I'm not surprised he wanted you. I do," Chris said, pushing a strand of hair behind Catherine's ear.

"I'm scared," Catherine admitted, looking into Chris' eyes, her own still watery and red-rimmed. "It's so fast."

"We aren't young kids, more's the pity," Chris said with his usual wide grin. "I certainly know what I want. I overreacted, and I'm sorry for that. I promise in the future I'll listen to what you have to say. Forgive me?"

"We both handled it badly," Catherine said. "You overreacted. I underreacted. I just want to forget the whole situation."

"Catherine. Stay with me tonight," Chris whispered, leaning over and kissing her nose, which was still red from the extended bout of crying.

"Are we sure about this?" Catherine asked, her heart hitching. Fear and excitement swirled inside her, pushing away the devastation she had been feeling.

"As sure as we can be," Chris said, rising to his feet, pulling Catherine gently with him. Holding her hand while she took the one step to return to the top of the landing, he opened his bedroom door.

Turning to Catherine, he asked silently for her agreement. Looking into Chris' eyes, Catherine was surer about this than she had been of anything for a long time. She nodded with a smile and squeezed his hand. It was time to start living again.

Chapter 19

Catherine woke with a stretch and a smile. They had spent days hardly moving from Chris' bedroom. They had gone out for food and returned to Catherine's room for her clothing and toiletries. He had been discreet each time she had contacted Megan and Andrew, but for every other moment they had been entwined together.

Chris folded himself around Catherine as she tucked herself into him. He didn't think he would ever tire of the thrill that rushed through his body every time she did that. Kissing her head, he breathed the morning scent of her.

"You realise what day it is today, don't you?" he asked, pulling her closer.

"No. What?" Catherine asked.

"The last day of the market," Chris answered.

"Oh, my goodness! It is! We've only one more night before we have to return home," Catherine moaned. She wasn't sure how she was going to cope with not waking up next to Chris each morning.

"Do you want one last trip into the past?" Chris asked.

"I'd never considered that," Catherine responded, wriggling around, so she faced Chris. "What do you want to do?"

"To stay in bed with you, but I'm happy to go back, if you'd like to say goodbye to Mrs Hayes and Mrs Edwards. I know you thought a lot of them," Chris answered.

"Why does the last day not last for two days?" Catherine asked.

"I've no idea, but it was stressed quite forcefully when I started coming through, if you aren't back at 5 p.m., the way is blocked," Chris responded. "I usually come back earlier just to be on the safe side."

"Yes, it would be awful to get stuck," Catherine said with a shudder.

"We can leave it if you'd prefer," Chris suggested. "There's no real need to go back, is there?"

"The money!" Catherine said, suddenly being reminded of her self-imposed task. "I need to give Mrs Hayes the money I've saved. It won't be as much because we've been really ungrateful for the opportunity and didn't spend every moment there, but I should give it to her. It'll be really useful towards improving her situation."

"You're too good," Chris said, nibbling her lips. "I'll join you on one condition."

"What's that?" Catherine asked.

"That we don't go quite yet," Chris said, before kissing Catherine fully, preventing her responding in the negative even if she'd wanted to.

*

Walking into the Pump Room on Chris' arm, Catherine felt happier than she had in years. He was special; she knew it already. In fact, the only scary thing about the whole situation was how suddenly and hard she had fallen for Chris. She was afraid to admit it so soon; he could run far and fast if she was open about the depth of her feelings. She would have to try to contain her overwhelming emotions, but she wasn't sure she could.

They had assured Eliza that they didn't need her help on their last day, and the woman had acquiesced with a smile of relief at their open affection, leaving them unaccompanied.

They headed over to Mrs Edwards who looked at them speculatively.

"We've come to say our goodbyes," Chris started after good mornings had been exchanged. "We're leaving Bath this afternoon."

Mrs Edwards smiled, "And is there to be an announcement soon?" she asked.

Chris chuckled at the direct question. "We are going to speak with our families first," he said.

Catherine had blushed but nodded at Chris' diplomatic answer. "Is Mrs Hayes joining us? I have something I need to give her before we leave."

"She should be here by now," Mrs Edwards responded, looking towards the doorway into the room. "She said she'd only be a few moments behind me. Oh my goodness!" Mrs Edwards exclaimed in horror.

Chris and Catherine turned to see the cause of her distress. Mr Parker was walking through an increasing number of shocked onlookers as his presence was noticed.

"What the devil?" Chris asked no one in particular.

Mr Parker was battered. His right eye was partially closed and his lip bloody. A bruise was already forming on his chin. His clothing was bloodied and dishevelled, and his stovepipe hat was missing completely.

He stopped when he reached their group. "Thank goodness, you're here!" he greeted Mrs Edwards, wincing in pain as his lip split as he spoke.

"What on earth has happened? Have you been attacked?" Mrs Edwards asked.

"I suppose I have," Mr Parker responded. "Where's Mrs Hayes?"

"I don't know. She said she would be following me, but I've been here this last half hour waiting for her," Mrs Edwards explained.

"We need to find her," Mr Parker said.

"Why? What's going on?" Chris asked.

Before Mr Parker was able to explain himself, the Master of Ceremonies approached the group. "Mr Parker, I must entreat you to leave and seek attention for your wounds," he started without preamble.

"I will. I just need a moment," Mr Parker responded.

"I'm afraid that won't be possible. Your presence is upsetting some of our more delicate visitors," came the uncompromising response.

"Can you not give him a minute to gather himself?" Catherine asked disgusted.

"No, Mrs West. I cannot. This place has standards to maintain, and no one is allowed to breach the rules."

"Fine!" Catherine snapped. "Come. Let's leave this place and find somewhere that is willing to provide a safe environment for someone who has clearly been attacked. If you hear screams, sir, don't worry, it's probably us being beaten by the same person who has carried out this vile act on my friend!"

"Madam," came the cool response, but the Master of Ceremonies used his arm to indicate they should be leaving.

"What despicable behaviour! You should be ashamed of yourself!" Catherine hissed as she stormed out of the room.

The group paused a few steps away from the Pump Room. Catherine muttered to Chris. "I'm feeling more and more that the grass isn't always greener!" to which she had received a quick smile.

Chris turned to Mr Parker. "Tell us everything," he demanded.

"Chorlton has gone mad," Mr Parker started. "He received a letter this morning from his mother, saying that the creditors have started calling in his debts. He's been living beyond his means for some time."

"What has this to do with Mrs Hayes?" Catherine asked.

"He blames her for his failure in securing your hand," Mr Parker explained.

"That's ridiculous!" Catherine said with feeling. "I'm quite able to make my own judgement, and he never had a chance! He's a lunatic to have even thought for a moment I could be with someone like him!"

Mrs Edwards looked shocked at the words, but turned to Mr Parker. "What can he do? My friend has nothing he could want. She has no fortune."

"Perhaps not. But he said if he was facing ruin, he was taking her with him. I think he's planning on doing some sort of exchange with Mrs West, for Mrs Hayes' safety. I tried to stop him. You can see how successful I was at that," Mr Parker shrugged.

"You need those wounds cleaned," Catherine said.

"We need to find Mrs Hayes first. Miss Chorlton is helping her brother. Poor Mrs Hayes won't be handled with care," Mr Parker said, moving to Mrs Edwards' side when he realised his words were upsetting her.

"Parker, you need medical attention," Chris started. "Tell me Mrs Hayes' address and we'll go check on her. Mrs Edwards, I think you should accompany Mr Parker. Dealing with Chorlton might not be pleasant."

"Oh dear! But she's my friend!" Mrs Edwards responded, clearly torn between the man she cared for and her friend.

"I want to give Chorlton the beating he deserves. It won't be a nice thing to witness," Chris said grimly.

"I should be with you," Mr Parker said, valiantly. "I know what he's capable of."

"You need to look after yourself. I can sort out that dandy. Don't worry! He might be younger than me, but I've been involved with enough rugby fisticuffs to be able to handle myself," Chris responded.

"What's that?" Mr Parker said in confusion.

Chris laughed, realising his mistake. Rugby hadn't been invented yet. "Never mind, it would take too long to explain. Now where are you staying with Mrs Hayes?" he asked Mrs Edwards.

Catherine knew why Mrs Hayes had been reluctant to declare where they were staying. Westgate Street was not one of the best streets in Bath. The group separated, Catherine following Chris silently. She knew Chris was ready for a fight, and although not one for violence, she couldn't help being of the opinion that Mr Chorlton deserved what was coming to him.

They arrived at Westgate Street, and after locating the rooms and knocking for some time, it became clear that there was no one in residence.

"What do we do now?" Catherine asked.

"We find them," Chris said. "I don't intend leaving that poor woman to that bully."

"Where shall we start?" Catherine responded, agreeing to the sentiments exactly.

"He's not likely to have gone to any of the populated places. He might even have taken her out of Bath. We can return to Parker and formulate where we should be searching. I don't like including him, but the more help we have, the quicker we find her," Chris said, already heading away from Westgate Street.

Mr Parker was having his wounds bathed in his room at the White Hart. Catherine had raised her eyebrows in shock when she discovered an unconcerned Mrs Edwards alone with a gentleman in his bedchamber, tending to his wounds.

Chris explained quickly what he was thinking, and they agreed two sets of two people would be more productive. Setting out from the White Hart, Chris turned unexpectedly, striding out along the road running past the Pump Room.

"Where are you going?" Catherine asked, struggling to keep up with Chris.

She received no answer, nor a slowing of his pace until he reached the end of Quiet Street that led into Wood Street.

"What are we doing here?" Catherine asked.

"You're going home," Chris said simply.

Chapter 20

Catherine came to a sudden stop. "What? No!"

"I'll be happier knowing you're safe on the other side," Chris said firmly. "The clock is ticking, and I need to concentrate on finding Mrs Hayes."

"Obviously," Catherine snapped. "And standing here arguing is wasting minutes. I'm not going back."

"Catherine, please," Chris said, holding her by the shoulders, in a shockingly open way. "I'm being selfish. I need to know you're through and safe. I don't know what plans Chorlton has. He's obviously a desperate man. If it's like Parker says and he's on some warped mission to kidnap Mrs Hayes and then exchange her for you, his heiress, it's going to take time, which we haven't got."

Catherine felt herself start to struggle for breath but tried to contain her panic. "But the clock is ticking for you as well," she said quietly.

"If I'm on my own, I'll barge in like the lunatic I can be on the pitch. Admittedly in my youth," Chris said with a self-deprecating smile. "I need to know you're safe. I'm old enough and ugly enough to look after myself."

Catherine nodded silently. She was afraid to speak because of the tears threatening. She was ashamed to admit it, but she had been inwardly worrying about the time. She was concerned about Mrs Hayes, but her overriding focus would always be Megan and Andrew. She had to get back to them before the gateway closed.

They walked to John Street and Chris paused. "This is it. Will you wait for me in Union Passage?" he asked.

"Yes, of course. I don't want to leave you," Catherine finally was able to utter.

"It won't be for long," Chris assured her.

He opened his arms, and Catherine immediately moved into them. Being enfolded in his bear hug, without a doubt, was the place where, if there weren't other considerations, Catherine would always choose to be.

"I'll be as quick as I can," Chris whispered, tilting her chin so Catherine looked into his eyes. "I love you, Catherine."

Catherine's eyes widened in shock, but then she smiled. "And I love you, too," she said, stretching up to kiss him gently on the lips. She didn't care if their action was shocking to the society of 1811.

Chris let her go reluctantly. "I need to go."

"Please be quick," Catherine begged.

"I will," Chris responded before turning away from her, turning the corner into Quiet Street without looking back.

Catherine turned away. He had to succeed. She couldn't bear the thought of any other scenario.

*

The discomfort passed, but it had been different. Catherine had heard a 'pop' and a flash of blinding white light from behind her as she had passed through the portal. She seemed to be able to get her bearings quicker than she had every other time she had been through the experience.

Seeing Eric and Eliza standing at the top of the alleyway, she walked quickly towards them.

"I hope you've enjoyed your experience," Eliza said with a smile.

"Sort of. As long as Chris makes it through and Mrs Hayes is safe, it will have been mostly pleasant," Catherine said with a long breath.

"What's happened?" Eliza asked, immediately on the alert.

Catherine quickly told her of the situation she'd left behind, noticing how both Eliza and Eric were looking alarmed. "Can you not help?" she asked finally.

"We can't interfere," Eliza responded, but she didn't look happy. "Why didn't he just come home with you?"

"Well, let's go around to Union Passage and see if he has," Catherine suggested. She was a little annoyed that neither herself nor Chris had caused this situation, but the people in charge seemed to be unwilling to take matters into their own hands.

Eliza and Catherine walked to Union Passage. The Passage was the complete opposite of John Street, with more shops and people in the vicinity.

"How does the disappearance work here? Surely, it's too public a place?" Catherine asked.

"It's surprising what people don't see when they don't want to. Anything strange is seen as threatening, so very often it's ignored," Eliza replied.

"Where should we wait?" Catherine asked.

"Just here," Eliza instructed.

"Where else?" Catherine asked drily. They stood at a pedestrian crossroads, probably the busiest place along the passageway.

They stood in silence for the next few hours. Catherine checking her watch every few moments, her only sign of discomfort being the occasional stamping of her feet against the cold that was seeping through their bodies.

The skies darkened and signs of the traders packing up for the evening became more obvious. This particular Saturday evening would see a mass exodus from the city as shoppers and Christmas Market traders all made their way back to their normal routines.

Eliza had noticed with every chime of the hour from the Bath Abbey that Catherine seemed to withdraw into herself further. The feelings of apprehension increased as nothing occurred to give either of them hope.

Five o'clock came and went. Neither said a word when the chimes finished or when a flash of white appeared and disappeared in the alleyway.

Eventually, Eliza decided she had to make Catherine acknowledge the truth. "It's over. He's not coming back," she said quietly.

"We need to help him. He won't have stayed willingly," Catherine responded.

"It's too late," Eliza replied.

"No! I'm not accepting that!" Catherine insisted. "Open up my way back. I need to return."

Before Eliza could answer, Catherine started to run towards John Street. Eliza had no option but to follow, but she didn't rush. There was no need; it was a futile excursion.

Eric had rested his sign on the ground. He could finally give-up his dreary role. Leaning against the wall waiting for Eliza's return, he was alarmed enough to stand upright when he saw Catherine barrelling along John Street. She paused at the point she had disappeared previously, walking backwards and forwards over the same piece of ground to try and recreate her passage into the other world.

Eventually, she ran up to the end of John Street, where Eliza had joined Eric. "Send me back!" Catherine demanded.

"It's not as simple as that," Eliza responded. "We can't just open and close as we wish. I told you when it would close. He knew that as well."

"So, he's condemned to goodness knows what kind of life because he was trying to help someone?" Catherine asked incredulously. "I suppose at least he'll be rich."

Catherine noticed Eliza's shifty expression. "What? Tell me why he won't be rich!"

"The money ends when the portal closes. It all finishes," Eliza said, not quite able to look into Catherine's eyes.

"NO!" Catherine shouted, not caring that she was making a spectacle of herself. "He has no means of support! You can't abandon him like that!"

"I can't do anything about it," Eliza said.

"That's completely irresponsible!" Catherine snapped. "You have a duty to care for people when you play around with their lives! I'm not accepting this. Do something!"

Eric finally spoke. "Wait here. I'll return as soon as I can." Before waiting for an answer, he disappeared into the wall as he had on other occasions.

Eric's action made Catherine rub her forehead. "I must be going mad," she muttered to herself.

"I'm sorry it didn't work out for you," Eliza said, trying to smooth what had turned into a nightmare of an assignment.

"What were you trying to achieve?" Catherine asked.

"For you to meet the hero of your dreams," Eliza tried to explain.

"Fine. So, when things moved beyond friendship for us, why didn't the opening close then?" Catherine asked. "So many things could've gone wrong. Wouldn't it just have been easier to make sure we were safe?"

"You had to make your own choices. There was always the chance you would pick Mr Chorlton," Eliza said defensively.

"There was never the chance I would have picked him!" Catherine responded in disbelief. "You can't know me very well if you thought that."

"But you spend so much time reading about the Regency," Eliza responded in self-defence. "I was giving you what you wanted."

"I read to escape," Catherine said with a sigh. "To pretend life was perfect in another time. But even I'm not foolish enough to believe it was."

"But you've often commented about the heroes in the stories," Eliza insisted.

"Because that's what they are — stories. I want to pick and choose my hero. Between the pages I don't have to pick up after his washing, I don't have to smell his breath after he's had a night out with the lads, and I don't have to face up to the fact that everyone is as flawed as I am," Catherine explained. "I'd much rather be with someone like Chris, with all his idiosyncrasies than someone who sees a wife as a commodity and rarely anything else. I love the stories, and I'll continue to read them. But if I'm to meet someone new, it would have to be someone I could call my equal. I would imagine there were few of that type of hero around then."

Eric prevented Eliza from replying to Catherine's revelations by reappearing. He looked at Catherine. "I've got good news and bad news," he stated.

"Oh, for goodness sake!" Catherine said with feeling. "Just tell me."

"You're right. She is hard work," Eric said to Eliza, which succeeded in him receiving glares from both women. "Okay!" he said, holding his hands up in defeat. "He'll continue to get daily funds but only until the end of December."

"And then what? The portal reopens?" Catherine asked.

"No."

"That's not good enough!" Catherine responded. "He won't know how long he has money for. When is the soonest I can return to 1811?"

"You can't. It was a one-time visit," Eliza replied.

"Why did Chris get access year after year, but I only get to go the once?" Catherine demanded.

"He was hurt very badly and needed a slower recovery," Eliza explained. "He wasn't ready to meet anyone for a few years."

"And I'm so shallow that I was?" Catherine asked in challenge.

"You've admitted yourself that there wasn't much love between you and your husband at the end, so you were more open to another relationship, even if you didn't realise it," Eliza pointed out.

"I really don't like you knowing everything about me," Catherine responded tartly. "Will Chris' portal open next year?"

"Yes," Eric said with authority. "I took the liberty of checking that."

"Finally, some progress!" Catherine responded. "So, if I'm here, I can go through and meet him?"

"Yours won't open," Eric said.

"Why not? You've shown me the man of my dreams and now you're keeping us apart?" Catherine asked. "That's not part of the deal. You'd better get it organised, so I can go back."

"It'll have been two years in his world," Eliza pointed out gently.

Catherine took a breath. "If he's forgotten about me then, so be it. I check he's happy and then I return, but I need to make sure he's well."

Eliza and Eric exchanged a look before Eliza nodded. "It'll be open on the first day of the market."

"Good," Catherine responded with feeling. "And I want you to accompany me," she said looking at Eric.

"Why me?" Eric asked in alarm.

"Because although I'm loath to admit such a thing, I might need the help of a man when I go through again. I don't know what I'm going to face," Catherine explained.

"He's a trainee! He can't go!" Eliza said heatedly.

"Well, he's going. You got us in this mess. You can damn well let me try and get us out!" Catherine said. "I'll see you both next year. Please don't interfere in my life until then!"

Catherine walked away.

"Tell me again why she needed our help?" Eric asked.

"She never would've stood up to anyone like this. Her husband had her brow-beaten into submission. She's finally asserting herself," Eliza explained.

"So her man being trapped in 1811 was all part of the plan?" Eric asked in confusion.

"Well, no," Eliza admitted. "But I'm sure he'll be fine."

Chapter 21

During the drive home Catherine shed tears for Chris. She was worried and afraid and unable to see ahead to the next week let alone the following year. Returning to her children was definitely like being faced with a bundle of mixed emotions, and she was not sure which one would emerge at what time. One thing was for certain, she wasn't sure how to get through the coming months.

*

The thing with having children — of whatever age — is that their lives and routines soon take over everyday life. Megan and Andrew returned the same afternoon that Catherine did, and she was soon absorbed in washing clothes, shopping and feeding her hungry pair.

A lot later in the evening, Andrew sought her out as she finally had a moment to unpack her own suitcases.

"You okay?" Catherine asked, as Andrew flopped on her bed.

"Yes," came the usual reply. "I think Megan believes in Father Christmas again," he responded with a smile that was probably supposed to be derogatory but didn't quite make it.

"That's because he exists," Catherine said. "If you want to openly announce his nonexistence, that's fine, but don't come crying to me when you have no presents on Christmas morning!"

"One day I'll test that theory, and we'll see just how soft you really are," Andrew teased.

Catherine smiled at him. "Foiled again! Did you enjoy yourself?"

"It was brilliant, although I don't think Dad was too pleased. I spent more time with the animals than I did with him or Danielle. I made sure Meg was happy enough though," Andrew said quickly.

"I wouldn't expect anything less. You're a good big brother," Catherine responded, ignoring the years of arguing they'd done when they were younger.

"Tell her that," Andrew said. "I've been thinking of getting a job, to try and save up until I get to uni," he said quietly.

Catherine closed the drawer she was folding shirts into and joined Andrew on the side of the bed. "I don't mind you getting a job while you're at sixth form, but you know all the prospectus bumf say that, if you get on the vet courses, there won't physically be enough time for part-time work."

"I do want to help though," Andrew responded.

"I know, and I'm forever grateful that you do. But I've got news on that score. At least for the start of uni life," Catherine said.

"What is it? You've won the lottery?" Andrew asked.

"Not quite. While I was away I learned a bit about antiques and managed to make a bit of profit buying and selling them," Catherine said, glossing over the reality. She dampened down the feelings of guilt she'd experienced when taking the last trinkets to the antique dealers on the morning of her return. She knew it would have been what Chris wanted, but it didn't stop her feeling disloyal by making money when he would be struggling.

"Oh?" Andrew responded, not really understanding the impact of her words.

"I want to show you something," Catherine said, before fishing her phone out of her pocket and accessing her online banking app. "This won't take you through the whole of the course, but with this, and my two jobs I think it gives us a head start don't you?" Catherine asked as she showed her son the balance in her account.

"Bloody hell, Mum, have you robbed a bank?" Andrew asked in disbelief, looking at the bottom figure on the statement.

"No, not quite," Catherine laughed. "It takes the pressure off a little doesn't it?"

"That's amazing, Mum!" Andrew responded with feeling.

"I'm glad it'll put your mind at rest. We can't go mad. There'll still be cost-cutting to do, but I think we'll be able to achieve it." Catherine was under no illusion that the next years weren't going to be a struggle, but if it gave her children the best start to their careers, she would work her fingers to the bone.

"Thanks, Mum," Andrew said flinging his arms around her in only the way a gangly teenage boy can do.

"You're welcome," Catherine said, clinging onto the rarely given treat. "There's just one thing …"

"Go on. There was always going to be a catch," Andrew said, preparing himself for disappointment.

"No! It's nothing to worry about. I'm going to need to spend some money — although only a small amount — on a trip to Bath next year," Catherine said.

"For more antiques?" Andrew asked hopefully.

"No," Catherine smiled. "I don't think there'll be time for that. I met someone in Bath, and I want to go back and see him," she answered in the most airbrushed way possible.

"Really? I didn't expect you to say that," Andrew admitted. "Does Megan know?"

"No. It's complicated. I will tell her but not yet," Catherine answered.

"Is he married?" Andrew asked, frowning.

"No! I'd never do that to another human being!" Catherine answered hotly. "He's had to go away and will only be back next December. I'm not sure if things will be the same when we meet again, but I need to give it a try," Catherine tried to explain.

"It still sounds dodgy to me, Mum. Why see him after a whole year if you like each other? As long as he isn't married, though, I'm fine with it. There's been enough grief in this family to make me and Megan completely risk-averse!"

"I should find that comment quite sad, but as your mother, I find it reassuring!" Catherine said with feeling.

Andrew smiled. "Maybe we need to give you a few scares just to keep you on your toes."

"No thanks!"

Catherine continued her unpacking, feeling a little lighter. Andrew had been more accepting to her having a relationship than she'd thought he would be, although showing him the money first probably was the right ploy.

She knew explaining to Susan, wasn't going to be anywhere near as easy.

*

It was nearly a week before Catherine had the opportunity to speak to her friend fully about what had happened. She had waited until they would not be disturbed.

Susan twisted her hair in her familiar 'I'm pondering' pose. Catherine knew from experience it wasn't a good sign.

"Are you being serious?" Susan asked her long-time friend.

"I know it sounds ridiculous, but it's all true," Catherine responded.

"I can wholeheartedly believe you've met someone new, but time travel and fairy godmothers are a little hard to take," Susan admitted.

"Try living through it!" Catherine said with feeling. "I've brought a few mementoes that might help convince you," she said, unloading her bag.

Giving each object to her best friend, Catherine explained what they were. "This is a card case, containing my calling cards," she handed Susan a silver box that had an intricate pattern on the front, made with mother-of-pearl. The cards inside were exquisite in their design, the lettering very ornate. "The case is worth hundreds of pounds in today's market, so you know I wouldn't have bought it purely as a joke. Here's the receipt. This shop no longer exists in Bath, so I suppose I could have forged it, but the antique shops have authenticated the receipts." Catherine waited while Susan examined everything closely.

"I want to believe you," the friend admitted.

"Thanks for listening so far," Catherine said with a smile. "I think if roles were reversed, I'd be calling the asylum by now!"

Susan laughed. "What else have you got?"

"I've got these three books," Catherine said. "I'm hoping this will completely convince you."

Catherine handed the books to Susan, who, the moment she realised what the books were, looked at her best friend in shock. "How did you get these?"

Catherine smiled. "I was disappointed when Eliza said that we were in 1811, because I knew there was no chance I would get to meet Jane Austen, but then I remembered she'd been published in 1811. It was lucky I was there in December, they were only released in October."

"The covers aren't bound very well," Susan remarked.

"It's called marbling," Catherine explained. "Apparently, people would get them covered themselves in leather to match their other books in their own library. It's a completely different way to how we buy books these days."

"Who's the little expert then?" Susan teased. "Have you had them valued? They're in perfect condition."

"It's because they're new," Catherine said gently. "I've looked on the internet. I thought they'd be worth a few thousand pounds."

"And?" Susan persisted.

"They're worth tens of thousands of pounds, especially because I have the receipt," Catherine said quietly. "I've made so much money buying and selling the stuff we brought back with us. It's really taken the pressure off me, financially."

"That's a lot of money! At least that's one worry off your mind," Susan said.

"I'm not sure I can actually part with them. Not yet anyway," Catherine admitted. "I was told there was a reason I'd been allowed into the past. I'd thought it was to help another woman who was struggling there then I thought it might be for myself."

"Couldn't it have been both reasons?"

"Possibly," Catherine smiled. "I did begin to hope that it was meeting Chris and then we went and magnificently messed it up!"

"I don't think it's safe for you to go back next year," Susan said.

"Does this mean you believe me?" Catherine asked.

"I don't know what I believe, if I'm honest," Susan admitted. "You're no liar though, so I suppose I have to believe you or admit my friend has gone completely mad."

"Perhaps a bit of both?" Catherine suggested with a laugh. "It still feels strange to me, but Chris was very real, and I need to go back."

"So, he'll have lived two years there?" Susan asked.

"Yes, but with only one month's money," Catherine said, chewing her lip. "I wish there was something I could do to find out what's happening to him."

"Contact the local archives," Susan suggested.

"To find out what?" Catherine asked.

"Anything," Susan answered unhelpfully.

"I suppose I have names and possible addresses," Catherine mulled. "I think it's a start anyway!"

"Hopefully, it'll give you peace," Susan answered, still wondering about the story she'd listened too.

Chapter 22

Something unsurprising caused a further dilemma for Catherine. Susan had asked for Catherine to visit one night, and Catherine had agreed, not suspecting her evening wasn't going to be quite the pleasant one she'd anticipated.

Susan sat next to her friend and put her own mobile in Catherine's hands. "I know you don't go on Facebook very often, so I've presumed this has passed you by," Susan said, knowing there was no gentle way to break the news.

Catherine stared at the unblinking screen, her face paling at what she was reading. "Oh! Good God!" she muttered. "They're looking for him."

The post that had shocked her was a picture of Chris, smiling out of the screen, with an appeal for information about the missing person. "I suppose it's no surprise really. You've been back nearly two weeks," Susan responded.

The appeal was from Chris' sister and was a heart-breaking tribute to her missing brother. "Of course he was going to be missed," Catherine said quietly. "What an idiot I was not to realise that before now. What can I do to help them?"

"There's nothing you can do," Susan responded. "If you start trying to explain, you will find yourself in a psychiatric ward."

"I know, but I need to let them know he's alive," Catherine said, clearly distressed.

"You don't know that," Susan said quietly.

Catherine slumped. "I don't, but I have to believe he's okay. Oh, damn it! Why did I insist on giving Mrs Hayes the money I'd saved? If I hadn't wanted to be someone's saviour we'd never have gone back!"

"You're a good person. You weren't to know," Susan responded, defending her friend.

"Thanks for the vote of confidence, but my actions have caused a family to suffer a year's worth of agony. I can't imagine what they must be going through."

"Just don't mention anything, even if it reaches the national news," Susan urged.

"I won't. I don't think I can watch the news until next December."

*

Catherine spent the next few months working hard on two jobs, being a mum to two teenagers and becoming an amateur sleuth/historian. She spent every spare moment on the phone or on the internet. She paid for copies of documents, justifying the expense to herself by acknowledging it was Chris who had given her the idea of bringing items into the present to sell as antiques. She could spare a few hundred pounds on trying to find out if he'd been safe during his forced stay. For once in her life she pushed aside the ever-ready feelings of guilt. This was for Chris.

It was mid-March before a school trip and college trip coincided and so, having a child-free evening, she invited Susan around for a catch-up and update of her findings.

They enjoyed a take-away and a large bottle of wine. When they'd moved into the lounge for comfort, Catherine sat down on the floor near her coffee table.

"This is the stuff, I've managed to trace. It isn't much," Catherine admitted.

"Let me see." Susan flopped onto the floor beside her friend. "Did you find him?"

"Yes and no," Catherine started. "First, let me tell you about Mr Chorlton."

"I hope he came to a sticky end!"

"He did," Catherine said. "I couldn't find anything out about him for years, so goodness knows what he did, but thankfully, it looks like he left Bath at some point after my visit."

"Did he take your Mrs Hayes?" Susan asked.

"No. But I'll come onto that," Catherine responded. "The only record of Mr Chorlton is an entry into a workhouse in 1856. He was in his seventies but classed as a pauper."

"From a gentleman to a pauper? That must have been hard to stomach!" Susan said, almost feeling as if she knew the man.

"Yes, it must've," Catherine agreed. "I feel sorry for him in a way. It can't have been easy to fall so far. Workhouses weren't pleasant."

"I expect not, but he didn't sound very nice, so I don't feel sorry for him!" Susan retorted.

"You cruel woman!" Catherine scolded her friend. "He died in 1858 of consumption. It's a really weird feeling, knowing he died at such an old age when he was so much younger only last December!"

"I've heard of first-world problems but never time-travel problems until today!" Susan chuckled.

273

"Welcome to my world!" Catherine grinned. "Anyway, I've not been able to trace any marriages to him, so it appears he never found his heiress after all."

"Once he'd seen you, he was spoiled for anyone else!" Susan offered like only a best friend could.

Catherine laughed. "Hardly! Eliza was shocked that I never would have considered him, but you'd have spent about an hour in his company before condemning him."

"I'm not that good. It took far longer with Paul," Susan pointed out.

"Yes, but he fooled all of us," Catherine said. "Including me, and what's hard to swallow is that it took years for me to realise what a self-centred prat he was!"

"At least you came to your senses. Now, what else have you found?" Susan asked.

"Something not so surprising," Catherine said. "Mr Parker and Miss Edwards married in January 1812, and Mrs Hayes and a certain Mr Dobson were their witnesses!"

"Really? How fabulous!" Susan exclaimed, grabbing the offered copy of a wedding certificate. The names of all parties mentioned could be made out clearly. "It says the married couple were living in the same place. Does that mean they were living together before they were married? I'm shocked!"

Catherine laughed. "Now don't you start condemning my Regency friends with your modern standards! Of course, they won't have been living together. She would have been ruined and ignored by society! Rooms were let to different people in the same house. It must mean they were in the same building."

"Was Westgate Buildings a good address?" Susan asked.

"No. Which is worrying," Catherine admitted, staring at the name of the man she longed to see, wishing it could give her a clue. "It looks as if Mr Parker didn't have much money either. I hope Chris is okay."

"Well at least you know he hadn't starved to death at least for the first month he was there without support, so there's a chance he'll still be well when you return in December," Susan assured her friend.

"Thanks for that. I think," Catherine responded dryly.

"Have you found anything else?" Susan asked.

"No. Which is both worrying and reassuring at the same time. It means he didn't end his days in a workhouse in the wrong century, but it gives me no other clues to how he was or where he lived. He must have been with our friends, but whether he lived with them or not is a mystery," Catherine mused.

"I will be on pins the whole time you're in Bath this year," Susan admitted.

"I might not even need to go back," Catherine said. "I'm going to wait at the location Chris came and went. If he comes through the opening, I won't be going through. It's a risk I'm not prepared to take after last year."

"And if he doesn't come through?"

"Then I have to try and find him. I can't abandon him."

PART TWO

Chapter 23

Bath – December, A Year Later

Catherine checked into a different hotel than she had stayed in previously. There had been a national appeal to try and find Chris. She had received a visit from the local police, who had been informed by the hotel that she'd spent some time over breakfast with Chris. No one had known of their developing relationship, and although it made her feel like the worst kind of person, Catherine had made it seem as if she had only spoken twice to Chris in the breakfast room. The police had seemed satisfied with her responses and had left her alone.

Now, though, she didn't want to face questioning by the proprietor of the establishment or spend time going over what had happened. A hotel in Queen Square was close to the address she'd stayed in when in 1811 and close enough to the opening should she need to use it.

She had faltered when she'd seen posters attached to lamp-posts, a picture of Chris smiling out at her. It stated he was missing, last seen in Bath. She'd seen this type of poster on previous visits, but she'd only wondered casually about the story behind the face being sought; now she knew the story, and it didn't rest easy. She had to hope he would be returned to his family soon.

Wandering around the city, watching the Christmas market chalets being set-up made her impatient for the following morning when she'd been promised there would be access to the past.

*

Hurrying to the Union Passage, Catherine was filled with hope, apprehension and nerves. It was 1813 in Chris' world. What he had done in the previous two years, she had no idea, but whatever it was, she hoped he was ready to come through to the future, a future she still wanted to share with him.

Pausing at the place she knew to be the opening, she saw Eliza walking from the opposite direction.

"I thought you'd be here," Eliza said.

"Just five minutes until nine," Catherine responded. Then the Christmas market would be officially open. "Have you any news about him?"

"No. We aren't able to accompany you after our time has come to an end," Eliza replied.

"It seems your rules change to suit your needs. You must have spent time watching me, to be able to quote words I'd uttered," Catherine said.

"That was in an effort to cater to your specific needs," Eliza defended herself. Their conversation wasn't exactly aggressive, but it certainly wasn't conciliatory.

The clock chimed the hour, and Catherine held her breath. Eventually, releasing it in a whoosh, she turned to Eliza. "He isn't coming through."

"No," Eliza responded, looking worried.

"We need to go to John Street," Catherine said, already starting to walk away.

"Would it not be better to give him some time?" Eliza asked, hurrying to catch-up.

"No. If he could have come through, he would be here already," Catherine responded with conviction. "I need to go to him."

They walked in silence until they reached the top end of John Street. For some reason, it was a one-way system into the time-travel opening. Catherine nodded to Eric, who had been standing at the top of the alleyway, this time without his sign.

"Are you ready to go?" Catherine asked.

Eric looked nervously at Eliza. "Yes."

"Do I receive the same funds as last year? I might need money," Catherine asked, being practical.

"Yes. Everything is as it was, even your accommodation. Don't forget it's two years since you visited," Eliza responded.

"That thought has kept me awake on more nights than I care to recall," Catherine said, already starting to move down the alleyway. "Hopefully, this won't take long."

*

The numbing nothingness was always going to be hard to bear after so long a gap between journeys. Catherine leaned against the wall in an effort to receive support while gathering her bearings.

Eric waited patiently, watching as Catherine ran her hands down her front, now covered in a cotton day dress. "There are some things I'd never get used to if I did this for ten years," Catherine said with feeling. "Doing a Superman-style clothing change is one of them!"

"We can't have the population of the nineteenth century being shocked by a woman in jeans. The repercussions could be insurmountable," Eric responded cheerfully.

"You're certainly a different character than Eliza," Catherine said with a smile.

"That's because I'm a trainee and haven't been turned into a corporate puppet yet," Eric responded.

Catherine closed her eyes. "I thought I wouldn't be surprised by anything anymore, but you've just managed it!"

Eric smiled. "What do you want to do first?"

"It's a long shot, but I'll check the rooms we're staying in, just in case there's been a message sent through."

The pair walked the short distance to the house Catherine had come to know on her last excursion into the past. She noticed that the buildings seemed darker than her last visit, another two years of soot obviously seeping into the limestone.

Entering the room, she found everything the same as it had been, which was strangely familiar. Invitations were stacked on a side table, and Catherine looked through them quickly.

"There's nothing from him in this, nor is there any other clue. I'm presuming the Master of Ceremonies knows of our arrival?" Catherine asked.

"Yes. As your brother, I've made sure of that."

"My brother? Not my servant? Whose idea was that?" Catherine asked.

Eric kept his expression blank, but there was an unmistakable twinkle in his eye. "It was thought me being a relation would cause less suspicion or intrigue."

"So, not Eliza's idea then?" Catherine pushed.

"No. Not really," Eric said, diplomatically not mentioning the heated exchange that had taken place when the news had been broken to Eliza.

"So, brother, let us visit the Pump Room and see who is listed in the visitors book," Catherine said grandly.

Eric offered his arm, and the two left the building.

Chapter 24

Catherine checked and double checked the pages of the visitors book in the Pump Room. She tried to scan the pages whilst appearing nonchalant, but the panic was rising in her chest. There was no entry of any of the people she knew.

It was a relief to know Mr Chorlton was not resident in Bath, but as for the others, if they weren't in residence, she had no idea where to start looking for them.

They were approached by the Master of Ceremonies, who welcomed them both to Bath.

"We are delighted to be here, aren't we, brother?" Catherine said pleasantly.

"We certainly are," Eric responded.

"I was wondering, sir, if you were aware of a Mr Dobson, Mrs Hayes, or Mr and Mrs Parker? I met them here two years ago and was hoping to see them again," Catherine said.

The Master of Ceremonies paused. "They aren't names I recognise, even in those who haven't subscribed to the facilities of Bath." People paid to take part in the entertainments, so the ones embracing Bath society would be known by him.

"Could they be here without your knowledge?" Catherine asked, desperately clinging on to a small hope.

"They could," the Master of Ceremonies acknowledged. "But only if they weren't part of polite society. From what you suggest, that wouldn't be an option?"

The words were asked politely, but it was a fact that the best in society would be the only ones interacted with. The general invalids who visited the spa town would not be of note to many beyond their immediate circle. It was clear the standard of the clientele was important to the Master of Ceremonies.

"No! Not at all!" Catherine responded quickly. "I met them within these walls. I'm sure they must've decided not to visit this year, which is a shame."

The Master of Ceremonies inclined his head and made his excuses, leaving the pair alone.

"I notice he wasn't keen to make introductions to us," Catherine said.

"I think you've put enough suspicion in his mind to give you a wide berth," Eric responded.

"Dread to think the tone of his establishment be brought down!" Catherine said in a huff.

"To be fair, he's struggling against the rise of other resorts," Eric said soothingly. "Bath continues to decline. It can't be easy for those whose job it is to promote the facilities."

"I hope Chris and the others haven't been tempted by those resorts or I'll never find them."

"Where would you like to try next?" Eric asked.

"The White Hart," Catherine said firmly. "And if there's nothing there, Westgate Buildings."

*

The White Hart proved fruitless. Catherine hadn't expected Mr Pickwick, the innkeeper, to remember anyone from two years ago, but she needed to check that they weren't in residence.

Walking towards Westgate Street, she felt a weight pushing against her chest. "If I don't find them here — ".

"There are a lot of lodging houses in Bath," Eric interrupted, not sounding hopeful.

"Yes. So how on earth do we visit them all?" Catherine asked.

"We'll have to hope for the best," Eric responded.

"You're now beginning to sound as deluded as your co-worker," Catherine said, raising an eyebrow.

"Don't!" Eric responded with a groan.

Entering Westgate Buildings was far different from entering a well-to-do establishment. The whole feel was different. The hallway was darker. There was more noise coming from the rooms, and the building felt damp. The street outside had been pleasant enough, but Catherine knew that some of the rooms were let extremely cheaply.

Catherine felt sympathy for anyone in reduced circumstances being forced to live in the building. She knocked on the first door which was opened by a woman older than herself; her appearance was reassuring as she was dressed, not in the finest clothes, but in clean, perfectly acceptable apparel.

Catherine made her enquiry, to which she received a negative reply. A Mrs Hayes no longer resided in the building.

"Have you any idea where she went when she left?" Catherine asked in desperation.

"Do you realise how many ladies and gentlemen pass through these doors?" The caretaker asked.

"I can only imagine," Catherine admitted. "I'm just trying to locate my friends. I know it is a vain hope. Mrs Edwards married from here to a Mr Parker. They had a friend, a Mr Dobson."

The caretaker paused for a moment, looking Catherine and Eric up and down. "I keep a good house here," she eventually said.

"I'm sure you do," Catherine acknowledged in confusion.

"I do remember your friends," the caretaker responded. "The lady that married Mr Parker was a decent one, but the pair left behind … well … I just couldn't accept it!" She folded her arms across her chest in disgust.

"What happened?" Eric said. "You can be honest with us. Sister, dear, prepare yourself. I have a feeling we are going to be shocked."

Catherine looked at Eric wanting to ridicule him but instead gasped dramatically. "I'm ready," she said.

The caretaker lowered her voice. "They were in two rooms initially. The ladies in one, the gentlemen in the other. After the marriage, the Parkers left the establishment, and one of the rooms was given up. I thought the other widow had left with her friend, but no! Them two. They were in the same room. Together!"

Catherine gasped, not needing to act in any way. Chris and Mrs Hayes living together. That was something she hadn't considered.

Eric put his arm around Catherine in a gesture of support. "What did you do?" he asked.

"Why, I threw them out! There's no funny business going on while I'm in charge! My master would cast me off without a reference if I was to allow behaviour like that within these walls! No. They had to go," the caretaker said with feeling.

"Have you any idea where they went?" Eric pressed.

"Not a clue, but the likes of them are not welcome around here!"

"Thank you," Eric said, passing a coin to the woman. "I'm sorry we have reminded you about an unwelcome experience."

"You seem respectable people. I'd stay away from the likes of them, if I was you," the caretaker advised, accepting the money and closing the door.

Eric and Catherine walked out in silence. "Come, you need some food," Eric directed. He led the way to

Sally Lunn's establishment, ducking his head as he entered the low doorway.

They were soon seated, and Eric ordered for them both. Pouring tea, he watched Catherine.

"Not what you expected to hear," he said gently.

"No," Catherine responded. "How arrogant am I? To think he might have waited for me."

"You waited for him," Eric pointed out.

"I did, but it was half the time. Perhaps he just accepted that he was going to stay here and lived his life accordingly?" Catherine mused. She had to be fair to Chris. He had been faced with a nightmare of a situation. If it meant her heart was breaking, that was her lookout not his.

"Perhaps. But we don't know what happened. Do you know where Mr and Mrs Parker went? We could send a letter to them, asking for information," Eric suggested.

"No. I don't know where they moved to. The census only started in 1841. Apart from trying to glean knowledge from parish records, which in their case would be births I suppose. But it's a long shot. I'd presumed Mrs Parker was too old to have children," Catherine admitted.

"It's a reasonable assumption," Eric said.

"It's such a shame that his family won't know what happened to him. At least I'll know he settled in this time, which is a slight consolation. I hope he's happy," Catherine said.

"Don't give up hope just yet. We haven't scoured the streets," Eric responded, tucking into his Bath bun with relish.

Catherine smiled at Eric's behaviour, despite her desolation at the realisation she might have lost Chris for good. "You eat like my teenage son," she said. "He always eats as if his current meal is the last one he'll ever eat!"

"We only eat when we're on assignment, so technically this could be my last meal," Eric said between mouthfuls.

"Really? How do you survive?" Catherine asked in surprise.

"We don't need food on the higher level," Eric explained.

"I wish I hadn't asked," Catherine said with a groan. "Most of the time I can persuade myself that I'm not going mad, and then you say something that convinces me I am."

Eric grinned. "Sorry," he said, completely unrepentant and ordered another bun.

Chapter 25

Catherine did feel slightly better after having her sweet tea. Eric had insisted she have sugar in it, which made her feel extremely indulged. Strange how something so taken for granted could be such a treat in another time.

They had decided to walk along Milsom Street just in case there was any sign of Mrs Hayes or Chris. Catherine knew it was a vain hope, but she had to try.

The street was bustling, but there was no sign of a tall, broad rugby player or the ever-cheerful Mrs Hayes.

They ventured farther out of the main shopping street before Catherine paused. "This is stupid. We aren't thinking everything through properly."

"What do you mean?" Eric asked, coming to a stop.

"As far as we know, neither of them had much income to sustain them. So, let's presume they didn't have enough money to leave Bath," Catherine explained.

"Fair enough, but I've already pointed out that the number of lodging places is huge," Eric responded patiently.

"But if we look at the type of lodging house they'd be able to afford — because they're clearly not out and about in the higher society — that should narrow down the area where they could be found," Catherine said, pleased she had thought of a way to focus their search.

Eric paused. "The types of areas you're talking about won't be pleasant."

"I know. But, as far as we're aware, they have what little money Mrs Hayes had plus the money I'd saved — which must surely have been spent by now — plus the money Chris had until the end of the first December. I don't know how much the cost of living is here, but it's going to be more than that," Catherine reasoned. Every time she thought about Chris, she felt sick. He must have suffered these last two years. She hoped it hadn't been all bad.

"True, but I think I should make enquiries while you wait for me in your room," Eric suggested.

"No! I might be able to help," Catherine said. "I'm forty-one years old not some naïve child."

"The poor areas are really poor. The only people who would willingly live there are ladies of the night and thieves," Eric whispered, not wishing to be overheard.

"I'll take my chances," Catherine insisted.

"I can understand why Eliza was frustrated," Eric muttered but tried to look innocent when Catherine glared at him.

"Where do we start?" Catherine asked, still glaring.

"Avon Street and the streets around it," Eric responded. "I think we'll start with the worst and work up."

Catherine followed her guardian, or whatever he was. She was certain her reasoning was correct, but it didn't alter the fact that she was walking into goodness knew what situation.

*

Walking into Avon Street, Catherine wouldn't have had to stretch her imagination too far to convince herself she was in a different city. The buildings were smaller than the towering grand Georgian houses that filled the streets from the Royal Crescent to Sydney Gardens, although those in Avon Street were by no means small structures. One thing was certain: They were hovels. It was obvious without the need to go inside any of the rooms.

The stench from the street made Catherine's nostrils flare in disgust. This was worse than the overpowering odour in a ballroom; it was the smell of life in the gutter, and it wasn't pleasant.

The streets seemed narrower, darker and more forbidding. The crowded chimneys on the buildings belched out their black poison into an atmosphere that seemed to envelope the pedestrians. Mists would gather here on dank, dark days, adding to the gloom of the unloved streets.

Late afternoon on a dull December day was probably not the best time to approach the streets, the darkening sky seeming to add to the gloom. As they walked farther down the street, the air seemed to become damper. Catherine knew they were approaching the river and shivered in the unwelcome environment.

Catherine was no coward, but she walked close to Eric. She watched surreptitiously as they passed the people who lived and worked in this less-appealing area of Bath.

Gone was the finery of those who frequented the assembly rooms and pump room. These folk looked world-weary, peering suspiciously out onto the world and seeking whatever chances they could use to their advantage, whether legal or not.

Eric cursed under his breath as he noticed a few interested glances aimed in their direction. Their clothes screamed out that they were intruders into this other world, easy targets for those waiting for every opportunity to gain a few extra pennies by fair means or foul.

"This is madness. We're going to Queen Square. We'll return in the morning. That'll be safer," Eric said.

Catherine didn't argue; she just remained silent until they had returned to a street that felt less threatening. "Surely they won't be living here?" she asked quietly, trying to keep up with Eric's purposeful strides.

"I've no idea," he answered honestly.

"Don't you have ways of finding out?"

"Afraid not. I wish we did. It would save us returning to that place tomorrow. Hopefully the undesirables will still be asleep if we go early enough," Eric responded trying to be positive.

"Thank you for helping me," Catherine said.

"From what I recall, I didn't have much choice. You demanded I escort you," Eric said, his twinkle returning.

"Oh, yes. I suppose I did," Catherine admitted with a small smile.

"You're welcome," Eric said quietly. "And for the record, I hope we find your man."

"From what's been said today, it doesn't sound like he is my man anymore."

The pair walked in silence until they reached number 13 Queen Square. Catherine faltered at the railings of the house.

"Are you staying here with me?" she asked, suddenly realising the implications of sharing a room with one chamber pot and a stranger.

"No. Eliza is inside," Eric said. "It was thought best to keep appearances as appropriate as possible."

"I suppose after the exchange at Westgate Buildings, I can't argue with that," Catherine acknowledged. "Will I see you in the morning?"

"Yes. As soon as you are ready, come onto the street, and I'll be waiting," Eric said. "Goodnight."

"Goodnight," Catherine replied and entered the house.

Eliza was already there, and although the atmosphere was a little strained, the two women fell into the pattern they'd developed the year before. Catherine settled into bed not sure if she would get much sleep, but the sounds of the Regency night soon sent her into a deep, dreamless sleep.

Chapter 26

Eric was waiting as promised the following morning even though Catherine had risen early. They had both dressed in far less good quality clothing than they had been used to. A battered woollen cloak protected Catherine's shoulders against the damp air.

The pair walked in silence towards an area of Bath neither wanted to revisit, but they knew they had to if they were to look for the missing couple. The tension eased between them when they reached Avon Street, and even on first glance, they could see that the street was far quieter than it had been the night before. Even the odour didn't seem quite as bad, although the smell was by no means agreeable.

As they walked the length of the road, Catherine looked at every building as they passed. Shutters were closed on many of the windows preventing any view into the rooms beyond the glass.

"I don't even know what we're looking for!" she said in exasperation. "We can't knock on every door."

"No. Look! There's a street seller. Perhaps she's heard of them," Eric said, walking over to a girl with a basket of bread.

A conversation ensued, but Catherine knew without asking that nothing positive came from it.

Eric returned, shrugging his shoulders. "Nothing," he said. "Let's walk down to the river and then up Clarks Lane. I don't think there's anything else we can do. I'm certainly not foolish enough to start banging on doors. Even fairy godfathers aren't immortal," he said with feeling.

They walked together, Catherine wrapping her cloak tightly around her shoulders in an effort to combat the damp air. This was a side of Bath she'd never imagined and didn't want to remain in for long.

If nothing happened to give them some sort of lead to the whereabouts of Chris and Mrs Hayes, she would have to accept that they were lost to her. The thought depressed her more than walking through the slums.

She remained quiet as they walked. She was aware Eric was sending her concerned glances. She presumed he was waiting for her to admit defeat. It seemed inevitable, but she couldn't face it just yet.

They turned into Clarks Lane after walking a short way along the river front. It was an area very similar to Avon Street, if not slightly worse. The roadway wasn't as wide as Avon Street, which was decidedly narrower than the wide roadways of the Crescent and Great Pulteney Street. Smart carriages were nowhere to be seen. The odd cart was the only vehicle on the road with no sign of fine people amongst these streets. Catherine tried not to think about what they were walking through underfoot, but she had to concentrate on keeping her footing, the pavement was so dirty. No one cared enough to clear up the detritus.

They turned left into Corn Street, to turn immediately right into Peter Street, which would bring them back onto Westgate Buildings. Catherine pondered the fact that yesterday she'd pitied anyone living in those lodgings. Today, though, they seemed positively regal compared to her current surroundings.

Catherine paused, reaching out to halt Eric with her hand. "It's her!" she said.

"Where?" Eric asked. The street was starting to come alive, a few people busying themselves in everyday life.

"There! Half-way down the street, standing at the doorway, talking to another woman," Catherine pointed out.

"Are you sure?" Eric asked, as he watched the woman accepting something from the one she was speaking to. Their conversation came to an end, and Mrs Hayes turned into the house, closing the door behind her.

"She looks older and more worn out," Catherine admitted. "And dirtier if that makes sense, but I'm sure it's her."

"Come on then! What are we waiting for?" Eric said, setting off at a fast pace.

Catherine didn't falter. Her heart had lifted at the thought that they'd found them! She couldn't wait to see Chris, no matter what he'd decided.

Before they'd reached the house, Mrs Hayes stepped out of the front door once more and started heading away from them.

Catherine increased her pace. She didn't want to shout and draw attention to themselves, but when she gained a reasonable distance she did call out.

Mrs Hayes turned at the sound of her name and the look of shock, pleasure and then shame on her face would have been comical if not for their location.

"Oh! I'm so glad we've seen you!" Catherine said with feeling, embracing the woman, even though she was grimy. It was clear Mrs Hayes was taken aback by the outward show of affection; not many would experience such an embrace in a public street.

"Mrs West! What are you doing here?" Mrs Hayes asked.

"I could ask you the same question!" Catherine laughed in response. "I've been looking for you since my return. I'm so glad I've found you. Is Mr Dobson with you?"

Mrs Hayes' eyes filled with tears. "He is," she said, clearly upset.

"What is it?" Catherine asked, all amusement gone. "Where is he?"

"He's in our lodging, but he's very ill. I don't think he'll survive this world much longer," Mrs Hayes said, unable to stop the tears. "I was just on my way to the apothecary to get him something to ease his pain."

"Oh my God!" Catherine gasped in horror.

"We need to see him," Eric said, immediately taking control.

"Prepare yourself. He's much changed from when you last saw him," Mrs Hayes warned.

She turned back the way she'd come and, upon reaching her lodging, led the way into the building. Walking up the stairs she turned. "I'm afraid we're on the second floor. The rents are cheaper the higher up we go," she explained with some embarrassment.

Catherine and Eric followed her in silence. Catherine could smell the musty-damp that indicated the house should probably be condemned rather than housing numerous lodgers within its walls.

The stairway was narrow and oppressive, but their steps did not cease in their purpose as they turned when the staircase turned and continued their climb upwards.

A doorway at the top of the building was opened by Mrs Hayes. Her cheeks were pink. Catherine didn't know whether it was from the exertion or embarrassment at where she was living. Catherine squeezed the woman's arm in reassurance as she entered into the room.

It was a small attic room. A bed dominated the space, placed in the only part of the room that had a straight ceiling. A chest of drawers, a chair, a large basket of fabric, a truckle bed and a small fireplace filled the spaces along the walls that the ceiling sloped above, restricting the height in the room. The shutters were open on the single window into the attic, but the glass was firmly closed against the cold December air. No fire was lit in the grate.

Catherine moved into the room, although her legs had buckled when she saw Chris. He was lying in the bed, a smaller, older, more drawn version of the strong man who had existed not so very long ago. His face was grey and covered with a sheen of sweat. His lower face was covered in a dishevelled beard. He had lost weight, she could tell, even though he was covered by a blanket. The broad, tall man seemed to have shrunk to half the size he had been.

She wanted to run to his side but managed to stop herself. "What's happened since we last met?" she asked Mrs Hayes, unable to stop her voice cracking.

Mrs Hayes slumped in the chair, not attempting to be a polite hostess in such an inadequate space.

"It was all a misunderstanding," she started. "Mrs Edwards … I mean Mrs Parker … along with Mr Dobson and Mr Parker, were looking for me. That awful Mr Chorlton was apparently out to get me because you'd seen sense, and he blamed my interference. Thankfully, I'd taken myself off for a walk to the Crescent. I was supposed to meet Mrs Parker in the Pump Room, but I felt a little melancholy, so I took myself off."

"That's why you couldn't be found," Catherine said.

"Yes. I felt so ashamed afterwards that everyone was searching when I hadn't let anyone know where I was, but sometimes it gets a little too much, you know? And I just wanted to be alone," Mrs Hayes explained. "Although I'm not sorry I missed an angry Mr Chorlton!"

"What happened to him?" Catherine asked.

"I've no idea. He must've left Bath by the time I'd returned to my rooms. I've not seen him since," Mrs Hayes responded.

"But it was too late for Chris to return," Catherine said almost to herself.

Mrs Hayes frowned at Catherine but didn't comment directly on her use of Chris' given name. "Mr Dobson and myself were in a financial pickle, so as two people can live almost as cheaply as one, it made sense to stick together."

Catherine swallowed before speaking. "Please forgive this impertinent question, but how have you managed?"

"We haven't really, have we?" Mrs Hayes said, opening her arms to encompass the room. "Mr Dobson told me about the money you'd sent for me, which was so kind of you, and he had some of his own. We moved immediately into cheaper lodgings but couldn't maintain them, so we took this room."

"It can't have been easy," Eric said with sympathy.

Catherine was struggling with the image of Chris being with someone else. Love had been given and received between them even during the short time they'd shared together, and it choked her to think he had left that behind. She couldn't condemn him though. He had had to live, and Mrs Hayes was a nice person, Catherine refused to blame anyone other than herself for insisting on seeing her friends one last time.

Mrs Hayes spoke, interrupting Catherine's thoughts. "It has been a struggle, but I've been taking in sewing, as you can see." She pointed at the basket full of garments to be mended. "Some of the dressmakers send out some of the smaller jobs. It isn't worth their effort to do them. I'd just received payment and was going to buy some laudanum for Mr Dobson."

Chris had not moved throughout their exchange, which worried Catherine. "What happened to him?"

"He's been working at anything and everything, labouring, any job he could get paid for without having references," Mrs Hayes explained. "Together we've managed to get by, just about. Three weeks ago, though, he started with a sore throat, and it's gone worse each day. His temperature goes from icy cold to raging hot, and he can't bear to be touched. It's as if his whole body hurts. The doctor saw white spots at the back of his throat, but he can barely open his mouth now. I've paid for him to be bled, to be given poultices and tonics, but nothing is helping. The doctor told me two days ago to expect the worst." Mrs Hayes' voice caught in her throat.

"There must be something we can do!" Catherine said, looking at Eric, but receiving no encouragement from him. She took a steadying breath. She was not going to give up without a fight. She had caused this, and if it took every idea she could think of, she was going to try to help Chris. "Right, Mrs Hayes. Forget about the laudanum. I'm going to get him some medicine that will help, but it will take me a little while."

"I've tried everything!" Mrs Hayes said defensively.

"I know," Catherine soothed. She rummaged in her reticule. "Here. Take this money. Get food, drink and fuel for the fire. Eric, you stay with Chris. I'll return as quickly as I can. Don't let him die in the meantime!"

"What are you going to do?" Eric asked, his alarmed expression never too far from the surface.

"I think I've an idea of what it is," Catherine said. "I'll be as fast as possible."

"But this is five pounds!" Mrs Hayes interrupted.

"Yes. Spend every penny! There'll be more tomorrow," Catherine said, already leaving the room.

Chapter 27

Catherine ran through the streets. She didn't care that it wasn't seemly for a woman to be running, let alone a woman running who was unchaperoned.

She had to get help and soon.

She ran to John Street. There was no time to lose, and what was available in 1813 was of no use to Chris.

Barely stopping to shake-off the effects of walking into the present once more, Catherine hurried off. She had to act quickly.

Returning to her hotel on Queen Square, she was relieved she'd booked into a place close to the time opening. Fishing out her mobile, she googled an address before moving to the window and making a call.

As the call connected, she wrapped a hand around her throat, pressing hard on her wind pipe.

"Hello?" she croaked when the call was answered. "I'm on holiday and need an urgent telephone consultation with Doctor Darla please."

"I'm sorry, all the appointments are booked up today, but if you phone back tomorrow at eight thirty, you might be able to book an appointment then," came the business-like voice of the receptionist.

"You're not listening. I need to speak to Doctor Darla urgently. Otherwise I'm going to be forced to phone for an ambulance and spend the day in accident and emergency. I'm phoning now to prevent clogging up the system," Catherine persisted. The pressure of her hand making her choke, but she did not let up.

"If I can take your name and date of birth, I'll just put you on hold," came the cool response. The person on the other end of the phone clearly not happy with being threatened with an unnecessary trip to the hospital.

Catherine gave the information and waited impatiently while the conversation between doctor and receptionist took place. She was relieved the threat of accident and emergency had done the trick. If she couldn't speak remotely to a doctor, her plan would fail.

The receptionist came back on line. "Doctor Darla will ring you back within the next thirty minutes."

"Thank you. I appreciate it."

Catherine ended the call, and taking a drink of water to ease the self-inflicted pain, she gathered her credit card and popped it into her pocket.

She made a list of all the items she would be buying and found a cloth shopping bag that always travelled with her but never seemed to be on her person when she needed it most.

Eventually, the mobile sprang into life, and Catherine picked it up, re-enacting her previous odd strangulation noise.

"Doctor Darla?" she croaked.

"My goodness, Catherine, that doesn't sound good! What on earth have you been doing?" came the reassuring voice of Megan's best friend's mother.

Catherine wasn't one for going to the doctor, but she was relying on her previous good character adding weight to the lies she was about to tell.

"Oh, it's typical me," she croaked, woefully. "Only I could have a week away from the kids and come down with tonsillitis."

"You sound bad," came the sympathetic response. "Describe your symptoms."

Catherine described exactly what Mrs Hayes said Chris had and offered a suggestion, thanks to google. "When I was sixteen I had septic tonsillitis and flu. It put me on my back for weeks, and I think this is a recurrence," she groaned.

"It does sound like it. I'd like you to see someone down there," the doctor responded.

"Please no!" Catherine pleaded. "I just want to curl up in bed. I'm here with a friend. Is there any chance you could fax a prescription through to a chemist? I arranged one once for Paul when we were away on holiday. I know it's unusual, but I really can't face trying to find a doctor and then sitting for goodness knows how long in a surgery. I just want to go to bed. My friend will pick up my prescription. I'm literally around the corner from a Boots," according to google, she finished silently.

"This once," the doctor said. "But if this doesn't start to improve in a few days, I want you to call a doctor. It can turn nasty, especially in adults."

"I will, I promise. Is there anything else I can do that will help?" Catherine asked.

"I'm going to email over a prescription for a week's course of antibiotics. Take paracetamol every four hours and ibuprofen. You can replace the paracetamol with co-codemol but don't take them both together. Lots of fluids and keep warm. And rest. Make sure you rest. I'm being serious, Catherine. If you don't see an improvement in three days, seek advice down there."

"I will. Thank you," Catherine responded. She croaked out the fax number of the chemist and assured the doctor she was being well cared for.

Catherine took the opportunity to ring her children. She hated to lie to them, but she had to let them know that she would be unavailable for the next few days. Her 'illness' served as a convenient excuse. She would miss speaking to them, but for once they couldn't be her top priority. Chris had to come first. It would also support her lie if Megan saw Doctor Darla socially.

Stopping at one chemist on Westgate Street, she stocked up with as many tablets they would allow her to buy in addition to cough medicine. It wouldn't hurt to be prepared. She also bought anti-bacterial wipes, soap and a flannel.

Entering Boots, she bought more tablets, a baby syringe — she presumed it would be easier to get medicine down that way— adding scissors and razors to her basket. She collected her prescription, bought some energy drinks and left the premises, feeling some shame at the amount of lies she was telling.

Stopping at the kitchen shop on Quiet Street, she bought a pestle and mortar and some hand towels. Stuffing everything into the already bulging bag, she quickly walked around to the opening and re-entered 1813.

Breathing a sigh of relief, Catherine tucked the bulging bag under her arm and hurried toward the room in which Chris' life was hanging in the balance. She was thinking through the practicalities of the situation when a man stepped out in front of her as she hurried along Peter Street.

"Would the lady like help in carrying her heavy load?" he asked, the grime on his face hiding the pale skin underneath.

"No. Thank you," Catherine said, stepping to the side. She frowned, looking closely at the stranger.

"Oh, I think you do," came the menacing response as he matched her attempt to move away from him.

"Mr Chorlton!" Catherine said in surprise. It seemed the last two years hadn't been kind to him at all.

"Recognise me do you?" Mr Chorlton snarled. "You owe me."

"I owe you nothing!" Catherine said hotly. "You were mistaken in your choice. I haven't the money you thought."

"I heard it from your own mouth," Mr Chorlton spat.

"When? Was I being serious?" Catherine asked in confusion. She couldn't remember telling him anything so personal.

"You were talking to Dobson."

"Ah, so, no. I wasn't being serious," Catherine said.

"You are rich. I can tell."

"How on earth can you tell? You were dressed in fine clothes when we first met. That means nothing," Catherine said, becoming impatient.

"You have all your teeth and no small-pox scars. You must have been given the finest care as you grew," Mr Chorlton said, not unreasonably.

Catherine paused. She had noticed the state of people's teeth, but hadn't realised what impression her good dental hygiene would say about herself. "Why are you here?" she asked.

"Where else would I be? In the slums along with your friends. They aren't faring too well. I'm going to make sure they never forget me," Mr Chorlton responded ominously.

"It's ridiculous! How can you hold onto something for so long?" Catherine asked in disbelief.

"Easy for you to say when it's not your family who has to sell everything to try and pay off debts. My children have gone hungry too many days to count, and the blame is on you and your friends," Mr Chorlton responded. "That tends to focus the mind."

"I'm truly sorry your children have suffered. But you built-up the debts. No one else. You should be trying to earn an honest living rather than looking for an opportunity to dish out some sort of misguided revenge.

"I need what's in that bag," Mr Chorlton said, stepping forward. "I'm sure it'll bring in some pennies."

Catherine stepped towards the man, a movement he obviously didn't expect with the look of surprise he gave her. Before he could speak Catherine pointed a finger into his chest and started to rant. "My friend is likely about to die because of my actions, but in this bag, there are items that might help him. They're of no value to you or anyone else. Don't think you can intimidate me into giving them to you. I spent years married to one of the worst kind of men you could possibly imagine! So, try to take my bag if you wish, but I promise you this: I will scratch, kick and bite with the last breath in me before I'll let you take it! Now get out of my way! As if I'm going to wander about alone with a bagful of valuables! Do I look completely stupid?"

Mr Chorlton looked about to speak, but again, Catherine stopped him. "Get out of my way before I have a bout of hysterics!"

He held up his hands. "Go. But we aren't finished."

"We never even started!" Catherine snarled and walked around the menace. She tried not to run the rest of the way to the house, afraid to show any hint of fear to her nemesis. But it took all her willpower to walk at a sensible pace.

Entering the building she took a second to close her eyes and breathe slowly and deeply. She had been a little unfair with the description of Paul, but it had served its purpose. With a slight smile at her audacity, she ran up the stairs, sending a small prayer to any God who might be listening to help her save Chris.

*

The fire was going, and there was a kettle on an iron rod over the flame. Catherine was relieved. At least she'd have hot water at her disposal.

There were signs Mrs Hayes had eaten something, and she looked brighter for it.

"There's food for you and Mr Atkinson," Mrs Hayes said.

"Thank you. I need to get started, but before I do, I need you to go with Mr Atkinson," Catherine said to Mrs Hayes.

"Go? No! I can't leave Mr Dobson at this stage!" Mrs Hayes responded heatedly.

Catherine put down her heavy bag and took hold of Mrs Hayes' hands. "How long have you been caring for him without help or support?"

"But ... "

"Please. I have rooms. Eliza is there. Let her care for you. Take a bath. Use some of my clothes. Have a rest. Sleep. I'll look after him for you to the best of my ability," Catherine assured her.

"And if he worsens?" Mrs Hayes asked.

"I'll send Mr Atkinson for you immediately," Catherine promised. She could understand why the woman would want to be with Chris. He seemed to inspire deep affection in those around him. A pity his wife hadn't felt the same; she seemed to have been the only one who hadn't loved him as he deserved to be loved.

Mrs Hayes seemed tempted, so Catherine pushed the point. "I don't want you to make yourself ill. You look fit to drop," she said gently.

"I feel it," Mrs Hayes said quietly.

"Then go."

Mrs Hayes nodded her agreement and left the room. Eric followed her, but Catherine pulled him back when she thought Mrs Hayes was out of earshot. "Be careful. Mr Chorlton is in the area, and he's still blaming us for his misfortune. When you return, I don't care how you do it, but bring clean bedding. Blankets and sheets and clean nightshirts. Oh, and clean clothing for me."

"I will," came the quiet response, and Catherine was left alone.

She picked up her bag, and using the windowsill as a medicine shelf, she sorted out the items. Breaking the first antibiotic in half, she filled the syringe with the powder contained in the capsule and adding some liquid from one of the energy drinks she moved to the bed.

"Chris, it's Catherine. I came back," she whispered, stopping herself from uttering 'for you'. "I need you to take this medicine. I know it'll hurt like hell to swallow, but you must."

Chris' eyes flickered, but he didn't open them. Catherine tucked one hand under his neck and tried to lift his head a little from the pillow. When she was happy with the angle, she gently forced the syringe through his lips. Chris moved his mouth slightly, and Catherine was able to insert the device to the side of his cheek. She didn't want to choke him by sending the liquid straight into his throat. Releasing the fluid and waiting until she felt him swallow, she found it was easier than she thought as he winced and moaned as he did it.

Catherine kissed his forehead. "I'm sorry. I promise not to kiss you again. I know you belong to another, but oh! How I've missed you!" she said quietly before laying his head back on the pillow.

Moving to the window, she took out co-codemol and ibuprofen and started to crush them in the pestle and mortar. When they were like fine powder, she mixed some cough medicine in with the dust, and using the syringe once more, filled it with the concoction.

Moving to the bed again, she lifted Chris' head. "As my Grandma used to say, this will either cure you or kill you," she said gently. "It probably isn't advisable to give you everything without food, but I'm not letting you die on me, Chris! If you're leaving your family behind and staying in this world, the least you can do is write them a letter to tell them you've gone away somewhere. It might help them stop worrying a little."

Once again, Chris winced as he swallowed. Catherine placed his head gently onto the pillow. She moved to the window and opened it a little. Now that the fire was going, she wanted to get some fresh air into the room, although in their environment, she wasn't completely convinced how fresh that air would be.

She had a lot to do but couldn't start anything until Eric returned. She sat on the chair, waiting impatiently and willing the man she had so quickly fallen in love with to live as he battled illness in a century of high mortality rates.

Chapter 28

Eric returned with two escorts, each carrying a bundle of sheets, blankets and a small box of items.

"I thought a portmanteau would take up too much room," he explained the unusual mode of conveying goods.

"That's fine," Catherine responded, indicating the items should be placed on the chair.

When the men had left with a coin each for their trouble, Catherine turned to Eric. "Did you see anything of Mr Chorlton?"

"No. It appears he's not made himself known to your friends," Eric responded.

"We can't leave Mrs Hayes alone. I've no idea what he'll do."

"She'll be safe with Eliza," Eric assured her.

"I'm not convinced," Catherine said bitterly. "This whole episode has been full of catastrophes."

"Not of our making!" Eric said defensively.

"Then who's? I accept my part in it. My foolish vanity was flattered by Mr Chorlton, but you must acknowledge that this whole experience was created by yourselves!" Catherine said. She decided it was best to concentrate on Chris. Recriminations could be voiced another time. "I'm going to need your help moving him. He needs to be cleaned up."

"Is it wise to disturb him?" Eric asked.

"Possibly not, but being so grubby can't be helping his situation, and washing might make him feel fresher. I'm going to do the work. I just need you to help reposition him. I want to put one of the blankets he's using now underneath him, to stop the mattress getting wet. I'll also need a steady supply of clean water," Catherine instructed.

"I feel I'm going to become well acquainted with the stairs," Eric mumbled.

"It'll help burn off those buns you enjoyed," Catherine responded, moving to the bed. "I hope the co-codemol has had the same effect as laudanum without the addictive qualities and he's in a deep sleep."

Together the pair worked, slowly rolling Chris, so the blanket covered the sheet and mattress underneath him. "The sheet is already soaked," Eric commented about the sweat-filled cotton.

"I know. I hope we can get his temperature down," Catherine responded quietly.

She used the scissors to cut his nightshirt off and his drawers. She left a small area of material intact on his body, more to protect Eric's modesty, as he'd looked at her in alarm when she'd started cutting material. When she'd removed the old clothing she started to wash his body with the soap and water. She took her time, trying to get as much of him clean as she could. It grieved her to think what difficulties he must have faced, but she pushed the maudlin thoughts behind. She was here to help not hinder.

Eventually Chris was as clean as he could be. He had moaned a few times, but apart from that, there had been no response. Eric and Catherine struggled to get a fresh nightshirt over his head. Tucking the new blanket around his body, Catherine was satisfied, that at least for now, he looked slightly better.

She started to crush the next set of tablets while Eric seated himself on the one chair in the room, exhausted from his exertions. She had been feeding Chris a syringe full of energy drink every fifteen minutes. She was sure it wasn't enough, but at least it was something. He needed calories, and it was the only way to get something into his system.

Once Chris had been given the second set of tablets, Catherine left him to rest. He'd had a traumatic morning. She turned to Eric once it seemed Chris was as comfortable as he could be.

"I'm trying to think if there's anything else we could be doing to help," she said quietly.

"You've done all you can. Time will tell," Eric responded.

"You mean you can't look into the future and put my mind at ease?" Catherine asked.

"No. We can give possibilities. You make your own choices, and from that, there are consequences that dictate the path you'll go down," Eric explained.

"It all seems too easy for things to go wrong," Catherine said.

"If people were simple, we wouldn't be needed," Eric said.

"One thing I've never understood, though. Why was my experience supposed to be only once and yet Chris has been coming for years?" Catherine asked.

"You were ready for possibilities when you came through. Chris needed longer to recover before he was open to the potential of a different future.

Although, because of events we couldn't control, it took longer than even we anticipated," Eric explained.

Catherine paused before speaking. "My mother's death," she said quietly.

"Yes," Eric responded. "We couldn't do anything to help. I'm sorry."

Catherine smiled a little. "She would've liked him," she said, looking with longing at Chris. "And she would've cursed me for messing it up."

"I think we've all messed up, although I'll probably get a telling off for admitting as much."

"The saying 'it's better to have loved and lost than never to have loved at all,' is the biggest load of codswallop I've ever heard!" Catherine said with feeling.

Eric thought it prudent not to comment.

*

Eric and Catherine took turns watching Chris through the night. Once he'd been given his last dose of tablets, Catherine admitted he needed an undisturbed sleep, if possible, and so restrained herself from giving him fluids during the night. He'd had two energy drinks over the day, so she was content that he was getting a small amount of fluids and nutrients.

Early morning dawned with Eric making a new fire and bringing up fresh water while Catherine gave Chris his first tablets of the morning. It was selfish of her, but she needed to touch Chris, and holding his head up was the closest she could be to him. She had restrained herself from kissing him again; she could not be so cruel to another woman.

They were interrupted from their ministrations by the arrival of Eliza and Mrs Hayes. Catherine noticed that her friend looked brighter and more herself, although she was thinner than she had been, a sad indication of some of the struggles she'd faced along with Chris.

"How is he?" Mrs Hayes asked, as soon as she was through the door.

"He's had a settled night, and his temperature seems to be more normal," Catherine said. "I'm going to give him another day of rest and then swap to the medication that won't make him so drowsy. I'm hoping the infection will have started showing some improvement after two days." Catherine had disregarded the need to return to her present to try and maintain an appearance of normality. Chris needed her, and that was all that mattered. The fact that she was in a larger, less personal hotel would help disguise her being missing — a fact she hadn't considered would be an advantage when booking her room.

Mrs Hayes walked over to the window sill and picked up the items that Catherine was still storing there. "What are these concoctions?" she asked.

Catherine looked at the alarmed faces of Eliza and Eric, but shrugged. She didn't care about affecting the future as long as Chris was well. "They're from a new doctor I found."

"I've never seen any of these before," Mrs Hayes said. "But he looks less fevered than he did, so they must be doing some good."

"I hope so," Catherine said with feeling.

"I slept too long. I'll stay with him now," Mrs Hayes said. "You get some rest."

Catherine felt defensive jealousy rise up in her chest, but tried to hide it. "I need to be here to administer the medication," she said firmly. She might not have any right to be with him, but she couldn't walk away just yet.

"We'll both stay then," Mrs Hayes said. "There's not room for us all though."

"We'll leave you for now," Eliza said. "We'll bring another bucket of water and some food when we return this evening."

Catherine smiled in thanks and relief. They left, but Eric returned within a few minutes, carrying a second chair.

"Thought this might be useful," he said to a grateful Catherine.

Mrs Hayes settled on the chair near the mending basket and picked up her sewing. She faltered when underneath the top item, there was a bundle of money. "There's five pounds here!" she said in surprise.

"I will be able to give you five pounds every day whilst I'm here," Catherine said. There was no point in trying to deny who had put the money there; Mrs Hayes was no fool. "I'm only sorry I can't send more when I'm not here."

"Why would you give us so much?" Mrs Hayes asked in confusion.

Us. Catherine swallowed. "I've faced hardship in my past. If I can help, I will. I wish there was more I could do."

There was more she could do. She had been working on it over the last year with the archives, but she wasn't sure if it was allowed or was the correct thing to do, so for the moment, she held her counsel.

"It's very kind of you and will help greatly. Thank you," Mrs Hayes said.

They settled down, watching Chris while Mrs Hayes sewed. Catherine knew there was no point in offering her services; she was no needlewoman. When Catherine made a warm drink for them both, she tried to find out what the future held if Chris recovered, which thankfully, all the signs seemed to point to.

"Do you think you'll stay in Bath?" she asked, starting to crush the next set of tablets.

"I would've have left before now," Mrs Hayes admitted. "But Mr Dobson was intent on staying. He knew you'd come back."

"Did he?" Catherine asked, warmth filling her insides.

"Yes. I wondered why it would take you two years, and why he didn't write to you, but he was sure you'd be here and able to help," Mrs Hayes said quietly, looking fondly at Chris. "He was steadfast in his belief in you."

Catherine blinked back tears at the faith Chris had in her and the implications of the look Mrs Hayes was bestowing on him. "He was very lucky to have you," she said eventually.

"We were lucky to have each other," Mrs Hayes said firmly.

"Yes," Catherine responded.

Chapter 29

On the third morning, Chris' eyes fluttered open when Catherine lifted his head to give him his medication. She could've wept with relief but instead smiled. "Hello, you," she said gently. "Have you finally come back to us?"

"I knew it was you," Chris croaked. "You came. I knew you would. I never doubted you for a moment."

If Catherine had needed to speak to Doctor Darla at that moment, she would've had no trouble in making her voice choked; her windpipe seemed unable to function.

"Oh! You're awake!" Mrs Hayes said, jumping from her seat.

Chris' eyes flickered to her, and he smiled a weak smile. "Have I been out of it for long?"

"Weeks! I thought you were lost to me! The Doctor had given you up!" Mrs Hayes said, tears leaking from her eyes.

"Here. Take this," Catherine instructed, feeling like an intruder but needing to give him his medicine.

"What is it?" Chris croaked, but accepted the syringe being put into his mouth.

"Good old antibiotics and energy drink. You've probably had more sugar in these last few days than you have in the whole of the last two years. I'm so very sorry about everything," she whispered at the end of her speech.

"It was my choice," Chris croaked back.

Catherine gently rested Chris back onto the pillows. "I think it's time we tried to get some food into you." She turned to Mrs Hayes. "Is there somewhere I can get some soup from that would be nutritious? It'll give you the opportunity to have some moments alone."

"If you go to market and buy whatever you need, in the basement there is a kitchen and a lady who will make anything you wish for a fee," Mrs Hayes explained.

"Good. I'll do that," Catherine said, unable to look at Chris again in case she saw those eyes staring at her. It had been hard enough when he was unconscious, but with him awake, she wasn't sure of containing her emotions.

She walked out of the room without looking back. She would be practical and helpful and make sure she was as useful to them as she could be. There was nothing else she could do.

She was unaware that Chris' eyes followed her as a starving man would look at a plate of food. He had believed she wouldn't abandon him. Throughout every day of the previous two years he had clung to the idea that she would return, that the portal would open, and if he couldn't get to her, she would come for him.

He had known there was a chance of being trapped when he had decided to stay and search for Mrs Hayes. He was no fool, hence he'd insisted that Catherine return to the present. He'd had to make sure she was able to get back to her children.

The feeling he'd suffered when he'd walked down Union Passage too late to be transported but still clinging to a tiny fragment of hope that the way out would still be open only to find he was stranded, had made him stagger. He was trapped in a world in which he was a virtual unknown with no viable means to support himself.

It had been hard to focus for the first few days. He'd gone round almost in a daze, but eventually he'd been determined to make some sort of life for himself and wait for Catherine come back.

He hadn't expected it to be quite so hard.

*

Eric appeared at Catherine's side the moment she left the building.

"I don't know how you do that," Catherine said, startled, and not for the first time.

"Practice," Eric replied. "I can't leave you alone with Mr Chorlton in the vicinity. We don't want any further complications. What are we doing?"

"Going to buy nourishing food for a sustaining broth, and I hope you've got money, because I've left today's funds with Mrs Hayes," Catherine responded.

"Why is it when people are ill, they're fed the most unappetising food imaginable?" Eric asked as they walked through the streets.

Catherine smiled but didn't reply. She appreciated Eric's lightness; it helped lift her spirit, which these days, was more likely to dwell on the doom and gloom of a situation. Spotting Mr Chorlton loitering at the side of a building, she prepared herself in case he decided to try to take her to task again, but all he did was shout, "Rather you than me mate," to Eric and let them be.

"I see you've been making friends," Eric said once they'd passed Mr Chorlton.

"I find it comes naturally," Catherine responded.

"He didn't seem too keen to approach us. Perhaps you scared him off when you last spoke. Whatever did you do to him?"

"Threatened to have hysterics and bite and kick to my last breath," Catherine admitted with the first genuine laugh in days.

"I can't understand his hesitation at all!" Eric said with feeling.

*

Catherine returned to the room. She'd purposely stayed with the woman, helping as much as was possible to cook the food. She could have done it all herself, in reality, but it was appropriate to maintain the illusion that she was a lady and unable to carry out such menial tasks, so she had asked for direction when fully aware of what to do.

In truth, she hadn't wanted to return to Chris' room immediately. Oh, she wanted to spend every moment in his company, but she couldn't face the prospect of seeing him with Mrs Hayes.

Eventually, though, it was time for the next round of tablets, and so along with a steaming bowl of broth, she entered the room.

Chris was lying with his eyes closed, and Mrs Hayes was sewing. The room was peaceful. Catherine carefully laid the bowl down and went to the windowsill to sort out the tablets.

Walking over to the bed, she touched Chris' shoulder gently, at which he opened his eyes. "Yes, nurse?" he croaked.

"Time for your medicine," Catherine said, unable to stop the smile reaching her lips at the realisation he was recovering. "I'm replacing co-codemol with paracetamol. I think it would be best if you were a little more awake, so you can try to eat something."

Chris groaned. "I don't think I could swallow anything."

"If you can't, I'll return home and bring back some meal supplements," Catherine said, trying not to give too much away to Mrs Hayes.

"They don't sound appealing either," Chris admitted.

Catherine lifted his head; he was still very weak. "You need sustenance. You've lost weight," she said quietly, inserting the syringe.

Chris swallowed with difficulty. "Stop worrying," he said but looked grateful to be resting his head on his pillow when she laid him down once more.

"I'll let the tablets take effect while the broth is cooling and then you need to at least try some," Catherine said gently.

"Fine," Chris acceded but closed his eyes.

"He's so weak," Mrs Hayes said, concern on her face as she joined Catherine at the foot of the bed.

"Yes, but each day the infection will reduce," Catherine assured her. "I think he's out of danger." She wanted to have him carried home, but knew he was still too ill to move, never mind that she had no authority to do such a thing. He was with Mrs Hayes now.

The women worked between them to lift Chris slightly and feed him the minimum of broth before he was too exhausted to do more. He fell into a deep sleep once he was laid on his pillow. Catherine watched him, chewing her lip in concern.

"I think I will get the meal replacements," she said. "They'll probably do him more good than struggling to get food into him."

"Can I get them for you? You've been rushing about all morning," Mrs Hayes offered.

"No, but thank you for the offer," Catherine said quickly, smiling slightly at the thought of trying to explain everything to Mrs Hayes. "I wanted to pick something else up from home anyway," she said, having made a difficult decision.

"When you return, I'll take this sewing to the seamstress. I've done it all," Mrs Hayes said. "He's been a good patient."

Catherine smiled a little and left the room once more. She would give them both the means to keep themselves in some sort of comfort. It was the least she could do.

*

Mrs Hayes, opened her eyes in surprise at the packages that Catherine placed on the now crowded windowsill. The packets of Complan were accompanied by a large bottle of milk.

"Where are you getting these things? I've never seen anything like them in my life!" Mrs Hayes asked.

"I give you my word that there's nothing illegal in this," Catherine assured her. "I can't explain it all though. It would take too long."

"I don't see either of us going anywhere for the foreseeable future," Mrs Hayes said drily.

"No. Perhaps not, but I'm afraid I'll just have to ask you to trust me on this one."

"As you seem to have offered nothing but help, financially and otherwise, I can hardly refuse your request," Mrs Hayes said. "I'm just glad he's recovering."

"As am I," Catherine said.

She mixed the powder with the milk to make the meal replacement formula. Catherine then made Chris drink all the mixture, ignoring his complaints. Mrs Hayes had left them to return her sewing, accompanied by Eliza. Chris mentioned one thing which made her pause.

"I need to use the pot," he whispered.

"Oh dear!" Catherine said, flushing. "How do we arrange that?"

"I'll be able to manage," Chris responded. "There are some things which shouldn't be shared."

Catherine smiled but shook her head. "You are as weak as a kitten. You won't be able to stand unsupported. I'll have to help you."

"Not a chance," Chris ground out, closing his eyes. He was so tired all the time. Two sentences, and he was exhausted.

"You could try and use it lying down?" Catherine suggested.

"No. I'm not risking wetting the bed. I've enough problems," Chris muttered, but he didn't actually know how he was going to manage to get out of bed. Every sentence took all his energy.

A tap on the door disturbed the discussion, and Eric entered the room. "I believe I can be of service?"

Catherine smiled gratefully. "Yes. Thank you. I'll wait outside the door. Call if you need me."

The last time Catherine saw Chris, Eric would never have been able to support him without help, but with Chris' reduced weight, she had no doubt the capable being would manage the sick man.

A few minutes passed before Eric opened the door. "All sorted," he said with a smile, holding a covered pot. "He's tired though."

Catherine re-entered the room and took a seat without saying anything. It was enough to watch him undisturbed while he slept.

Chapter 30

Catherine had agreed to return to Queen Square the previous evening. She hadn't had a decent night's sleep in days and was flagging. Promising to return in the morning to administer the fourth day's tablets, she sank into bed, grateful for the comfort. A dreamless exhausted sleep soon overtook any disturbing feelings that she was constantly pushing away in an effort to be a good friend.

The following morning Eliza woke Catherine with a cup of steaming hot chocolate. Tensions had eased a little between the two women, although Catherine would always feel like more could've been done to help Chris.

Getting ready, Catherine took a bundle of papers out of her drawer. Eliza paused in passing Catherine her bonnet. "That's modern paper," Eliza said.

"It is," Catherine acknowledged, struggling to fit the bundle in her reticule.

"What information does it contain?" Eliza asked.

"The opportunity to provide Chris and Mrs Hayes with the means to support themselves in the future," Catherine said, a challenge in her eye.

"You know you can't interfere with history," Eliza said.

"*You're* interfering with history," Catherine stated, her tone sharp.

"That's different," Eliza insisted.

"I'd say it's worse," Catherine responded. "I'm giving them this. They're entitled to some help after what's happened."

"Why would Chris need it? Surely he'll be coming back with you?" Eliza asked, changing tack.

"He's spent two years with Mrs Hayes. He won't leave her and quite rightly too," Catherine responded.

"I was wrong about you," Eliza said.

"In what way?" Catherine asked, her curiosity piqued.

"I thought you were a fighter, but you aren't. You're too quick to give up. I'd be fighting for something I wanted so much," Eliza said with a shrug.

Catherine bristled. "How dare you!" she spat, finally losing her temper. "I've followed him to a different century, for God's sake!"

"But you're not making any effort to show him how you feel. You're too busy being a martyr," Eliza said.

"He's been unconscious for most of the time I've been here!" Catherine snapped. "Apart from that, if you think it's acceptable to try and steal a man from under another woman's nose, you really haven't understood me. If he loves her, I'd only be making a fool of myself, in the process. And I've done enough of that over the last couple of years to last me a lifetime!"

"Oh, stop the pity fest and see what's actually under your nose!" Eliza snapped in return.

"You're unbelievable!" Catherine shouted. "Don't come near me ever again! I've had enough of this farce!"

"In that case run back to the twenty-first century and mourn the loss of the man you're supposed to be with!" Eliza shouted in return before disappearing into thin air.

Catherine blinked a few times. She had known that they appeared as if from nowhere, but it was hard to see someone actually disappear before her very eyes. It shocked her enough to deaden slightly the anger the argument had caused.

Sitting down for a moment, she rubbed her hand across her forehead. How could a forty-one-year-old — a sensible forty-one-year-old — be involved with time travel and fairy godpeople, if that's what they were?

She sighed. She had accepted that she would be returning to her own century and grieving over Chris. She was slightly unnerved yet again that Eliza seemed to know Catherine's thoughts before she'd actually thought them.

Eliza was trying to point out that all was not lost. Was she right? No. If Chris turned his back on Mrs Hayes, he could just as likely turn his back on her. She'd had enough disappointment with Paul; she couldn't risk it with Chris.

She set her shoulders. She had no choice but to forget him, whatever Eliza said.

*

Entering the room on Peter Street, Catherine was relieved that Chris was awake and looking a lot better. She was confident enough to allow him to try to swallow the tablets without the syringe and was buoyed that he managed it.

"Would you mind if I looked down your throat?" she asked. "Megan had tonsillitis when she was young, and although it didn't turn septic, I did see what it was like."

"My breath will be awful," Chris admitted with a groan.

Catherine smiled. "I promise to hold mine then!"

She looked down the open mouth, and although his throat was swollen, it didn't look as bad as she'd imagined.

She made the Complan and although Chris grumbled at her, she insisted he drink the mixture. She had been supported by Mrs Hayes.

When Chris had closed his eyes to rest, Mrs Hayes whispered to Catherine. "Do you mind if I go out? I feel in desperate need of a walk."

"Of course not. I'll stay here as long as I'm needed. Take Eric, he'll be waiting downstairs. If you feed him at some point, he'll be delighted!" Catherine responded.

"I'll see you in a little while," Mrs Hayes said, and wrapping her shawl over her pelisse, she left the room.

"Take as long as you need," Catherine said.

Silence descended, and Catherine took the opportunity to look at Chris while he slept. She had brought razors with her a few days ago but hadn't thought he would be able to spend so long shaving. She didn't want to suggest it for fear it would tire him, but she longed to see his smooth face again. The square jaw and dimpled chin were just not the same covered in scraggily hair.

Eventually, after a couple of hours had passed Chris stirred. "Are we alone?" he asked.

"Yes, Mrs Hayes has gone for a walk."

"I've lost track of time. How many days are left of the market?" he asked. "I don't want you getting stuck here because of me."

"Like you did because of me," Catherine said.

"I've told you. It was my decision," Chris said, rolling his eyes.

"We've still got days yet," Catherine assured him. "You might want to return to see a doctor before the portal closes again. I'm not sure a week of antibiotics will be enough to completely get rid of the infection. You've been really ill."

"Yes. I thought I was done for. My mates would have found it hilarious if I'd died of tonsillitis!" Chris croaked, mortified.

"Talking of your mates," Catherine started. "They, along with you family and the police have been looking for you."

Chris groaned. "I thought they would. Oh, how can I explain all this?"

"I can take a letter back and post it. Perhaps saying you're safe and well but don't want to be with them anymore? If you act as if you've had a breakdown of some sort, they might accept that you're somewhere in the world but not with them," Catherine suggested. It was an appalling idea, but the only thing she'd been able to think of to put his family's mind at rest.

Chris frowned. "Why would I not want to see them again? I know we talked about me moving to the north to you, but it isn't *that* far away from London!"

"Yes, but that was before you set-up home with Mrs Hayes. I don't blame you, Chris. In fact, I've got something that will give you both the chance to live a better life than you have been doing," Catherine said quickly.

Mrs Hayes walked into the room just as Chris was about to speak, but he waited until she had closed the door behind her before he continued.

"Is everything well?" Mrs Hayes asked, looking between the pair, confused at the tension in the room.

"Mrs West, was just about to tell us how she's worked out a get-rich-quick scheme for us," Chris said, but his tone was cold.

"Oh really? I'd like to hear that scheme!" Mrs Hayes smiled. "I hope it's nothing illegal though. We're not desperate enough to go down that path!"

"It's not illegal," Catherine said. She took out the bundle of papers. "These are lists of companies that have been successful from 1813. I know you haven't got a lot of funds, but there's also a list of winning horses at the next big races at Newbury. I thought that, with the money I've been giving you, you could place some bets and increase your pot substantially. Then, you would have enough money to invest. I've made two lists, one of long-term success, one for short-term gains," she explained.

"How do you know this?" Mrs Hayes asked, astounded.

"From a lot of research," Catherine answered truthfully.

"Why do you want to help us so much?" Mrs Hayes asked.

"Because I like you both. A lot," Catherine said, unable to stop herself from glancing quickly at Chris. His face was inscrutable, but he was watching her closely.

"But we aren't staying in the same place. How could we work on this together?" Mrs Hayes asked Chris, looking baffled.

"It seems Mrs West wants us to stay together," Chris said, looking at Catherine, his tone not giving anything away.

"Why would she do that?" Mrs Hayes asked.

"You've been living together for two years. You need money to set-up a proper home," Catherine said.

Mrs Hayes suddenly realised what Catherine was hinting at. "Oh! My dear Mrs West! We've only been living together out of necessity! I wanted to leave Bath as soon as Mr and Mrs Parker married, but Mr Dobson was determined to wait for your return. I couldn't leave him to his own devices after you'd been so kind to me. He had confessed about his straightened circumstances, and believe me, one knows one's friends when one is in dire need!" Mrs Hayes said with feeling.

"But living together … " Catherine started.

"Is cheaper than living apart, especially as I would have needed a companion," Mrs Hayes explained. "It's safer when living in areas such as we are in. But," she said, looking annoyed. "I'll have no aspersions cast on either of our characters, if you please! Whether you are a generous friend or not!" Mrs Hayes said, her tone tart.

"I slept on that truckle bed," Chris said quietly.

"It isn't big enough!" Catherine couldn't help the disbelief sounding in her voice.

"No. It isn't," Mrs Hayes said. "But he insisted even though I'd have been fine with it. When he became ill, I forced the situation to change. I was somewhat stubborn over the matter."

"I was too weak to argue," Chris admitted with a slight smile.

Catherine sat down. "I thought you were a couple," she said quietly.

"But you didn't ask. I'd have told you straight away," Mrs Hayes responded.

"So, are you still intent on abandoning me?" Chris asked Mrs Hayes.

"Do you mind?" she responded. "I'm ever so happy you're recovering. It's nothing short of a miracle."

"And modern medicine," Catherine said quietly. "Are you leaving Bath?"

"I'd promised my cousin I would stay with her when things settled here," Mrs Hayes continued. She turned to Catherine. "I agreed to stay until you returned. Mr Dobson was certain you would."

"He appears to have had more faith in me than I did him," Catherine said, shamefacedly.

"He explained you hadn't had much time together before your family took you away. But I suppose, when true love is there, nothing can stand in its way. Now, hark at me! Getting misty-eyed and silly! Miss Cuthbert said she would sort everything out for my transport when I was ready," Mrs Hayes said, turning to Chris. "I think it's time I left isn't it?"

"Are you abandoning me so soon?" Chris asked.

Mrs Hayes smiled, and exchanged a look that was full of affection. "I would never leave you if you still needed me, but your lady has returned, and a third is never a desired party in such a grouping. You'll do very well without me."

"You stood by me so steadfastly. I couldn't have survived without you," Chris said quietly.

"We helped each other. You've supported me and shown me that there is always hope. I needed to see that. After Mr Hayes died and left such a mess, I was so desolate and believed everyone was selfish and out for themselves. You've shown me that isn't the case, and I won't ever forget that," Mrs Hayes said, her eyes filling with tears, but they were happy, hopeful tears.

"I won't ever forget you," Chris admitted.

"You don't need me here anymore do you?" Mrs Hayes asked, reaching out and squeezing his hand.

"I'm going to miss you," Chris said quietly.

Mrs Hayes' ever-ready tears trickled down her cheeks. "I'd rather miss you than have lost you the way I thought I was going to only a few days ago. I wish you all the very best."

She handed the bundle of papers back to Catherine. "I don't think I'll need these, thank you."

"But it would make your life so much more comfortable!" Catherine said with feeling.

"I know it's been a struggle these past few years, but my cousin has told me of a lady who needs a companion. She says it would be perfect for me. In reality, I just need enough funds to get by. I'm not greedy. My husband was, and it brought nothing but pain and sorrow," Mrs Hayes said with a sad smile.

Catherine embraced the woman, who was so much younger than herself, but her struggles and the time she was born in had aged her beyond her years. "Thank you for looking after him," she whispered.

Mrs Hayes smiled. "I'm glad I could help. Now make sure you take care of him from now on."

"I will. I promise."

Chapter 31

The door closed, and silence descended. Catherine eventually looked at Chris. He was staring back at her, but he looked drained.

She immediately gathered his next set of tablets and took him a drink. "Here, have these. I don't want you having a relapse."

"I want to go home," Chris said after taking the tablets. He looked exhausted; the exchange with Mrs Hayes seemed to have worn him out.

"You will. Very soon. But rest now," Catherine said quietly, moving his hair from his forehead gently, relishing that she could touch him once more, and she couldn't hold back. She had missed him so very much.

"You doubted me," Chris said, his eyes fluttering shut.

"I didn't. I just knew you were too decent to leave her if you'd decided she was the one."

Chris shook his head slightly. "There's only one for me."

Catherine's stomach fluttered. "Those are big words to utter, Mr Dobson," she said quietly, kissing his forehead gently.

Chris sighed. "I love you."

Catherine choked back her tears. "And I love you. Sleep now."

She curled into him, her arm across his chest and held him while he slept. Not wanting to be anywhere else.

*

Chris woke and kissed Catherine's head. She raised herself off his shoulder and smiled into his eyes. "Feeling better?" she asked gently.

"A little."

"It's time for your next tablets," Catherine said, reluctantly getting off the bed.

"So soon?" Chris asked in surprise.

"You've been asleep nearly five hours!" Catherine responded with a smile. "Here, take these. You've got a bit of colour back in your face. You were grey before. I was worried you were going to deteriorate again."

"I want to go home," Chris said quietly, his eyes appealing far more than his words.

"Chris, I don't think you're strong enough to mo — "

There was a sudden knock on the door, and without waiting for an answer, it was flung open forcefully. Two stocky men walked into the room.

"What on earth are you doing?" Catherine demanded, scrambling off the bed.

"We're here for Mr Dobson," one of the men said, ignoring Catherine. "It seems you've been living beyond your means."

"I've never used credit," Chris said, trying to shuffle himself up the bed but not having the strength to move.

"They all say that," the second man said. "We're here to escort you to the debtor's prison unless you can pay us the thirty pounds you owe."

"Thirty pounds!" Catherine groaned. She had no money on her person, having given Mrs Hayes her daily five pounds.

"I owe no one. There's been a mistake," Chris ground out.

"You can sort out the mistake when we get you settled," the first man said, moving towards the bed.

"Stop!" Catherine almost shouted. "He's been seriously ill! You can't move him!"

"His debts have been called in. He's coming with us," the second man towered over Catherine.

"Is there a problem?" came a voice from the doorway.

Catherine turned to see Mr Chorlton standing in the doorway, looking extremely smug. "You've done this!" she spat at him.

"Tut, tut, Mrs West! How can I have run up debts in someone else's name?" Mr Chorlton asked with glee.

"Easily, I'd imagine. You low-life!" Catherine said and launched herself at Mr Chorlton.

Mr Chorlton knocked her with some force out of the way, and Catherine landed in the corner with an almighty thud. Pushing the pain of the impact aside, she immediately jumped to her feet and looked as if she was going to attack once more.

Eric appeared from behind Mr Chorlton. "I believe I can be of service?" he said pleasantly as he entered the room.

"These men are accusing Chris of running up debts, and it's him!" Catherine said, pointing at Mr Chorlton. Her tone was almost hysterical. She couldn't let them take Chris away. He would be stranded forever.

"I see. Gentlemen, could we adjourn outside? It appears to be a little crowded in here," Eric said.

"We want no funny business," the lead man said, looking reluctant to move.

Eric smiled. "As you can see, Mr Dobson is in no fit state to escape. I'm sure if we step outside, we can arrange this to our satisfaction."

"He's going to prison."

"Yes. He's leaving with you," Eric soothed, and the two men followed him downstairs. Mr Chorlton did not move, looking pleased with himself.

"You're evil!" Catherine said. "I won't let you win!"

"I already have," Mr Chorlton responded.

"I'm glad you'll end your days in the workhouse! You deserve nothing less!" Catherine snapped.

Mr Chorlton moved towards her menacingly. "I'm sick to death of you. Let me show you what happens to women who I tire of!"

Catherine was focused on the expression of hatred on Mr Chorlton's face when the door once more burst open behind her.

"I believe someone needs a Sedan Chair?" Eric asked as he walked through the doorway.

"Don't you ever knock?" Catherine asked, his entrance having made her jump.

Eric paused. "No. I don't think I do," he responded. "There's a sedan and two impatient men waiting downstairs. I thought we could manage you between us," he looked questioningly at Chris and Catherine.

"You're letting them take him?" Catherine asked, sagging with defeat.

"I promised them he would be leaving here today," Eric said, looking directly at Catherine.

"I'll get his medication!" Catherine said, quickly filling her bag with tablets, medicines and meal replacements.

When she'd collected all the paraphernalia, she went to Chris' side; he was sitting on the edge of the bed, thanks to Eric's help.

Between the three of them, they struggled their way down the stairs, taking each step slowly but steadily. Mr Chorlton watched them with pleasure from the top of the staircase. Every groan uttered by Chris made his smile widen.

Finally, when they reached the outside door, the two sedan bearers moved to help Chris into the chair.

"In you get," Eric said to Catherine as she stepped back, ready to run alongside the chair if need be.

"We won't fit!" she exclaimed.

"Needs must, as your grandma used to say!" Eric said with a grin, holding the door open for Catherine.

Glaring at him in half annoyance, half amusement, Catherine clambered into the vehicle. She tried to take as little room as she could, but was forced to hold onto Chris as the chair was carried at a speedy pace.

Chris closed his eyes as the box moved along. "We can't be going to debtor's prison. I'm sure Eric has a plan," Catherine whispered, trying to support him.

*

As the sedan turned the corner, a figure emerged from the shadows and moved towards the open door that the previous occupants had left behind. He was dishevelled and dressed in poor quality clothing. He walked up the stairs and entered the top room where the door was standing open. Mr Chorlton was waiting for his accomplice.

Looking around the room, Mr. Chorlton noticed a small bundle lying discarded on the floor. Picking it up, he studied the pages for a few minutes, trying to figure out what the words meant. Smiling to himself, he took the top page, flinging the others into the remains of the fire. Checking around the room for anything else of value, the pair left the property.

"Is that the only thing of value?" the second man asked.

"Yes. There was nothing else. Just this, along with a lot of other useless writings," the first answered.

"What is it?"

"Looks like it's a list of horses for the next few race days at Newbury."

"So, how's that useful?"

"One horse named in each race. I think it might be a little suggestion as to who might be winning," came the educated guess.

"Oooo. What were the other writings? More races?"

"No. Just a list of names and companies. Nothing useful in them. I burned them, but this could be our ticket out of here!"

"We need money for bets," the man pointed out reasonably.

"We'll get some from somewhere. I think we need to get ourselves to Newbury."

"Well, Mr Chorlton, if you're that confident I'm sure I could steal us the coach fare."

"Excellent. I won't be returning anytime soon. Now he's in debtor's prison, I've no need to hang around. It's enough to know she'll be broken-hearted over him. She can't give me the funds I need, but Newbury can," Mr Chorlton said, pleased with his morning's work.

*

Eric opened the door of the sedan chair, keeping pace with it as he ran along, along with the two debt collectors. "Prepare for a bump!" he said cheerfully.

"What! More than we've had already?" Catherine asked, her tone sharp due to worry about Chris. His pallor was grey again, and he had his eyes closed in pain.

"It'll soon be over!" Eric responded, before shutting the door with a bang.

Within moments Chris and Catherine were lurched forward and a blinding flash stunned them for a moment. When Catherine opened her eyes, she blinked, trying to make sense of where they were. They were no longer seated in the sedan chair.

She rushed to Chris' side. "We're in my room in Queen Square," she explained, amazed that Chris was actually standing.

"What happened to the debt collectors?"

"I've no idea, but they aren't here!"

"How did they manage that?" Chris groaned.

"Chris. You don't understand. I took a room in Queen Square this year for the Christmas market. I didn't want to return to where I stayed last year. It felt too odd going back there with all the questions that had been asked. We're home, Chris! We're in our own century!" Catherine said, hardly able to believe it herself.

Chris sank to the floor. "Thank God," he said with feeling.

"Come. Let's get you to bed. You're exhausted," Catherine said, half-dragging, half-pulling Chris onto the bed.

Chris tried to work with her, but he was so weak, he could barely do anything. Eventually, due in the main part to Catherine's efforts, he was settled in her bed. Catherine covered him and then busied herself with sponging down his forehead. It was too soon to give him more medication, but he was hot and sweaty.

After a half hour, he opened his eyes. "I never thought I'd get back," he said, his eyes glistening.

"I would've never given up trying to reach you," Catherine said.

"I know. It's the only thing that kept me going," he said quietly. A teardrop rolled out of the corner of his eye, falling onto the pillow.

Catherine wiped what was left of the trickle of water away. "You're safe."

"I wanted to come back so much it was a physical pain. I couldn't bear the thought of ending my days there, of never seeing you again if you couldn't return," Chris admitted, the normally strong man unable to stop the tears dampening his pillow once he'd started to release the fears that had been almost physically debilitating.

"You came through it, Chris. You're here in the present, and your family will be desperate to see you," Catherine soothed, but didn't try to stop him from crying. He'd been through so much, it was only right he was able to let go his inner worries. "All you need to concentrate on now is getting healthy again."

"I don't think I'll ever be the same as I was. Too much has happened," Chris said.

"It doesn't matter. I fell in love with you, and that hasn't changed. Not for one moment. Not even when I thought you were lost to me," Catherine admitted. "We're both different from who we were last year, but I know for certain we're meant to be together."

"I just felt so helpless. So absolutely alone," he admitted. "I thought I was going to die, and I would disappear into history. Two hundred years away from you."

"I don't know how you survived. I don't think I could have," Catherine admitted.

"I took every job I could, but at first I was laughed out of businesses, being mistaken for a useless toff," Chris explained, remembering some of the frustration laced with fear if he didn't find a way to earn some money.

"How did you convince them?" Catherine asked, gently stroking his face. Her heart breaking for the tears that Chris was shedding.

"I didn't really. The shoddier I became, the more convincing I was that I was one of many labourers, scrounging for work. If I managed to get a few weeks of work, it was such a relief. I couldn't do much that was respectable. I didn't have references, and I would have been put into single-men's accommodation working in any of the houses who needed staff, which would have left Mrs Hayes alone," Chris continued, feeling release as his words and tears spilled forth.

"She could've gone to her sister," Catherine pointed out.

"She refused to leave me. We never really talked about where I came from, but I think she sensed I wasn't really of her time in some way. I made so many mistakes in those first weeks. It was hard to keep up the pretence when it was going to be a permanent thing. I don't think I would've managed so well without her, which is laughable when I think of how we lived," Chris admitted.

"I'm glad we knew her," Catherine said. Even when she had been jealous of Mrs Hayes, suspecting her of securing Chris' affection, she hadn't disliked the woman.

"There was one doubt I had," Chris continued. "You'd mentioned yours was a one-time visit, and I was terrified you wouldn't be allowed back. I just had to hope you were mistaken."

"They said I wasn't going to be able to return, but I put them straight on that point the moment I knew you'd been trapped," Catherine said with feeling.

"I prayed you'd find a way," Chris said with a small smile, extremely tired from his exertion.

"You're home Chris, and I'm never going to let you go again," Catherine soothed. "Everything will be well, I promise you."

"Thank you for coming," he said, sleepily, the effort of moving and the emotion of the day exhausting him.

"Thank you for waiting," Catherine said. "It might have taken us a long time to find each other, but we're here, back in the present, and we're never going to go backwards again. From this day onwards, we're moving forward, never looking to the past."

Chris smiled, his eyes remaining closed. "That sounds good," he whispered. "I love you. Have I told you that?"

Catherine kissed his forehead. "Nowhere near enough times, my darling man."

"I'll have to do it more," Chris whispered.

"You will," Catherine said. "I'll expect it every day, shall I?"

"At least," Chris mumbled before falling into an exhausted sleep.

Epilogue

It took Chris more than three months to recover fully from his ordeal. His tonsils had turned septic and were slowly poisoning him. Eventually, after two more courses of medication he started to recover fully.

His appearance and illness went some way to him being able to excuse his disappearance. A few lies were told, but his family were eventually convinced that he had collapsed in a small village in South Wales and only after months had he been able to tell the doctors he'd been staying in Bath. To the police, he had to pretend he'd had a minor breakdown and disappeared, as hospital records could be checked by the authorities, but not by his family. His relatives were so relieved to have him back in their midst, any doubt over his whereabouts were forgotten in the effort to help him recover fully.

Catherine stayed with Chris initially, returning home a week later than she had been expected. She was able to blame her so-called illness for the delay. It had been a wrench to separate from Chris after that week, but he'd promised to join her as soon as he was able, and until then, she visited him on as many weekends as she could. Catherine did sell the Jane

Austen first editions. Needing funds to travel to Chris she sold them without regret.

They introduced Catherine to Chris' family as someone who had been volunteering in the hospital where affection had developed between them.

Chris never really returned to his old life. His priorities had changed during the two years he'd been away, and although his family was precious to him, his love for Catherine was stronger than anything else he had ever felt. He had spent so long waiting that he wasn't about to waste a single moment once he had the opportunity to be with her.

He proposed to her six months after returning, and Catherine said yes without a single doubt. They married in a quiet ceremony, only close friends and family present, but it was a happy day for all in attendance. Everyone witnessed how much in love the bride and groom were.

As for Catherine, she had thought she'd been in love with Paul. She was to find out that a young infatuation wasn't as strong as this almost overwhelming, supportive, second chance at love. She'd never been happier and adored Chris more than she thought possible.

Chris did become his old self again. It took months, but little by little the old Chris emerged. He once more became the person who relished life and loved a joke. He never returned to the rugby pitch, not feeling physically quite as strong as he had been but became an avid supporter of rugby league when he moved north, or 'proper' rugby as Catherine called it.

Andrew did eventually become a vet. He spent some time in New Zealand after his studies finished, but his relationship with Paul broke down. He returned to England upset, but he was to find that stepdads could be as good, if not better, in the role of father to a young man just setting out on his own path.

Megan accepted Chris immediately. She claimed it was because he kept her mother focused on other things, so she couldn't concentrate on what Megan was doing quite so much. In reality, they would plot and plan together, making family occasions extra special with the little touches they'd created or concocted between them. When Megan eventually married, it was Chris who walked her down the aisle, at her request, and Chris who had become choked with emotion when giving the father-of-the-bride speech.

Paul eventually left Danielle for a younger woman. He'd informed her that she was no fun anymore, even though she'd tried to give him everything he wished for. Her sons never forgave him for hurting their mother. He moved to Australia with his new partner but was to return to New Zealand when she left him because she decided he was too old. He tried a reconciliation with Danielle but to no avail.

Susan married Adam Jones. She'd eventually met her Mr Right, although she did complain bitterly that he'd only married her so she would arrange the fayres the school had. Adam would smile at his spirited wife and kiss away any complaints, leaving Susan unable to continue arguing.

Years later, Catherine tried to find out what had happened to Mrs Hayes. She was delighted when after a lot of research it was discovered that she had indeed been a companion to an elderly woman and a romance had developed with her widowed son. Mrs Hayes was to become Mrs Anthorn and have an immediate family of six step-children and a comfortable income. She lived until she was eighty. Catherine imagined her friend being surrounded by people who loved her for the rest of her life.

Mr Chorlton did indeed travel to Newbury races and won a substantial amount on the horses. True to form, though, he squandered his money and ended his days in the workhouse, as Catherine had discovered years before.

*

Bath, Present Day — the end of the Christmas market.

Eric stood at the top of John Street, leaning on the wall. He didn't need to be there but was waiting in the hope that Eliza would pass.

Eventually, she appeared.

"So, that's it for another year then," Eric said, his hands in his pockets.

"I'm glad that assignment is over!" Eliza said with feeling.

"Are they all so complicated?" Eric asked.

"Not usually, thankfully," Eliza responded, mirroring Eric's stance, leaning against the brickwork.

"I suppose I'll see you next December then," Eric said.

"You won't. There's been a change of plan," Eliza informed him.

"Oh? Sounds interesting."

"We're going to be at the Jane Austen Festival next year," Eliza said with a smile.

"There's a lot of people who visit the festival," Eric pointed out.

"Yes. All who love everything Regency and some who are looking for their own Regency hero," Eliza said with a smile.

"So, we're going to be helping more than one couple?" Eric asked looking interested.

"Well, as you're now an official fairy godfather, it was thought, together, we'll be able to handle more than the usual number. Who knows how many people we'll help working together?" Eliza asked with a smile.

"I like the thought of that!" Eric said with his trademark twinkle.

"Helping more than one couple?" Eliza asked.

"No. Together. I like the thought of us. Together," Eric grinned. "Eliza!" he laughed. "I do believe you're blushing!"

The End.

About this book

Since reading Tom's *Midnight Garden* as a child I've been smitten with the idea of time travel. Each time Tom heard the Grandfather clock chime thirteen times, his adventure would start, sending him back to the Victorian era.

Two years ago, I finally bought a Grandfather clock (made in 1820 in Wigan, my home town! My very own Regency clock!) But I've yet to hear the thirteen strikes. And yes, I do count the chimes, just in case.

In the 1980's we had the *Back to the Future* series. I loved the original but don't think the others maintained the charm and fun of the first.

Then of course there's *Doctor Who*, travelling to all parts of history but usually involving aliens.

In the eighties, there was the series *Quantum Leap*, which I watched addictively. Christopher Reeves *Somewhere in Time*, was a sweet film.

The only series that almost beat my love of *Tom's Midnight Garden* was *Goodnight Sweetheart,* a 1990's series where the lead actor travelled back in time and lived one life in the war and one in the present. As the world wars are a real interest for me, I loved that series and thought Nicholas Lyndhurst was great as the slightly dopey, permanently torn Gary.

I always thought if I was to write a story about time travel it would have to be set in my beloved Bath. It is my favourite place and, if only I could afford to live in one of the grand Georgian apartments that now make up the large houses, I'd be there in a shot! But, in real life I'll continue to live in my home town of Wigan and travel to Bath as often as I can and enjoy its pleasures to the full.

Visiting Bath is almost like visiting a living history museum (especially during the Jane Austen Festival, when I, along with hundreds of others, dress up in Regency costume and attend events!). There are other towns in this lovely country which have as much history as Bath does, but I've never been able to connect to them in the same way. Walking along the streets of Bath, it's easy to imagine the carriages trundling along the roads. Looking into the windows of properties (yes, I do!), I see signs of features still in existence from those heady times when Bath was *the* place to go. The road layout, in the main, is still the same in the centre, and it's so easy for someone with an over-active imagination like myself to get carried away.

So, time-travel has been all around my formative years and, with my love of history, this book was destined to be written. I hope you enjoyed it. If you did, and you're fortunate enough to visit the Jane Austen Festival, just look out for Eliza or Eric. They might be about to help you find a real Regency hero!

Thank you, as always, for your support.

Audrey

About the Author

I have had the fortune to live a dream. I've always wanted to write, but life got in the way as it so often does until a few years ago. Then a change in circumstance enabled me to do what I loved: sit down to write. Now writing has taken over my life, holidays being based around research, so much so that no matter where we go, my long-suffering husband says 'And what connection to the Regency period has this building/town/garden got?'

I do appreciate it when readers get in touch, especially if they love the characters as much as I do. Those first few weeks after release is a trying time; I desperately want everyone to love my characters that take months and months of work to bring to life.

If you enjoy the books please would you take the time to write a review on Amazon? Reviews are vital for an author who is just starting out, although I admit to bad ones being crushing. Selfishly I want readers to love my stories!

I can be contacted for any comments you may have, via my website:

www.audreyharrison.co.uk

or

www.facebook.com/AudreyHarrisonAuthor

Please sign-up for email/newsletter – only sent out when there is something to say!

www.audreyharrison.co.uk

You'll receive a free copy of The Unwilling Earl in mobi format for signing-up as a thank you!

Novels by Audrey Harrison

Regency Romances

Return to the Regency

My Foundlings:
The Foundling Duke – The Foundlings Book 1
The Foundling Lady – The Foundlings Book 2

Mr Bailey's Lady

The Spy Series:
My Lord the Spy
My Earl the Spy

The Captain's Wallflower

The Four Sisters' Series:
Rosalind – Book 1
Annabelle – Book 2
Grace – Book 3
Eleanor – Book 4

The Inconvenient Trilogy:-
The Inconvenient Ward – Book 1
The Inconvenient Wife – Book 2
The Inconvenient Companion – Book 3

The Complicated Earl
The Unwilling Earl (Novella)

Other Eras
A Very Modern Lord
Years Apart

About the Proofreader

Joan Kelley fell in love with words at about 8 months of age and has been using them and correcting them ever since. She's had a 20-year career in U.S. Army public affairs spent mostly writing: speeches for Army generals, safety publications and videos, and has had one awesome book published, *Every Day a New Adventure: Caregivers Look at Alzheimer's Disease*, a really riveting and compelling look at five patients, including her own mother. It is available through Publishamerica.com. She also edits books because she loves correcting other people's use of language. What's to say? She's good at it. She lives in a small town near Atlanta, Georgia, in the American South with one long-haired cat to whom she is allergic and her grandson to whom she is not. If you need her, you may reach her at oh1kelley@gmail.com.

Made in the USA
San Bernardino, CA
17 January 2018